The Minstrel and the Prophet

Book One of the Chronicles of the Lawbreaker

Larry Z. Daily

Publisher's Note: This is a work of fiction. Names, characters, places, and incidents are a product of the author's imagination. Any resemblance to actual people, living or dead, or to businesses, companies, events, institutions, or locales is completely coincidental.

The Minstrel and the Prophet / Larry Z. Daily – 1st ed.
ISBN: 979-8-9913879-1-0 (eBook)
ISBN: 979-8-9913879-0-3 (paperback)

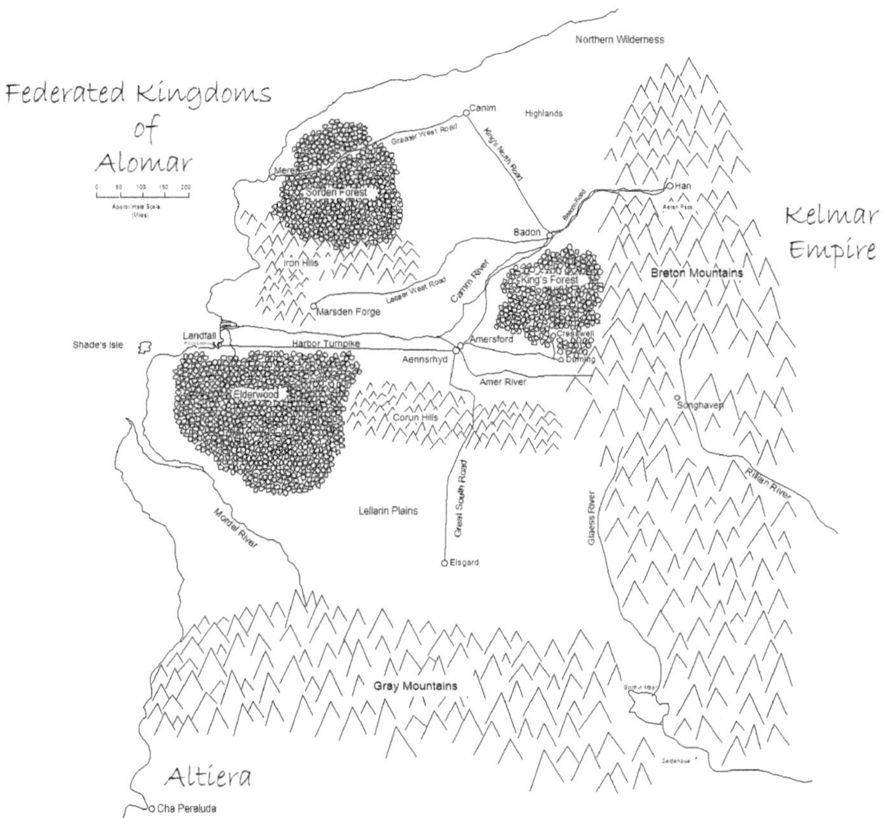

Federated Kingdoms
of
Alomar
Kelmar Empire
Altiera
Northern Wilderness
Canim
Highlands
Han
Aeran Pass
Badon
Breton Mountains
Greater West Road
King's North Road
Mere
Sorden Forest
Iron Hills
Lesser West Road
Canim River
King's Forest
Creswell
Durning
Amersford
Aennsrhyd
Amer River
Marsden Forge
Landfall
Shade's Isle
Harbor Turnpike
Elderwood
Corun Hills
Songhaven
Mortal River
Lellarin Plains
Great South Road
Glaess River
Rillan River
Elsgard
Gray Mountains
Cha Peraluda
0   50   100   150   200
Approximate Scale
(Miles)

This book is dedicated to the memory of Dean Burgi, who introduced me to Middle-Earth and Earthsea back in 1973. He started me on this journey.

And to Sandi, for just about everything.

Part One

The Minstrel

And so it has been that the handful of people out of a thousand, and the hundred thousand out of a nation step away from the things they know, clinging only to a whispered promise in some half-remembered dream of themselves – something to be found in another valley or over another mountain. These are the minstrels.

- from In Search of the Wild Dulcimer
- Robert Force and Albert d'Ossche

CHAPTER ONE

"*The real story?" I asked as I looked across the table at the young minstrel who just walked up and sat down at my table. She was smiling and her eyes sparkled with reflected firelight. "No one ever wants the real story."*

She looked at me steadily but didn't speak again as I took a sip of my wine. I shook my head slightly.

"No one ever wants the real story," I repeated. "They all want the tales of frantic gallops across the Federation trying to forestall treachery and murder or they want stirring songs of epic battles against an implacable invader." Even I could hear the weariness, the frustration, and the bitterness in my voice. "If it's not that, then they want the presumably salacious details of my relationships with two princesses. No one ever wants the real, human story. No one ever wants to hear about the pain and the loss and the overwhelming weariness. They don't want to hear about having everything you love taken away or broken in service of someone else's all-consuming ego. And they certainly don't want to hear about m..." I couldn't finish that thought. "They don't want to hear how it was all ended."

For a moment she just stared at me with the wisest, most sympathetic eyes I'd seen since... I fought to hold back the tears that memory threatened to unleash.

"I do," was all she said.

In my memory, it all began on a warm sunny day in the third moon of *Tymnagena*, the Season of Birth. I was nearing the completion of my thirteenth round of the seasons and the fourteenth anniversary of my birth, but that and the solstice and my Rite of Accession were still a few weeks away. The weather so far that spring had been ideal, but the adults of our village went about their business with strained looks on their faces; the relatively few visitors who came to Cresswell brought tales of strange events from all across the Federation. In the Highlands north of Canim, sheep gave birth to lambs with two heads or five legs or – one traveler said – the head of a dog. In the hills around Marsden Forge, hunters reported that they had seen deer attacking bears. Everywhere, healthy crops were suddenly blighted overnight. And just the week before, one of our own hunters staggered back to the village, his face and body swollen from what seemed to be thousands of bee stings. He claimed that he had just been walking through the forest when a huge swarm of honeybees boiled out of the trees and attacked him. Visiting minstrels, the most reliable sources of news, told of Kelmar raids on Federation towns and villages and the adults all whispered of war.

The stories, troubling as they were to the adults, merely sat at the edges of my consciousness. I was almost fourteen and had lessons to learn and chores to do. Further, I was rebuilding the fence around the village pastures to prove my worth to the community as part of my Rite of Accession, the ceremony that marked the transition from childhood to adulthood. That day, the day that it all started, a group of us children were gathered near the well, listening to a minstrel, though it wasn't lesson time. He was playing one of the teaching songs; I forget now which one it was. My aunt Keri had sent me to the well for a bucket of water, but I never could resist listening to a minstrel.

As the final chord of the minstrel's song was dying away, I heard my name.

"Lauren!"

I turned toward my home. Keri stood in the door.

"Lauren," she called again. "Come. Your father wishes to speak with you."

I stooped down to pick up the water bucket. I'd overfilled it and had to use both hands and I spilled a bit down my leg. I didn't stop to wipe it off, though. It wasn't wise to keep my father waiting. As I hurried toward the house, I let go of the bucket with one hand and tried to straighten my knee-length brown tunic with the other.

"What is it, Keri?" I asked as I neared the house. "Have I done something wrong?"

I was puzzled. My father never called me away from my lessons or chores without a reason, usually one that resulted in my being disciplined.

"No," she replied with an enigmatic smile. "You've not done anything wrong." She took the pail. "But get inside now, and be quick, he's waiting for you."

I tried brushing my hair into some semblance of order as I entered the house. It was built like most houses in Cresswell: a foundation of stone supporting a structure of whitewashed wood. Ours was larger than most of the other homes; for as long as anyone could remember my family had been the generally acknowledged leaders of the village. Though most of the houses in the village consisted of a single large rectangular room, my father had added interior walls to create a square main room at one end and two small bedrooms at the other. I slowly walked through the main room to the room in the left rear of the house where my father slept.

The shutters were open, and my father was staring out the window. He was leaning forward, his massive forearms resting on the windowsill. At that time, my father was a solid rock of a man in his mid-thirties, a warrior retired from the High King's army. His face was tanned from long rounds of the seasons in the sun, his coal black hair now touched here and there with gray. The rounds had not sapped his strength, however. When he trained with the men of the village, he held his great two-handed broadsword in one hand as easily as most men would have in two. Suddenly he seemed to become aware of my presence and turned, smiling.

"Lauren," he said. "Come in. Here, sit on the bed."

Feeling a bit confused, I joined him on the bed.

"Child, do you know what the *magenahr* is?"

"It's the wizard's adeptness test, isn't it?"

My father nodded and said, "That's right. And since you'll soon be fourteen, you must be presented to the wizards for the *magenahr*."

Excitement flooded through me, and I just had to stand up. I could feel myself smiling as I asked, "Is a wizard coming here? to Cresswell?"

"No. You are to be presented to the wizards at Amersford. We leave for the city at dawn tomorrow. Before we leave, though, I need to know where you stand on your Accession project."

"I finished rebuilding the pasture fence yesterday," I answered. "I wanted to finish up a couple of weeks early so that I could keep an eye on it as it settles. I want everything to be in good shape for the Rite."

My father smiled, one of the few times that I'd ever seen him do so. "That's very foresighted, child. I'm proud of you. Now, get back to your chores."

The first gray light of dawn was just beginning to steal in around the door when Keri woke me the next morning. I mumbled a word of thanks to her as I got up from the straw pallet where I slept near the fireplace in the main room of the house. As Keri tended the fire, I removed the loose robe that I slept in and pulled on my trousers. Then I padded barefoot across the room to the corner where my aunt was stowing food into a pair of backpacks.

"Keri, where's Father?"

She looked up and smiled.

"He went over to the smith to have his sword sharpened. He said you should be ready when he got back."

She went back to her packing, and I stepped outside to the wash basin near the door. Though it was spring, there was still a chill in the air and fog drifted amongst the houses. I spent a moment just looking at the village.

Cresswell was built atop a low, flat-topped hill. To keep out wolves and the occasional Kelmar raiding party, the villagers had – in the long-ago past – ringed the hilltop with a ditch. They used the excavated soil to build a low dirt wall inside the ditch. Those rudimentary fortifications enclosed a roughly oval shaped area with the long axis running approximately east-west. The wall was pierced by a gate facing to the northwest. Just inside the gate on the north side stood the inn, easily the largest building in the village, though it wasn't large as inns go. On the south side was the blacksmith's shop. The rest of the village buildings were storage sheds and an odd collection of rough built houses, most of which were clustered on either side of a broad open space that led from the gate to the opposite end of the enclosure. That's where my family's house was.

Somewhere in the distance, an early bird called once and then fell silent. That woke me from my reverie, and I turned to the wash basin and splashed water over my face and hair. The cold water washed the last traces of sleep from my eyes. After cleaning my hair, I moved on to scrubbing my face and body. There were tiny drops of dew clinging to the worn blue towel hanging next to the basin. I dried myself as best I could and then went back into the house.

Keri had finished the packing; the two packs now leaned against the wall near the door. She looked up from the fireplace as I pulled on my tunic and said, "Here, sit down. I've warmed some sausage roll for you and brewed some tea. Quick now, finish before your father gets back."

As I sat down to break my fast, she busied herself baking the day's bread. The tea, brewed from herbs I had gathered myself, was strong. The sausage roll was excellent, packed with meat, spices, and cheese. Not wanting to still be eating when my father returned, I ate quickly.

While I ate, I watched my aunt, noting the way her golden hair caught and held the firelight. It was amazing to me how unlike her brother she was. My father was broad and dark haired, medium height, with a gruff manner and a quick temper. Keri was the opposite, slender, almost tiny, with hair the color of wheat. She was almost always quiet and calm and in the rounds since my father had returned from the army to take up his role as leader of the village, she had often intervened when his means of disciplining me went a bit too far.

I had just finished eating and was lacing on my sandals when my father returned. When he saw that I was up, he nodded.

"Good to see you up at last, child. Are you almost ready to go?"

Without waiting for an answer, he turned to Keri.

"Did you get my sword belt mended? I'll be needing it now."

Keri stood up from her bread making, wiping her hands.

"It's there with the packs, and your sash also. I cleaned it for you."

"Good!" my father boomed and turned to the packs. He strapped on his sword belt and sheathed his sword. Then he knotted on his sash of warrior's red. He turned to me.

"Ready, Lauren?"

"Yes, Father." I said as I stood, wiping the last of my meal from my mouth with a worn napkin. "I'm ready."

My father bent, picked up a pack, and handed it to me. We strapped on our packs and took one last look around the room. Now that the moment was on us, I began to feel excited and anxious. I had spent days roaming the forests around the village, but I'd never been away from Cresswell before, had never slept anywhere but my father's house.

My father started toward the door, but then stopped and turned back to me.

"I almost forgot. I've got something for you, child."

He went to his room and returned with a sheathed dagger.

"Here. I got this from the smith. The roads from here to Amersford are mostly clear, but there's no use taking chances."

I pulled the dagger from its sheath and looked it over. It was of a plain, functional design, with a leather-wrapped wood grip and a steel quillon and pommel. When I tested the edge with my thumb it was far keener than I would have expected. Without intending it, I drew a small bit of blood. I looked up at my father.

"It's very sharp," I said.

He nodded.

"I had Govran sharpen it. It may not be fancy, but it's made of Marsden steel. Take care of it and it will serve you the rest of your life."

As I fastened the sheath onto my belt, my father spoke to Keri.

"We'll be gone maybe ten days. If you need anything, call on Jarl. I spoke with him, and he said he'd be glad to help you if you need anything."

"Safe travels, wayward traveler," Keri began the ritual parting. "May Garth bring you quickly home and put you on the path back to Mar."

She turned to me, and I saw, for the first time, that her eyes were brimming with tears.

"Take care, child of my heart. May you come swiftly home."

With that, I suddenly remembered that there was a chance that I wouldn't return. If a child was found to be an adept, he was kept with the wizards until he was trained. Sudden sorrow blunted the edge of my excitement.

"Take care, Keri. I'll be back soon. I know it."

We embraced and neither of us seemed to want to let go, but Keri finally did. As I stepped back, I could see the light of the fire shimmering on the tears in her eyes. I felt tears welling in my own eyes and gave Keri another quick hug. Then my father and I stepped out to meet the morning.

We stopped at the well and filled our water skins. The village was sleeping. At this hour only the innkeeper and the smith were likely to be up and about their business. No lights showed in the windows of the inn, though, as we passed it and stepped out through the gate. It stood open now; in this season wolves were scarce and when Kelmar raiding parties crossed into the Federated Kingdoms they seldom ventured so far from the main roads. We paused just outside the gate for a moment to drink in the cool morning air. Gray clouds hung low overhead, and a white mist swirled among the trees and lay thick in the low places.

My father started off at a good pace, and I had to push to keep up with him. Soon, even in the cool air, I was sweating, and I had a stitch in my side. I had never used a backpack before, and the straps began to rub sore spots on my shoulders. The road here hardly deserved the name. It was rough and uneven and overgrown with grass, littered with rocks, and marked mostly by a faint pair of parallel dirt tracks, worn by the wagons that sporadically brought outside goods to the village. My father was wearing boots and had no problems, but in sandals, I had to choose my path with care.

Gradually, though, I became accustomed to the pace. I got the pack settled in so that the straps didn't chafe, and I was getting better at choosing my path. As I came out of myself, I found myself filled with a sense of wonder. The forest, normally so familiar, had been transformed by the mist and the dim silver light and in my mind, there was magic in the air. I had never been in the forest when it was like this before. My mind was already on magic and wizardry and this only added to the feeling that, if I watched hard enough, perhaps some creature of magic would peer out from behind a tree.

That boyish fancy kept my mind occupied while my body adjusted to the walking. The sun was rising higher now, dispersing the clouds and burning away the mist. Oak and hickory became merely trees once more and, as the last traces of night wafted away on the morning breezes, the forest began to wake. Birds chitted all around and a far-away crow called and listened to its faint echo. Squirrels darted across the track and scrambled around in the branches overhead.

I took it all in in silence. My father had not spoken in over an hour, so I was surprised when he stopped abruptly with a muttered curse. I stepped up beside him.

"What is it?" I whispered, looking around for the threat.

Without bothering to be quiet, my father pointed and said, "Look."

A narrow, nearly overgrown path crossed our road. Across the clearing from us was a hollowed out tree stump. Something rested inside. It looked to me to be some kind of carving. I started forward to see what it was, but my father grabbed my arm in a grip of steel and hissed "No! It is one of the Dark Ones. The heathens set it here to watch the crossing. I had not known such a place was so close to home. Stay as far away from it as possible."

"Father, I don't understand. Why would anyone build a shrine to one of the Dark Ones?"

My father glanced at me, clearly irritated that I'd ask such a question. Then he returned his gaze to the shrine.

"Out in the hills and forests, some uneducated people still do not accept that Mar is our true Goddess, and they resist the guidance of the Keepers. They cling to the beliefs that made us the Alomar, the outcast of Mar. They believe that the Dark Ones are the true gods of our people, and they set up shrines like this one to curry their favor."

Muttering under his breath and keeping to the far side of the road, he stomped off. As we passed the shrine, I risked a glance at the carved figure. It seemed to me that glittering eyes watched from within the shadows inside the hollow. As my gaze locked onto those eyes, it seemed that a voice spoke in my mind.

It said, "*Vorath, Endollin.*"

Startled, I ran to catch up with my father. As we walked away, I had an uncomfortable feeling of being watched from behind, but when I looked back, I saw nothing there.

At midday we halted. The road had entered a clearing and there was a wide, grassy area on both sides of it. We sat in the grass by the side of the road and enjoyed the sun as we took a midday meal of jerky and hardtack.

I was quiet at first, grateful to be sitting down. I'd been thinking, though, and asked, "Father, what is the *magenahr*? What will I have to do?"

My father took a drink of water and then answered.

"I do not know," he said. "When I was a youngster, the wizards did not need to seek out the adept. They had more students to train than they could handle. It is only recently that their numbers began to dwindle, and the Keepers imposed the *magenahr*."

That wasn't what I was looking for and I wasn't sure how to respond, so I said nothing. We finished the meal in silence and then resumed our journey. Before long the forest thinned and gave way to grasslands. The road was smoother here, more defined, and with fewer rocks, but it had rained recently, and wide puddles lay across our path. As we left the shadow of the forest, I spotted a doe and her fawn grazing in the waist-high grass and stopped to watch them. My father continued walking until he noticed that I had stopped.

"Come on," he snapped.

Startled, the deer bounded back into the forest. I turned back to the road. We walked in silence until the sun was halfway to the horizon. We paused then for the evening meal. When we had finished eating, my father pulled out a surprise: a full skin of Cresswell's ale. He undid the seal, took a long swig, and passed the skin to me. I just looked at it for a moment; I had never been allowed ale before.

"Go ahead," he said. "I brought it just for this."

I put the skin to my lips and drank. The liquid hit my stomach like fire and a strange tingling warmth rushed out to the ends of my fingers. My eyes widened and my father laughed.

"That was a mighty swig for a first try, but no more for now. We've got a few hours of daylight left and I'm not wanting to carry you."

Once again, we continued. The sun had set in pastel pink and blue and the last light of day was fading when my father called a halt for the night. We spread blankets on the grasses, out of sight of the road, pulled more blankets over ourselves and lay back to sleep.

I lay silent, watching the stars. There was a gentle breeze whispering through the tall grass and I felt warm and secure in my blankets. I was comfortable and my mind began to drift. From habit, I began naming the constellations: the Huntress, the Hound, the Seven Sisters. Just as I was drifting off, two stars, like glittering eyes, caught my attention. Faintly, as if from far off, I heard the voice in my mind.

It said, "*Vorath, Endollin.*"

Instantly, I was wide awake. But all around was only the soft sigh of the breeze in the grass. I could no longer find the two stars that had looked like eyes. Listening for that far off voice, I drifted into sleep.

I woke with the dawn. My father had obviously been up for some time; his bedding had been packed and he was breaking his fast with jerky and hard tack. Fog once again shrouded the land. I quickly packed my blankets. As I finished, father asked, "Would you mind eating while we walk, child? I would like to get started."

I didn't want to hold him up, so I agreed, and we started walking. I nibbled on hard tack as we walked. Within an hour the fog had burned off. Our track – I just couldn't call it a road anymore – ended at an intersection with a true road, the first I'd ever seen. It was slightly elevated and paved with gravel. At its side, across from our track, stood a milestone. We crossed over and examined it.

"It says that twenty miles this way lies Durning." My father pointed left, to the east. "One hundred and fifty miles the other way is Amersford. We go that way."

Two more days passed as we travelled west across the plains. My father was silent most of the time, speaking only when we passed milestones and at mealtimes.

In truth, I didn't mind his silence because I was silent, too. My anxiety about what lay ahead was growing. I thought about magic and wizardry and found myself half hoping to be found an adept. Wizards were held in much esteem in the Federated Kingdoms, and they had magic. The tales of ancient wizardries fascinated me, and I often imagined myself a part of the stories.

Besides, I knew that there would be conflict if I returned home after the *magenahr*. More than anything I wanted to be a minstrel, one of the itinerant musician scholars of the Federated Kingdoms of Alomar. My father, however, wanted his son to be a warrior, to follow in his footsteps, something I simply did not want to do. But the possibility of being found to be an adept scared me, too. Cresswell was the only home I had ever known. The unknown, being a wizard, called to me, but it was frightening.

On the third day since our path joined the road, in the late afternoon, we met a man whose bright blue sash marked him as a minstrel. He was on horseback, riding out of the west. We stopped and waited until the man reined in his horse before us.

"Well met, Warrior of Alomar," said the minstrel.

"Well met, Minstrel of Alomar," my father replied.

The minstrel relaxed in his saddle. "I am Dermot, son of Perrin," he said.

"I am Dalach, son of Egan."

"Dalach? Of Cresswell? He who was…"

"A warrior in the High King's army," my father finished for him. "Yes, I am that one."

Dermot looked puzzled. For a moment, the minstrel looked as if he were about to speak, and then he noticed me standing slightly behind my father. He looked quickly between us a couple of times and then shut his mouth on whatever he had been about to say.

"Where are you heading, Dalach?" he asked instead.

"We are bound for Amersford," my father said, civilly, but without warmth. "Have we far to go?"

"You should be there before midday the day after tomorrow."

Dermot spurred his horse forward.

"Safe travels, wayward one," he said as he passed.

I watched him go. Then I turned to my father.

"Father, what was that about?"

"Some other time, child. Let's go."

We passed a few other travelers that day, mostly farmers with wagons of produce, bound for the town of Durning. As the sun set, we came to a short bridge over a small stream. We turned off the road and followed the stream until we were out of sight of the road. There, we made our camp under a large willow tree.

The next day dawned clear. Once again, we broke our fast with hardtack and jerky. Soon after we began the day's walking, we passed through the village of Kerith. It was of a size with Cresswell and its people were also farmers. One of the village dogs followed us for a while, growling and barking the whole time, but it turned back before the village was out of sight. That night, I couldn't sleep. The next day would possibly change my life, and I had no idea what to expect and no control over what would happen. The stars wheeled through the sky overhead and I found myself listening for that quiet voice, but nothing spoke to me that night. Long after moonset, I slept fitfully.

My father had to wake me the next morning. I felt groggy and a bit disoriented as we broke camp. Soon after we started walking, my father stopped a farmer and purchased some bread, cheese, and apples to break our fast. We ate as we walked. Just before the sun reached its zenith, we topped a low ridge. In the distance stood the city of Amersford and, beyond it, the Amersford Bridge.

Amersford was one of two identical cities – the other called *Aennsrhyd* (*Aenn* was the Elvish name for the Amer River and, in the Elven tongue *rhyd* meant crossing) – located at each end of the Amersford Bridge. The Twin Cities had been built in the days of friendship between Men and Elves, long before the Keepers came to lead the Alomar back to Mar. The cities had been a joint effort, whose purpose was to tend the great Amersford Bridge. The Bridge, also a joint effort, was built to span the Amer River which was, at this point, three quarters of a mile across. The Bridge allowed the crossing of the Great South Road, which joined the kingdoms of Elves and Men.

The cities, and the Bridge, were built of a white stone, resembling opal in appearance, but stronger than steel in strength. This stone was the favorite of the Elves. I had heard that they built their own capital city of it. The north and south walls of Amersford were pierced by the Great South Road. Where the Road passed through the walls were gates of iron, wrought by Phelan, greatest of the Smiths of Man. A tower stood on either side of the gates. The east and west walls were identical, each warded by a single tower in the center of the wall. The banner of Amersford, a white cross on a light blue field, topped every tower.

We stood gazing at the city for long minutes. I had no words for what I was seeing. I had, of course, heard descriptions of cities from the minstrels who came to Cresswell, but in my mind, they always looked like my village, but a bit bigger. Amersford dwarfed anything I had ever imagined a city to be like. The dumbfounded look on my face drew a quick snort of a laugh out of my father.

"Are you ready, child?" he asked.

Some part of me felt like I might be swallowed up by Amersford and never be able to get out, but, hesitantly, I nodded. The road we were on joined the Great South Road about half a mile north of the city. Within half an hour, we reached the city.

Amersford's massive iron gates stood open. Two guards, in the white and blue livery of the City Guard, stood on either side of the entrance. They eyed each person leaving the city and spoke briefly to each person entering. We joined the line of people waiting to enter. As we approached, the guards crossed their spears over the road.

"Who would enter the city of Marc?" one challenged. "And why would he do so?"

We stopped. I stood gaping at the guards. They were more lavishly dressed than any men I'd ever seen. Their tunics and trousers were of white linen with blue piping at the collar and cuffs, and they wore breastplates of blue painted steel. Upon their heads were steel helms, with inlay of white stone in the sign of the Bridge. Around their waists they wore their sashes of warrior's red.

Raising his empty right hand in a gesture of peace, my father answered the challenge.

"I am Dalach, son of Egan, of the village Cresswell. My child, Lauren, is now of age for the *magenahr*, and we have come to present him to the wizards."

"Your purpose is good," the guard replied formally. "You may pass."

As we started forward, the second guard said, "Dalach, it has been too long. I haven't seen you since..."

He trailed off at an intense stare from my father, who finished for him, "Since the army. Perhaps we'll have time to catch up while I'm here."

The exchange reminded me of the one with the minstrel Dermot. There was something about my father's service with the High King's army, something he didn't want me to know. I tried to remember what Dermot and the guard had said to try and figure out what I was missing, but my thoughts were interrupted as my father took my arm and propelled me through the gate.

And so it was that I first entered the ancient city of Amersford. On a day in which I had already seen so many things that surpassed my experience, I was suddenly face to face with a scene that beggared them all. Inside the city, the Great South Road ran in an arrow-straight line from Northgate to Southgate. An enormous amount of traffic – wagons, mounted men, pedestrians – flowed in both directions on the Road. To my immediate right were rows of houses and, further down, a low stone wall topped with an iron fence. I learned later that the wall surrounded King Marc's estate.

It was the view to the left, however, that amazed me. The east side of the city was its commercial district, a jumble of inns, shops, and stalls. A great sea of humanity flowed into, out of, and around these places of business, dressed in a multitude of colors never seen in Cresswell. The sheer numbers of people – far more people than I had seen in my entire life – overwhelmed me and I stopped and gaped in astonishment at what I was seeing.

"Quite a sight, eh?" my father asked. I nodded, my eyes still wide, and he continued. "There's an inn nearby, just off Trader Street. Let us see if we can bespeak us a place."

With that he plunged into the tide of people on a side street. I followed closely, afraid to be lost in this place. To either side, street vendors hawked their wares. An old man rushed at me, bearing a tray of jewelry.

"Jewels, young master," he cried. "Priceless gems, cheap."

I just stared at the man in confusion and rushed by. Ahead, I saw my father turn onto another street. I followed and found myself in an oasis of quiet.

The street was not a street at all, but a courtyard. Ahead of us was a large brick building. The sign above the door proclaimed it to be the Inn of the Dancing Bear.

My father looked down at me.

"This is a good inn," he said. "I've stayed here before. The rates are reasonable, and the food is good."

He put his hand on my shoulder and led me toward the inn. The door stood open, as it should, and we entered. The interior was dim after the bright sunlight of the street and, as my eyes adjusted, I could begin to make out the long dinner table. Beyond it, the innkeeper was changing the straw in the sleeping pallets. We watched in silence a short while, then my father spoke.

"Innkeeper, we need lodging for the night."

With a start, the man straightened from his work. He was short and fat, bald, with pink, puffy cheeks. He smiled and walked toward us, wiping his hands on his apron, and said, "Dalach! It has been far too long. How may I serve you?"

"Well met, Paul. As I said, we need lodging for the night. We'll also want the evening meal and the morning meal tomorrow."

The innkeeper reached into the pocket of his apron and pulled out a handful of tokens. He nodded to himself and turned back to Dalach.

"That will be three crowns for the lodging and another for the meals," he said. "Your room will be on the second floor, second door on the right."

"Done," my father replied and reached into the money pouch hanging from his belt. The innkeeper held out a chubby hand with three wooden tokens, one dark and two light. My father took the tokens, replacing them with the required coins.

"My thanks to you, Paul. Before you go, this is my child Lauren. We are in the city for his *magenahr*."

"Pleased to meet you, Lauren. Welcome to the Inn of the Dancing Bear. I wish you well with your test. Excuse me now, please, I've things to attend to."

He turned and hustled away. My father turned to me.

"Here, child," he said. "You hold onto these. But do not lose them; they are proof of our payment for the lodging."

Wide-eyed at this great responsibility, I took the tokens. I had a money pouch of my own, with but a pair of irons in it. Each of the copper crowns that my father had just spent was worth 25 irons. I hadn't known that he had that much. I was just a little awed. I added the inn tokens to my own meager sum and asked, "What do we do now, Father?"

"Now we try to get an audience with the wizards."

After we dropped our packs in our room, we went back into the bright sunlight and the tempest of the marketplace. Trader Street was the busiest area of the city, saving only the shops off the Great South Road. We made our way through the throngs toward the city's east wall.

A wide, tree-lined cobblestone street ran along the wall. This was a residential area, and quiet. We strolled down the street, soaking in the fragrance of trees and flowers.

"This is Wall Run," my father explained. "It runs the entire length of the east wall and ends in the southeast corner of the city. That's called Wizard's Corner, for the wizards keep a house there."

I nodded. I felt a growing sense of fear now that the test was so close. My chest felt funny, constricted, and my palms were sweaty. Silent and withdrawn, I followed my father toward the Wizard's Corner.

Wall Run ended in a quarter circular court. The wizard's house was built in an L-shape in the corner, its dull gray stone in decided contrast to the shining opalescence of the city walls. We approached the house, my father proudly, head held high, me silent, my eyes down, each step hesitant.

We climbed the few stairs to the porch and stood before the massive oak door of the wizard's house. With a final look at me, my father raised the brass ring and knocked. A second knock was required before the door was opened by a young novice in a gray robe. He looked expectantly at us.

"Well met, Wizard of Alomar. My name is Dalach, son of Egan. My child Lauren has nearly completed his thirteenth round of the seasons, and I have brought him here for the *magenahr*."

"This way" the novice said softly and led the way down the dimly lit hall. He showed us into a plainly furnished room. Again, he spoke.

"Master Crom will join you in just a few moments. Please, make yourselves comfortable."

With a nod of his head, he left the room.

I looked around. The room was small, with a plain wood floor. My father crossed the room to look out a window at what was, perhaps, a garden. A fireplace stood at one end of the room, the fire unlit. The walls were gray stone, adorned with two wall hangings. One was of Badon, the capital city of the Federation, the other of a silver and white tree. Four wooden chairs stood near the fireplace; they were all the furniture the room contained. Nervously, I sat down.

And then the man was there. He wore a black robe belted at the waist by his white wizards' sash. He was tall and thin, his hands bony, their veins knotted. His face was thin, sharp, almost hawklike. He was bald but for thin wisps of white hair over his ears. His eyes were pale blue and piercing and in his right hand he held a polished staff of dark ash wood.

"Well met, Warrior of Alomar," he said.

"Well met, Wizard of Alomar," my father replied, bowing slightly. I stood and quickly moved to his side.

"I am Master Crom," the wizard said in a voice which was full of vigor. "What do you want of us, warrior?"

"Master, my child will soon be fourteen. In accordance with the Keeper's Decree, he must be presented for the *magenahr*."

The alarming blue eyes came to rest on me. For a moment the wizard's face was creased with a frown, as if he saw something wrong with me. Then it passed and he said, "What is your name, child?"

I tried to meet his gaze and could not. I couldn't say why, but the wizard's pale blue gaze seemed to see right into me and that frightened me. I struggled with an odd feeling that something deep inside me was trying desperately to hide. Still, I managed to answer.

"I am Lauren, child of Dalach, sir."

"Lauren," the wizard commanded. "Look at me."

I raised my head and at last met that ice-blue gaze. For just a moment, just as our eyes met, Crom frowned again.

"Return here at the third hour past mid-day," he said. "We shall be ready then. You may go now."

Crom turned on his heel and strode out the door. Within seconds the novice was back, motioning for us to follow him. He led us back to the door, opened it and let us out. As I passed, he whispered, "Good luck later."

Then the door was closed, and we were back on the streets of Amersford.

"Would you like to see more of the city, Lauren?"

I nodded and added, "I'm hungry though. Could we get something to eat first?"

"Certainly," my father replied and started back the way we had come. Just outside the courtyard a street led back toward the center of the city. My father turned onto it, and then, shortly after, he turned right toward the shops. Before he continued, however, he stopped and pointed across the street to a quiet garden.

"That is Sanctuary Garden," he informed me. "Beyond it stands the Temple of Mar. We shall eat in the Garden. Then I want you to see the Temple and the King's Palace."

"And the Bridge?" I asked.

"And the Bridge," he confirmed.

Then, with me firmly in tow, my father waded into the marketplace. Minutes later we waded back out, laden with sausages, cheese and, as a treat, peaches. We returned to the Gardens.

The Sanctuary Gardens had been planted to keep the marketplace away from the Temple, and to provide a place of beauty for meditation and prayer before entering the Temple. Cobbled walkways wound between finely manicured hedges and flowerbeds, shaded by fragrant cherry and dogwood trees. Wooden benches had been provided and we sat on one of these to eat.

The sausage was fiery hot with spices and the cheese aged to perfection. We ate them quickly and then sat back, savoring the sweetness of the peaches. Parts of a large white building were visible through the trees.

"Is that the Temple?" I asked, juice from my peach dribbling down my chin. I wiped it off with my sleeve.

"Yes," my father replied. "Come, we'll finish the fruit as we walk."

We stood and began walking toward the Temple. As we cleared the trees, I gasped.

The Temple was made of white marble. Broad steps leapt up to where massive columns supported an intricately carved cornice. It was the largest building that I had ever seen, bigger than any I'd ever imagined. I was awestruck.

Men and women, their heads bowed in a prayerful attitude, were climbing up and down the stairs. One man, on his way down, wore the black robe and gold sash of the Repentant, the priests of Mar. My father took me by the arm and crossed to the foot of the stairs. There we waited for the Penitent. As he approached, my father spoke to him.

"Penitent, a moment, if you please."

The black-robed Penitent stopped, smiling.

"Yes, wayward one?"

"Holy One, I am Dalach, son of Egan and this," he said, drawing me to him, "is my child Lauren. He is to be presented for the *magenahr* later today. Would you please give him your blessing?"

"Certainly, wayward one. Lauren, bow your head."

I did as I was bid, and the Penitent raised his right hand, extending it over my lowered head. Slowly, he brought it down, till it covered the top of my head.

He spoke.

"I, as a true and faithful servant, call down upon you, Lauren, child of Dalach, the blessing and favor of the Keepers of the Alomar. May they keep you in penitence until

Mar grants you Her mercy. Most especially I beg the favor of Mancier, patron of wizards. With His intercession and if it pleases Mar, may you be found to be adept."

As he finished, it was as if lightning flashed through my head. For a brief moment, it felt like thousands of insects were crawling over my head where the Penitent's hand rested. A look of pain flashed across his face and my vision blurred. The Penitent withdrew his hand, holding it stiffly, as if it hurt. Then he forced a smile and turned to go. My father, though, was not finished.

"Penitent?"

The Penitent turned back, cradling his hand. My father noticed.

"Is something wrong with your hand?"

"Just the stiffening of age, I believe," the Penitent replied, but he looked troubled. "Is there something more?"

"Yes, Holy One. On our journey here from Cresswell, we passed a shrine of the Dark Ones. I thought you should know."

I raised my head and tried to listen, but it felt like giant fingers were trying to crush my skull. I couldn't get my eyes to focus, and I could barely think through the pain. The normal daylight seemed too bright to bear. I hung my head and closed my eyes as tight as I could.

"Where is this shrine?" the Penitent asked. He was speaking gently, but the sound of each word was agony. "We shall send a party to destroy it and purify the site."

I'm sure my father described the location to the Penitent, but I simply couldn't focus on what was being said. I felt cold, but sweat was running down my face.

"You should have thanked him," my father said reprovingly.

I couldn't reply.

"Lauren?"

When I still didn't answer, my father moved to stand in front of me and put one hand on my shoulder. With the other, he tilted my head up. My vision blurred and I swayed slightly.

"Lauren, what's wrong? You're white as the moon, boy."

"My head hurts," I said quietly. "It hurts so bad I think I might be sick. Can we go somewhere that I can lie down?"

My father nodded.

"We'll go back to the Gardens. You can lie on a bench. We've got an hour before we must be back to the wizard's house."

With my father half carrying me, we returned to the bench where we'd eaten, and I laid down. I fell asleep almost the moment I laid my head down. It felt as if no time at all had passed when my father woke me with a gentle shaking. I sat up, rubbing my eyes. There was no trace of the pain left.

"My headache's gone," I said. "Is it time to go?"

My father nodded and we set off. Within minutes we once again stood before the heavy oaken door, waiting for a response to our knock.

Again, the young novice answered and showed us back to the small room. Heavy drapes had been hung over the window, shutting out the light. A table, with a single lighted candle on it, stood in the center of the room. Crom sat at the table. Across from him was an empty chair. Only the tabletop and Crom's face were lit. The rest of the room was dark.

"Lauren," Crom intoned. "Enter now for the *magenahr*. Dalach, remain outside and close the door."

I entered, then heard the door softly close behind me. Crom motioned for me to sit, and I took the chair across from him, anxiety making me feel suddenly clumsy.

The wizard smiled.

"Lauren, relax. I am just going to ask you some questions. I want you to answer as best you can. Do you understand?"

I nodded.

"Good. What is your name?"

Why was he asking that? He knew my name. Perplexed, I looked through the flame at Crom.

"My name?"

The aged wizard nodded.

"I am Lauren, child of Dalach."

"Who is your mother, Lauren?"

I tensed.

"Her name was Elinore."

"Was?" Crom's voice softened. "She's dead?"

Suddenly, fantastic images exploded into my mind, threatening to overwhelm me. Dragons fought mail clad knights. Wizards battled one another with staffs of flame. I struggled to answer Crom while trying to keep my face neutral. Something told me not to let Crom know what was happening.

"Yes."

"I'm sorry, child. We must continue, though. Where are you from?"

"The village Cresswell."

I fought the images exploding in my head. For just an instant I ignored Crom and concentrated on suppressing a vision of a King's coronation. Abruptly something in my mind shifted, like a door closing, and the images stopped.

"Have you ever been here before?"

"No, sir."

Good, I thought, I didn't miss anything.

""Do you like Amersford?"

"Yes."

"Would you like to be a wizard, Lauren?"

My heart lurched. Could I have passed this easily?

"Yes. I mean no. I..."

My voice faltered and I hung my head.

"I love my family," I started again. "I don't want to leave them. But I think I would like being a wizard."

"I see."

There was a rustle as Crom moved, then a faint guttering sound.

"Lauren, look at me."

I looked up. The candle had been extinguished. Crom's staff, which had not been apparent before, was again in his right hand, glowing with a faint silver light. I hadn't noticed a change in the light and was surprised at the sudden show of magic. I met Crom's ice-blue gaze once again.

"Is there something else you'd rather be?" the wizard asked.

For a brief instant the images broke through. Quickly, I shut them out again, ignored the pressure I felt on my mind.

"A minstrel," I replied without hesitation.

"Very well. The *magenahr* is ended. Wait outside with your father."

Being careful to be quiet, I stepped outside to join my father. Together we anxiously watched the closed door.

Behind that door, Crom gestured with his staff. The drapes drew aside, and the shadows fled. He let the silver light die away. Another man stood in the corner by the unlit fireplace. Like Crom, he was wearing a black robe, but he also wore a hood and a black veil over his face. As the curtains opened, he removed the hood and veil, then picked up his white sash from a nearby chair and tied it around his waist. Then he stepped forward.

"Well, Master Crom, was there any reaction?" he asked.

The Master shook his head.

"No, Master Olen, there wasn't."

The younger man joined Crom at the table. He peered intently at the Master's face.

"Are you sure?"

Crom hesitated. Then he shook his head.

"Yes, I'm sure. He did not react at all. I don't understand though. There is some shadow of power around him. Did you send the images with all your strength?"

"Yes, I used as much force as I could. If he did not receive them, he is among the most insensitive people I have ever met. For just a moment, though, when he first entered, I also got a vague impression of great power. But, when I looked more intently, there was nothing there."

Crom sat lost in thought for a moment.

"Could it be," he asked at last, "that he was shielding against you?"

"How could an untrained youth shield against a fully trained wizard?" Olen replied. "Even if he was, I would have sensed the shields. He has no magic. That is all."

"I am not so sure that is true," Crom said. He paused just a moment more. Then he said, "No, you must be correct. Let me tell Lauren."

The door opened and Crom came out, closing it swiftly behind him. He turned toward us, his face stern. My heart started to pound.

"Lauren, child of Dalach," he said gravely, "you have been judged not to be an adept. You have no magic."

I sighed and felt all the tension in my body drain away. My father gave another of his rare smiles, reached out and ruffled my hair.

"Thank you, Master Crom," he said. "May Mancier favor you."

"Thank you, Dalach, son of Egan. May Garth watch over your homeward journey."

"Thank you, Master Crom," I said.

The wizard nodded in response, then left us in the hallway. A young novice appeared and led us back to the door. As we went down the steps, my father asked, "Are you ready for a tour of the city now?"

I nodded eagerly. We returned to the Great South Road and followed it north to the center of the city. My father explained that the stone wall and fence that I had noticed as we entered the city the day before surrounded the estate of Marc, the petty king who ruled Amersford. For a while we leaned on the fence and my father – who had visited Amersford while serving in the army – described the king's manor. Then we returned to the temple and went inside. The temple nave was enormous; over one thousand worshipers could be accommodated in its cold marble pews. An aisle way, broad enough for five men abreast, stretched from the narthex to the chancel and was carpeted in the deep purple favored by the Goddess. In the chancel, the huge altar was ablaze with the lights of hundreds of candles, kept perpetually alight in honor of the glory of Mar. Behind the altar hung a massive portrait of Mar herself, surrounded by the hooded forms of her chief servants, the Keepers of the Alomar. We paused to each make a brief prayer to Mar and then left the temple.

After a short walk we reached Southgate. Few people were leaving the city through Southgate this time of day; south of Amersford the Great South Road led only to the docks at the foot of the Amersford Bridge and across the Bridge to *Aennsrhyd*. Before the Great War, *Aennsrhyd* had been a great city, the Elven half of the Twin Cities. Now, it was largely empty, though King Marc kept a garrison there and a handful of the larger town homes had been taken over by well-to-do families who wanted more privacy than they could get in Amersford.

As we stepped out of the gate, my father paused to speak with the guards. I stood just outside the gates and looked at the Bridge a quarter of a mile away. The ground sloped gently down to the banks of the Amer River, where several ships were rocking gently at the docks. The view was dominated, however, by the great Amersford Bridge. The bridge was built of the same white stone as the city walls and in the late afternoon sun the play of colors on its surface was breath taking. The foot of the bridge began halfway between the wall and the bank of the river. From there it rose to its apex, 150 feet above the river. In the distance I could see *Aennsrhyd* gleaming in the sun.

It took us a quarter of an hour to reach the center of the Bridge. We stood there for a time, leaning on the rail and watching as the crew of one of the ships finished bringing their lading aboard and cast off. We stayed until the ship disappeared from view down river. Then we returned to Southgate and, after speaking briefly to the Guards, re-entered the city.

Together, we returned to the inn. On the way, I noticed that I wasn't having to struggle so hard to keep up with my father. My body was growing accustomed to the exertion, and I felt some small amount of pride at that. At the inn, I fished one of the lighter tokens out of my pouch and presented it to the girl who was serving, and we sat down to a fine evening meal. The stew was everything my father had promised it would be and, in celebration, I was allowed a whole mug of ale. Another followed that, and another after that. Before I knew it, the room was spinning around me, and I felt as if the slightest movement would result in my spewing my dinner all over the floor. My father just laughed and helped me up the stairs to our room.

It was a plain room, with just a pair of beds and a wash basin with a pitcher full of water. As we were preparing to sleep, someone knocked gently on the door. I heard my father get up and open the door, but I couldn't force my eyes open.

"Dalach," It was the innkeeper. "I recall that you said you were heading home tomorrow. You'll be returning to Cresswell?"

"You recall correctly."

"Then I have a gentleman who would like to have speech with you."

"Oh? Who and on what business?"

"He is a merchant, bound for Durning. He proposes to offer you a ride, as far as you wish, for a crown and your Vow of Protection."

My father was silent a moment.

"Bring the merchant here. I would meet him."

Paul hurried away only to return moments later with a richly dressed man of, perhaps, thirty-five.

"Well met Warrior of Alomar," the man said, bowing. "I am Kendal, dealer in fine cloth and jewels. The innkeeper undoubtedly presented my offer to you?"

"He did," my father said stiffly.

"And?"

"I find the terms agreeable. When do you leave?"

"At dawn, brave Dalach."

"We will be ready."

Kendal and the innkeeper left. My father closed the door, and I had the sense that he was standing over my bed.

"Riding with the merchant will cut our return trip to just two days," he said softly, but whether he was speaking to me or to himself I wasn't sure. "And now you're free to begin training to be a warrior."

Dawn came far too early. When my father shook me awake, I had an aching head and a nauseated stomach. My bones felt like rubber. For several minutes I lay staring intently at one of the ceiling beams, trying to keep the room from spinning around me. Then I rolled over and, with shaky arms, pushed myself up.

We gathered our belongings and went down to the common room. The inn was empty, save for a handful of men breaking their fast at the long table. Kendall was in the corner, near the kitchen, talking to the innkeeper. Seeing us up, Kendall waved us over.

"Good morning," the merchant said. "How are you feeling this morning?"

"Terrible," I replied. "I think I'm sick."

My father and the merchant both grinned.

"Dalach," Kendal asked, mock surprise in his voice, "have you been allowing this child ale?"

"He is nearly fourteen," my father explained. "It does appear, though, that he got quite drunk."

Kendal peered intently at me.

"He does appear a tiny bit green," the merchant observed. "Perhaps he would like to sleep it off in the back of one of the wagons instead of riding a horse. What say you to that, young Lauren?"

I did not speak but nodded. For an instant the room reeled, and I decided against nodding again soon.

"Yes," I said. "I would like that very much." I turned – carefully – to my father. "The ale did this to me?"

"Aye."

Smiling, Kendal suggested, "Why don't you go outside? The fresh air might revive you a bit."

As I walked away, I overheard Kendal say to my father, "One would think your child, mighty warrior, could hold his ale better."

My father was laughing as I stepped out the door. Two wagons, little more than boxes on wheels, stood in the courtyard. Each was drawn by a team of two horses, and several more horses, with their riders, stood nearby. The wagons were brightly painted in red, yellow, and green. My overly sensitive senses were pained by the glaring colors, and I stood watching the trees that overhung the courtyard wall until my father and Kendal emerged.

My father went immediately to one of the horses, while Kendal addressed me.

"You," he said, "can ride in the second wagon. There are furs on the floor that you can sleep on; please leave the other cloth alone."

While Kendal was talking, we had moved and now stood by the second wagon. The merchant spoke to the driver.

"Robeson, this is Lauren, the warrior's child. He took rather more ale than was good for him last night and would like to sleep it off. He'll be riding with you."

The merchant and the driver both laughed, and Robeson replied, "Yes, sir. I'll be ever so careful and try to avoid any bumps for the young master."

They laughed again and Kendal went to mount his own horse. Robeson gave me a hand up. I muttered my thanks and half stumbled through the curtain into the dim interior of the wagon. I quickly found the promised furs and curled up in them. When the wagons began to move, I was still awake. For a short time, I was aware of the clatter of the iron rimmed wheels on the cobbles, then I lost myself in the forgiving oblivion of sleep.

When I woke, the wagon was still. The dim light of early evening shone under the curtain. I felt as if someone had shouted, and the shout was what woke me. Then there was another yell and a loud "thok" as if something had struck the side of the wagon.

"Robeson!" I called and got no answer. Outside, though, I heard my father's voice raised in a sudden battle cry, and the ring of steel on steel.

I cautiously crawled forward and pulled the curtain aside. Robeson was sprawled across the seat, an arrow in his chest, his eyes wide and unblinking. In the half light I saw a man running toward the wagon from the left, a torch in one hand, a sword in the other. Suddenly, my father darted into view, guiding his horse with his knees, his great sword already red as it flashed toward the attacker. The sword connected and my guts lurched as the man fell, half clove in two by the force of the blow.

Fighting sounded to the right and then abruptly ceased as my father spurred his horse in that direction.

"They're running!" Kendal cried. "Thanks be to the Keepers, they're running."

Carefully sliding past Robeson's body, I climbed down from the wagon. I looked around in the gloaming and saw my father, Kendal, and three others still on horseback, and then, on the ground, the dead. My stomach heaved again; this time I couldn't fight it down. I dropped to my hands and knees next to the wagon wheel, vomiting. I was dimly aware of hoof beats as someone walked a horse toward me, the jingle of the stirrup and harness as the rider dismounted.

"Lauren, are you injured?" my father asked.

"No," I managed to croak.

My father said nothing for several seconds and then asked, "Is it the sight of the fight?"

I nodded as I slowly stood. My stomach felt empty, and the sweat was beginning to cool on my face. Still, I avoided looking at the bodies. Instead, I stared off into the distance.

"Father?"

"Yes?"

"Now that I've seen it, I don't think I can do this."

I wrapped my arms around my stomach and fought back sudden tears.

"You will if you have to," he answered gruffly. I heard him mount and looked up. My father sat erect on his horse, his bloodied sword resting across the saddle horn. For an instant I saw the brilliant young commander who had, at the age of twenty-five, risen to command an entire division of the High King's army. Then my father spoke, and the vision passed.

"I'll leave you alone for a while. Try to pull yourself together."

My father rode back to join the others. I waited quietly, breathing slowly and deeply to try and settle my stomach. I had a feeling that I knew what was coming and just the thought of it threatened to bring up what little was left in my stomach. After a few moments, the men walked their horses toward me.

"Thanks to the Keepers that you were with us," Kendal was saying as they rode up. "I've never seen a Kelmar raiding party so far west. Even with your might in arms, brave Dalach, we lost Robeson and four other men. I am sorry about that; Robeson was a good man and a good friend."

The men dismounted.

"You're not wounded are you, Lauren?" Kendal asked.

"No, sir," I answered.

"This is his first fight," my father noted.

"Lauren, I am sorry to have to ask this of you," Kendal said, pity in his voice. "But we need your help in clearing the road."

I nodded, my throat suddenly dry. This is what I had feared was coming. I helped drag the bodies of the Kelmar raiders – twelve in all – well off the road into the grasses. All of them were hacked and bloody and several times I stumbled to the side, fighting the uncontrollable heaving of my stomach. Then I helped move all the merchandise from one wagon to the other, and the now empty wagon became a funeral cart for Robeson and the four other slain Alomar men.

After we finished, we moved down the road until we reached the milestone standing across from the trail to Cresswell. We camped there, for in the morning Kendal and his party were to continue on to Durning, while my father and I would turn north to Cresswell. I spread my blanket out in the grass and fell at once into a deep sleep.

The morning came bright and clear. I woke feeling refreshed, despite the fact that I had vague memories of troubled dreams throughout the night. As I looked around, I noted that Kendal's men were mounted and ready, so I hastily rolled my blanket and hurried to where my father and the merchant were talking.

"Keep it," my father was saying as I joined them.

"No, Dalach," Kendal replied. "I asked for the crown in the belief that you would not have to fight. You did fight, though, and you saved us all. I feel that you should take your coin back."

"The price stated to me," my father insisted, "was my Vow of Protection and one crown. You owe me nothing because I fought as I agreed. The money is yours."

Kendal looked exasperated.

"Is there no merchandise I can give you then? Dalach, I truly only asked for money because I believed that you would not have to fight, and I wanted to turn a profit. Had I known otherwise, I would never have asked for payment."

My father said nothing for a moment, a thoughtful look on his face.

"There was a pair of boots," he said at last, "which looked to fit young Lauren. Perhaps those."

"Done!" Kendal cried, smiling. The boots were swiftly fetched, and I put them on as the merchant mounted. I had never worn boots before. After I put them on, my father probed the sides and the toes.

"These fit like they were made for him," he said.

"Safe travels, wayward travelers," Kendal said. "May Garth speed your way home and put you on the path back to Mar."

"And to you, wayward traveler," my father replied. "Travel thee well, friend Kendal."

With a wave of his hand, Kendal set his party in motion. My father turned to me.

"If we push, we can be home before nightfall," he said. "I don't want you to mention yesterday's battle to anyone. Keri and the others would worry that the village isn't safe, but there's no need for that. The Kelmar would never come to Cresswell." I nodded and we started up the track toward home.

The journey back took less time than I expected. I was wearing far better footwear and our journey had built up my endurance, so we were able to keep up a better pace. Long before I looked for it, we were within sight of the Dark One's shrine. From a distance it seemed taller than I remembered. As we got closer, I could see that the extra height was a large eagle perched on top of the stump housing the carved figure. The eagle watched us intently as we approached but did not take flight. I tore my gaze from the eagle when I heard my father swear softly. My father was warily scanning the forest around us. I turned to see what he was looking at and was shocked to see that the trees and bushes were filled with birds of all kinds. There were jays, thrushes, crows, falcons, hawks, sparrows, and wrens, all silently watching us. The air was heavy with menace. My breath caught in my throat. My father's hand was on his sword hilt. For a long uncomfortable moment, we stood back-to-back, scanning the forest around us, then my father hissed, "Let's get out of here."

We half ran up the track toward Cresswell. I fought the urge to duck down as I jogged along behind my father. We kept up the pace until the shrine was out of sight, then slowed to a walk. An hour later, the walls of Cresswell were in sight. Suddenly, an ache that had been in my heart, unnoticed since we left, was laid to rest. In joy I bounded up the hill ahead of my father and through the open gate.

A minstrel played at the well, a small group of people gathered around him. As I joined them, I quickly recognized the minstrel's song as the *Ballad of Maxim's Peace*, which tells the tale of how the High King Maxim ended the Lost Rounds by driving the Kelmar invaders back across the mountains. Then I got a small surprise; I recognized the player. It was Dermot, whom we had met on the road. The minstrel raised his eyebrows as he recognized me in return and then went back to his playing having never missed a beat. I listened with the others as I waited for my father to catch up. When he did, we stood listening to the end of the ballad. As the minstrel finished, my father said, "Child, go let Keri know that we are back. I must speak with Dermot."

I waved shyly to the minstrel as I turned to leave. Dermot nodded an acknowledgement, then stood as my father approached. I quickly crossed the dozen yards to the house. I looked back just before entering. Dermot was nodding at something that my father was saying and both men were watching me. Puzzled, I turned and entered the house.

Keri was overjoyed, but unprepared, to see us. We were back days earlier than she had expected, but she soon had a hot meal ready. The rest of the evening passed quickly as we talked of the past week's events. That night, as I lay on my pallet, I was happier than I'd ever been. For a while I lay drowsing, replaying in my mind the sights and sounds of Amersford and my first interaction with real wizards. Then it hit me: I had failed the *magenahr*. After my Rite of Accession, my father was going to expect me to begin training as a warrior. At that realization, dismay flowed like ice water through my veins. It took me a long time after that to fall asleep.

The next five days passed in a blur. Though the villagers still tended the fields and livestock and the routine tasks of daily life continued, more and more effort went into preparing for the summer solstice and the Summer Day of Passages. The Alomar observed a Day of Passages on each of the solstices and equinoxes. To the extent that it was possible, life transitions – naming ceremonies, marriages, coronations – were timed to coincide with the transition of the world from one season to the next. Because it was so small, Cresswell often had no one undergoing a life transition and so the Days were usually observed as general celebrations of thanksgiving. This time, however, there were two events: a marriage and my Rite of Accession.

On the morning of the sixth day after our return from Amersford, Keri roused me out of bed just before dawn. As was custom for those going through a transition, I wore nothing but a black hooded robe. The bottom of the robe just barely cleared the ground, and the sleeves were so long that they reached well beyond my fingertips. The hood hung low and kept my face in shadow. Just as I finished settling the robe into place, my father came out of his room pulling a deep green tunic over his head. Together, then, we all went out and joined several other families at the well.

One by one the other families joined those already at the well. We were all looking expectantly to the northeast, waiting for the arrival of the first summer sun. Those who spoke did so in hushed tones. No one spoke to me or the couple to be married who, like me, were clothed in hooded black robes. Then the first sliver of the sun appeared above the horizon and Dermot lifted his voice in the first verse of the Summer Song of Thanks. Dermot's clear voice echoed slightly in the hush of the new morning. Then, as he began the second verse, the whole village joined in, voices twined in the simple harmonies that best expressed the simple gratitude we felt for the fact of our existence and the bounty of our fields. With my voice joined with the others in that song, I felt as if we had ceased to be separate individuals and had somehow become one larger being. Then the song ended, and I felt that little sense of loss and emptiness that marked becoming just myself again.

We all went back to our expectant waiting. The first of the rituals – the marriage – would occur when the sun stood clear of the horizon. When all but a tiny sliver of the sun's disk was above the horizon, the couple to be married and I left the group and went out through the gate. Once outside the gate, we dropped our hoods. I looked at my companions. Clay was from Cresswell. He was tall and muscular, with leonine features and shoulder length hair that was somewhere between blonde and light brown. Like most of the village men, he'd left to join the High King's army after his Rite of Accession. After six rounds away, he'd returned in the early spring with Amie. She was a few inches shorter than Clay, with a thin face and wide, brown eyes that reminded me of a doe. Her long light brown hair was caught inside the neckline of her robe, and it took her both hands to free it. After the wedding, they planned to make a marriage trip to Amersford, and then, while Clay returned to the High King's service, Amie would return to Cresswell and move in with Clay's parents.

Clay, who had been looking back through the gate, turned to Amie and me.

"The sun must be fully up. Everyone is in place and they're all looking this way," he said quietly. "They should call us any minute."

Without another word we pulled off our robes. To the Alomar, all life transitions were experienced unclothed, the way the first transition – birth – was experienced. The cool morning air raised goose bumps all over our bodies.

Just then, the villagers called out together in one voice, "The Alomar are met. Are there any to come before us?"

Clay took Amie's hand, and the couple led the way through the gate with me following behind. Over the rounds at previous ceremonies, I had seen plenty of naked people – men, women, boys, and girls – before, but never a girl so close to my own age. Walking behind Amie, I became very aware of the sway of her hips, and I suddenly found myself thinking of girls in a whole new way. I had to force my attention back to what I was about to do.

The villagers had arranged themselves in a broad semicircle with the open side facing the gate. When we reached the point where the line of the circle would have been, I stopped while Clay and Amie continued into the center. There they stopped and faced my father and the other elders of the village, still holding hands. The other villagers shifted position, completing the circle. For a moment, all was quiet, then Clay spoke.

"I am Clay, son of Dyfed and Dian of Cresswell," he said.

"And I am Amie, daughter of Celos and Tian of Badon," said Amie.

As one, the villagers answered, "We are the Alomar. We hear you. What would you have of us?"

"We wish to be joined in marriage," the couple replied as one.

"Clay, have you come into this relationship of your own will and desire?" my father asked.

"Aye, I have."

"And are you already married or otherwise beholden to another?"

"No, I am not."

My father then turned to Amie.

"Amie, have you come into this relationship of your own will and desire?" he asked.

"Aye, I have."

"And are you already married or otherwise beholden to another?"

"No, I am not."

My father now addressed the villagers.

"Does anyone present know of any reason that these two should not be married?"

He waited a few moments and, when no one spoke, he said, "Villagers of Cresswell, you have heard these two state their intent to marry. To the best of my ability, I have determined that their intent is true and that there is no cause to deny their request. What say you?"

As one, the villagers responded, "We are the Alomar. We say they are husband and wife!"

My father turned to Dermot, who was standing next to him.

"Minstrel of Alomar, you have heard the intent of Clay and Amie and you have heard the will of the Alomar. Will you carry news of this marriage to the capitol?"

"I will make it known to the clerks in Badon that Clay, son of Dyfed and Dian, and Amie, daughter of Celos and Tian, are now husband and wife."

"Then may you find your way back to Mar together," my father said to the couple to conclude the rite.

Clay's parents came forward then with tunics and wedding rings for the new couple. Clay took one of the simple gold bands and placed it on the ring finger of Amie's left hand; she placed the other on the ring finger of Clay's left hand. Then they each put on one of the sleeveless, knee-length, undyed linen tunics. Finally, grinning from ear to ear, they kissed and joined the circle next to Clay's parents.

Now I stepped into the center of the circle. For a moment, no one spoke, then as one the villagers said, "We are the Alomar. What would you have of us child?"

I responded, "I am now beginning my fourteenth round of the seasons. I ask for the Rite of Accession."

"Then tell us who you are," the villagers replied.

"I am Lauren, child of Dalach and Elinore," I answered. "As part of his Rite, Dalach my father reworked Cresswell's wall and gate to make the village safer and more defensible. As part of her Rite, Elinore my mother put a new roof on the village warehouse. Dalach is the son of Egan and Dawne..." I continued my recitation until I had named and told the deeds of all of my great- great-grandparents.

"Child, your family has contributed much to the Alomar. What have you done for your people?" the villagers asked.

"I rebuilt the entire pasture fence," I responded.

"Was the job well done?" my father asked. "Can anyone speak to the quality of the work."

"Aye," answered Creighton, who had charge of the care of Cresswell's livestock. "I checked out the fence myself. I've never seen one so solid. You'd think the posts grew in their spots instead of being planted in holes. He done a really good job."

My father addressed the villagers.

"Villagers of Cresswell, this child has asked for the Rite of Accession. In your sight he has completed the Telling of his ancestors and he has given of his own heart and hands to the community. What say you?"

"We are the Alomar. We say that this child is a child no longer. He is now Alomar, possessed of all the rights and responsibilities of the Alomar. You are well come among us, Lauren son of Dalach and Elinore."

Keri stepped forward then and presented me with a sleeveless, knee-length tunic. After I pulled it on, Keri gave me a quick hug and a kiss on the cheek. Then I joined her in the circle of the villagers.

My father addressed the circle of villagers one last time.

"Villagers of Cresswell, the necessary Rites are concluded. Let us spend the rest of the day in thanks for our lives and the bounty of our fields, but especially for this new family and for our newest citizen, my *son* Lauren."

The villagers cheered. After a few moments, Helori, the innkeeper, stepped into the circle and held up his hands. It took a bit, but everyone eventually quieted.

"My friends," Helori said, "a feast is laid out in the main room of the inn. Let us eat, let us drink, let us celebrate this Summer Day of Passages. Take as much as you like, have fun, but please do have a care with the crockery."

At that, everyone laughed, and the circle dissolved. Everyone was milling around, congratulating Clay and Amie and me, but generally moving toward the inn. Dermot recruited a few of the villagers to sing harmony and they began playing lively songs of thanksgiving. Several couples began to dance. I looked around at my home, my family, and my friends. The joy I felt swelled to the point that it filled my chest and brought tears to my eyes. Then I felt a firm hand on my shoulder.

"Come on, *son*," said my father, again emphasizing the word son. "Let's go get something to eat."

CHAPTER TWO

I was just sitting down to breakfast on the morning after my Rite of Accession when my father staggered into the house. His unshaven face was pale, his eyes red-rimmed and bloodshot, his hair unkempt, and his clothes wrinkled. He smelled of stale ale and wood smoke.

Keri looked up from kneading dough for the day's bread. "Again, Dalach?" she asked, her face wrinkled in a frown and a note of disapproval in her voice.

"I was celebrating my son's Accession," my father answered, his speech faintly slurred.

"And what about two nights ago? And the night before that? Dalach, since you've been back from Amersford, I swear you've been drunk as much as you've been sober. Brother, what is happening with you?"

"There is nothing happening with me, Sister, and even if there were, it would be no concern of yours. Leave off." He turned to me and said, "Son, I have something for you. Wait here and I'll get it."

I glanced in Keri's direction, but she kept her face blank. A few moments later, we heard a thud and a soft groan from my father's room. Keri put down the dough and wiped her hands on her apron and, together, we rushed to the door of my father's room. He was lying face down in an untidy heap next to the bed, snoring softly.

"Well," was all Keri said.

We stood in the doorway for a few long moments, neither of us speaking, and then Keri said, "I suppose we should get him onto the bed. Can you get past him to lift his shoulders?"

My father's room was not much wider than his bed, so I had to step carefully to avoid treading on him. Then Keri and I lifted him onto his bed and returned to the main room.

I returned to my breakfast, but Keri sat down at the table with me instead of resuming her breadmaking.

"Lauren, we need to talk," she said.

Her tone was serious. I, with my mouth full, simply nodded.

"Lauren, I need to know what happened on your trip to Amersford. I know that there is something that you haven't told me. Am I right?"

I swallowed, remembering my promise to my father.

I peered intently at Keri for a moment, taking in the determined set of her mouth and the rare hardness around her eyes.

"Yes," I said, very quietly.

"Well, what is it?"

"Father told me not to tell anyone."

Keri's pursed her lips, and her blue eyes showed a sudden flash of anger.

"I need to know what happened," she stated in an uncompromising tone. "Lauren, your father – my brother – is in trouble. I've only seen him like this once before, about one round of the seasons after he returned from the army. The winter after you were born was a hard one for the Federation. It started just before harvest time. Crops that had been growing well all summer suddenly withered. A sickness began spreading among the livestock. The cold and the snows came early and hard and then people began to get sick. Here, in Cresswell, your grandfather Egan was one of the first to die. Then your mother came down with the sickness."

I was listening intently, and my heart was pounding. This was the most that I'd ever heard about my mother's death and my father's return to Cresswell.

"Your father came home to a village that was starving. Every family had lost someone to the sickness. Your father had lost his father and his wife, and he had you – a tiny baby – to care for, but he also had to lead the village. Eventually, it took its toll. He started drinking heavily then. The more he drank, the more disagreeable and unreliable he got. It got so bad that the villagers were beginning to talk about stripping him of his chieftainship. Even Jarl, who cares so much for your father that he resigned his commission in the army to come here with him, was talking about leaving. It was a big fight with Jarl that made your father realize how bad things were getting. He managed to straighten himself out and everything has been fine until now. I don't want things to get that bad again."

She paused just a moment, then repeated, "I need to know what happened."

The room was silent except for the crackling of the fire. Keri's words had filled me with anxiety.

"There was," I started, then my voice faltered in a throat gone suddenly dry. My father was not going to be happy if I talked, but Keri wasn't going to be happy if I didn't. I took a quick sip of water, glanced at the door to my father's room, and then started again. "There was a battle. We were riding with a travelling trader and a Kelmar raiding party attacked. Almost all of the raiders and five of the traders were killed."

"Your Father fought?"

I nodded and said, "He had traded a Vow of Protection for the ride back."

Again, we sat in silence, eyes locked, with the fire crackling and popping.

"Keri," I finally said. "For a while after the fight, Father seemed different. He seemed relaxed, almost happy."

Keri's gaze unfocussed and tears welled up in her eyes as she looked toward my father's room.

"Oh, Dalach," she whispered.

Then she focused on me again.

"Lauren you're an adult now. You need to hear this, and you need to understand that it doesn't mean that your father doesn't love you."

I felt like I could barely breathe. I nodded silently.

"Coming back here to Cresswell wasn't easy on him. He had earned a very high position in the High King's army. Very high." She paused for a moment, her face thoughtful, as if weighing how much to tell me. Then she continued, but I had a sense that she was leaving something out. "In that position he'd travelled to every city in the Federation. He'd supped with all of the Kings at one time or another. And he fought. The truth is your father is a warrior born. The Kelmar were always raiding, and your father was always in the thick of the fighting. After your Grandsire died, he had to leave all that and come back here. Ever since he's been stuck; a farmer leading a bunch of other farmers."

She paused.

"That fight reminded him of all that he had, of all that he gave up."

"What can we do, Keri?"

"I'm not entirely sure, but I do know this. For a while, you need to play along with his plans for you."

I started to object, but she cut me off.

"Lauren, I know that you want to be a minstrel, that you don't want to be a warrior. But play along for now, play at being a warrior, at least until I can figure out how we sober your father up permanently. Will you do that for me and for your father?"

I was torn. I wanted to help my father, but I could not forget how I felt seeing the bloody, mutilated corpses of the Kelmar raiders. I felt tears welling up in my eyes but nodded my assent.

Keri let out a sigh of relief and gave me a forced smile.

"Thank you," she said. "Now, you had best get to the fields. You have work to do."

I spent the morning tending the fields with the other men of the village. At midday, we broke for a meal, and I returned home. My father was sitting at the table eating his midday meal when I entered the house. He'd cleaned himself up a little but was obviously still feeling the effects of too much ale. His eyes were still bloodshot, and his movements were slow and careful. He was picking at his food as if the slightest mouthful would trigger a round of vomiting. As I joined him at the table, Keri served me a plate of cheese, slices of cold beef, and apples, and then returned to mending a tunic that had been torn while my father was cutting firewood in the forest.

"Son," my father suddenly said, "I know you've had a hard go of it, without your mother and all, and because of that I've been a bit loose with you."

I glanced at Keri, knowing that she would find my father's words hurtful. She had been the only mother I had ever known. At my father's words, she stopped her sewing and glanced at her brother, her mouth set in a hard line, but tears in her eyes. Keri set the sewing aside and, without a word, slipped out of the house. I tried to protest, but my father cut me off and continued.

"You are no longer a child, and I must get stricter with you if you are to be made a man. So, no more do I want to hear of your hanging with the minstrels. You may still attend the required lessons and you may listen to them at the seasonal ceremonies, but no more than that. Tomorrow you will begin training to be a warrior, and for that I've got you this gift."

My father bent to one side, overbalanced, and barely kept himself from falling off his chair by catching the edge of the table with one hand. With the other hand, he reached under the table and brought out a long object wrapped in oiled cloth. Smiling, he handed it across the table to me. My nose wrinkled at the smell of oil and burnt metal. Under the cloth the gift turned out to be two gifts: a wooden training sword and an actual sword. The sword was relatively plain. Its blade was iron, with a hilt of bronze set with a pommel stone of polished rose quartz. It was heavy and, in my untrained hands, unwieldy. My heart sank. Despite Keri's talk, I'd been hoping for more time before this conversation.

"Well, what do you think, son?"

I carefully composed my face, trying to conceal my dismay, before facing toward my father.

"Thank you, Father," I said in a flat tone. I immediately regretted that and hoped my father didn't notice.

"I've arranged for you to begin training with Jarl's class tomorrow," my father explained happily. "The other lads started a month ago, but if you work at it, you'll catch up."

"Thank you, Father," I repeated, trying to smile.

My father's smile suddenly disappeared, and he peered intently at me, his face clouded with anger and suspicion. He clenched his massive fists.

"Is there something wrong?" he asked, his tone indicating that the answer had best be "no."

I didn't answer. I was frantically searching for something I could say that would calm him down. I could feel myself beginning to sweat.

"Boy, I will not let my son become a minstrel. I will not let my son end up a farmer. My son will wear a warrior's red!"

I'd always been taught to tell the truth. Perhaps some version of the truth would work. I again forced myself to smile.

"I understand Father," I said. I forced myself to stammer. "I, uh, it's just this gift... I don't know what to say."

There was a brief silence. My father's face was red, the muscles of his jaw knotted with violent emotion. He stood, and I thought he was going to hit me. Then he visibly forced himself to relax.

"Well," he said. He looked a little confused. The anger seemed to drain out of his face. "Good. I mean, look at you. Fourteen and already as tall as I am. You've broad shoulders and arms like trees. There's strength in them if you'd a mind to use it. You're a warrior born, son. Like me."

We simply looked at one another for a moment, then he asked, "You will join Jarl's class tomorrow, right?"

I felt like something inside me was breaking as I nodded. With an uncertain smile, my father left the house.

I stood. It was time for me to get back to the fields. Keri was near the well and she watched me as I headed for the gate. I ignored the question on her face as I passed. Neither of us spoke.

My thoughts were jumbled. I didn't want to risk my father's anger, and I wanted to help him and Keri. I'll train, I thought, but I won't kill. I'll never kill anyone. I started to feel angry myself, angry and frustrated. As I tried to think of a way out of training, I began to feel trapped. I was nearly to the base of the hill when a voice calling my name caught me up short.

"Lauren! Hey, Lauren, wait!"

I turned. The voice belonged to my only real friend in Cresswell, Dane, the blacksmith's son. We were the misfits in Cresswell. I was the warrior's son, built in the very image of a warrior, but who dreamed of being a scholar. Dane was a blacksmith's son who wanted to be a blacksmith, but who simply didn't look the part. He was tall, at least a head taller than me, but thin as a sapling despite eating enough for two. The other boy was scrambling down the hill, his long arms and legs flapping wildly, as if he were about to come tumbling uncontrollably down. He, too, had returned home for lunch and was returning to the fields for the afternoon's work.

"Lauren," he panted as he came up. "How was your... What's wrong?"

"What do you mean?"

"You look upset. What's going on?"

"My father was there. He gave me a sword and told me I have to train to be a warrior. He's not going to give me a choice."

Dane frowned.

"We were in a fight on the way back from Amersford," I continued. "I saw..." I gagged on the memory. "I saw men sliced open like butchered pigs, their guts spilled out on the ground. I just cannot do that to someone. It makes me sick just to think about it."

"Well, what are you going to do? You're not leaving, are you?"

I looked down the road past the fields. The thought of leaving had occurred to me. I started toward the fields again and Dane fell in beside me.

"No, I'm not leaving. At least, not yet. I want to, but I have nowhere to go."

Dane looked sidelong at me, a frown on his face.

"What?" I asked.

"You know where you want to go."

"Right now, I'm thinking more about where I don't want to go."

"Where's that?"

I grinned at him as I answered.

"The fields. Do you forget that we'll be spending the afternoon hauling muck to the fields?"

Dane groaned. We walked in silence for a minute or two. All around birds called, and the calls seemed to echo. An occasional breeze stirred our hair.

My thoughts were in a turmoil. Visions of the roadside fight flashed in my mind: My father's sword cleaving a living man and the twisted bodies of the dead I had dragged away. I did not want to be a warrior; as I had said to Dane, I loathed the thought of killing. I truly wanted to be a minstrel, to roam the wilderness, to sing in all the cities of the Federation. My heart stirred as I imagined leaving Cresswell, following the road to some other place, some other town, or maybe even Badon, the heart of the Federated Kingdoms.

"Dane," I asked, "would it be so bad to be a minstrel?"

"No, Lauren, it would not."

Something clicked into place in my mind at that and I smiled. Dane noticed.

"Lauren?" he said, making it a question, a smile playing on his own lips.

I looked around the only place I had ever really known, the village atop its hill, the fields and pastures. I felt sure of myself.

"I am leaving. I don't know when, or how, but someday I am leaving. I will be a minstrel."

Dane grinned.

"I am glad, my friend. And I think you'll make a good minstrel. You've a fine voice and imagination, you tell a good story, and you're smart. You're too good to make a warrior. 'One does not make a warrior of gold, nor a singer of steel.' You're gold Lauren, true."

Surprised, I gazed intently at my friend.

"Where did you hear that? About gold and singers?"

"It's an old saying of my father's. Being a blacksmith, he thinks in terms of metals. Gold is too beautiful for warfare and steel is too rough for fine arts."

"Like minstrelsy?"

"Like minstrelsy," Dane agreed.

We'd reached the barn, and our wheelbarrows and spades were waiting.

"Lauren?"

"Yes?"

"When are you leaving?" Dane asked, speaking quietly so the others in the barn would not hear.

"I don't know," I answered.

"But what until then?"

I smiled grimly.

"I'll train to be a warrior."

I spent the afternoon hauling manure to the fields with my nose wrinkled from the smell and my teeth gritted from my determination to leave. As the sun began to sink in the west, we parked our wheelbarrows and laid aside our spades and headed for home. Dane stayed to talk to some of the other boys, so I headed back alone. As I prepared to climb up to the gate, I paused and looked up at the village perched atop its hill. The light of the setting sun fell on the dirt wall, causing it to seem to glow red. For just a moment, I felt a pang of remorse at the thought of leaving. It was the only home I had ever known. Then the moment passed, and my grim determination returned. I started up the path to the gate with a scowl on my face.

A group of children were playing in front of the inn. As I entered some of the children left their game and ran to the gate, but lost interest when they recognized me as a villager. They returned to their game as I passed. Keri was just lighting the lamps as I entered the house. My father was seated at the head of the wooden table that was built as massively as himself. He stared at me with an expression wavering between a frown and a smile but said nothing. I noticed that my sword now hung next to the door alongside my father's. I took it down. It was heavier than I remembered, and I almost dropped it. Carrying it awkwardly, I went to stand before my father.

"I didn't say this properly before, but my thanks to you for the gift, Father. I will surely be at the training tomorrow."

My father's face exploded in a smile, and he turned to Keri.

"Hear that, Keri? I told you the boy would come to his senses. Here, boy, sit, have some supper."

I returned my sword to its new hanger and seated myself next to my father. Keri had prepared a huge pot of stew, thick and steaming, and bread and butter to go with it. She smiled at me as she filled my bowl.

"Here, Lauren, eat this. It will give you strength for tomorrow."

The stew was excellent. I especially liked dipping a piece of buttered bread into it and then sticking the whole dripping mess into my mouth. I ate without speaking. My father and Keri chatted, occasionally glancing sidelong at me but I pretended not to notice. After the meal, while Keri cleaned the dishes, my father sipped ale, and told me of his time as a soldier. I listened half-heartedly, smiling occasionally, hoping to find a way out soon.

That night, as my father was snoring in his room, I got up from my pallet and went to sit by the window. I could not sleep. To my eyes the village almost looked pretty, the unfinished wood of the houses silver in the cold light of the near full moon.

I sensed a movement and turned to find Keri sitting next to me.

"Lauren?" she softly said. "You should be sleeping. Tomorrow will be a trying day."

I just looked at her. A single tear slid down my cheek.

"You really don't want to do this, do you?"

I shook my head. She reached out and softly touched my cheek.

"Lauren, be patient. We need to get your father sober. I know it's hard but please wait."

"But how long will that take, Keri? What about what I want now?"

She smiled indulgently. I felt a flash of anger at that.

"What do you want?" she asked.

"You know what I want. I want to be a minstrel."

"I know, Lauren. I hope that we can get you off to Songhaven soon."

We sat staring into the night. I turned and looked at my aunt. I had never noticed before how pretty she was. She had never married.

"Keri?" I asked very quietly.

"Yes, son?"

"Why did you never marry?"

She looked at me with a puzzled frown and then took my hand in hers.

"I promised your mother that I would take care of you. In doing that, I found that I didn't need my own family. I love you as a son, Lauren. Indeed, in my heart you are my son."

Again, we sat and looked out at the sleeping village, listening to the night birds calling. Once again it was me, still troubled at heart, who broke the silence.

"Father loves me, doesn't he Keri?"

"Of course, Lauren. He cares very much about you and your future. It's just that his love is sometimes a little rough."

Relief flooded through me, followed quickly by exhaustion.

"Thank you, Keri." I looked toward my pallet and yawned. "Good night."

"Goodnight, Lauren."

The straw of my pallet rustled as I laid down. Almost at once I fell into a deep and dreamless sleep.

Keri woke me before sunup the next morning. The smell of baking bread lured me to the table. I was just washing down a breakfast of eggs and bread with a mug of fresh, warm milk when my father entered the house.

"Lauren!" he cried; spotting me at the table. "So, you're finally up, eh? Jarl was just getting the other boys together as I came by. You had best be getting along if you don't want him to come looking for you."

I stood, crossed the room, and took my sword down off its hangers.

"Take the wooden training sword, son," my father instructed.

I quickly rehung the sword and grabbed the training sword instead. Then I hurriedly joined the group of ten boys in the center of the village. They looked at me with a mix of curiosity and disdain. Within moments our trainer joined us.

Jarl son of Merik was a short, heavy man whose upper body was covered with old scars. On his left cheek was a long, jagged scar he would not talk about, but the others he bore proudly, and could tell where and when he got each one. His flame red hair and beard were cropped close, making him look fierce and snarling, even when he smiled. He had served with my father in the High King's army. When they retired, he accompanied my father to Cresswell and, since his own village had been burned in a raid by the Kelmar, he offered to stay and teach the village boys swordplay. The villagers, urged by my father, accepted.

As he passed by me, he stopped and glared at me, his gaze shifting back and forth between my face to my training sword. I was holding it loosely, with the end resting on the ground.

"Boy," growled Jarl, "pick that thing up. Use both hands if ya haft'a, but get it up! No warrior would be caught dead carrying a weapon like that."

The others laughed as I raised my sword. Jarl ran an appraising eye over me, chewing his lip as he regarded me. Then he drew his own wooden training sword.

"This is just a test, boy, t'see what ya already know."

He swung his sword, and I moved my own to block it. The wooden blades met with an impact I felt to my core. The shock set my palms to tingling. I tried to counter the instructor's next swing, but the stroke was only a feint and the flat of Jarl's blade whacked me across the ribs. It knocked the breath out of me and, stunned, I dropped my sword and sat down with a thud. Jarl stood over me, shaking his head.

"You're out of shape, son. Start the exercises with fifty sit ups." He turned to the others. "All of ya, fifty sit ups."

The exercises continued for an hour. I was hot and sweaty and the muscles of my arms and legs were trembling when Jarl called a halt. I was just beginning to catch my breath when Jarl barked out another command.

"Twenty laps around the village, lads. Be quick about it, too."

The first few laps were torture. After those, the running became a test of my will. When we finished and I stumbled back to stand before Jarl, my breath was coming in ragged little gasps.

"Alright, boys. Pair up and spar."

I was paired with a boy named Denny. He was one of seven brothers, the sons of Harl, one of the village field hands. Harl's sons terrorized the children of the village, but always out of sight of the adults, and they had no compunction about ganging up on children smaller than they were. Denny and two of his brothers, one older and one younger, were now training with Jarl. Denny was my age, and he was smaller than me, but he'd been training for a moon already and he shared his brothers' vicious tendencies. Without a word, he swung his sword at me. I just barely blocked it.

"Wait," I said. "Isn't there going to be some instruction?"

"Don't let me hit you," he snapped. "There, you're instructed."

He swung again. I moved my sword to block, but at the last second Denny altered his swing and his wooden blade hit my sword hand. The pain was intense, bringing tears to my eyes, and I dropped my sword. As I tried to protect my hand, Denny laid into me with his sword and beat me to the ground.

"You're dead," he announced and laughed.

"Denny," Jarl snapped from across the field. "I didn't train you to be like that. What makes you think that's even close to a proper training method?

"It ain't my fault he sucks," Denny replied as Jarl glared at him. "Well, it ain't."

"You gotta lot to learn," Jarl growled at him. "Gimme that sword. You'll get it back when you've convinced me you know how to use it right. Now, twenty laps around the village."

Denny just stood there, his mouth hanging open.

"Now," Jarl snapped.

Denny glanced at me, and his look was pure malice. Then he turned and began jogging around the village. Jarl turned his attention to me.

"Well, son, I guess you're with me. Maybe that's how we should have started anyway, eh?"

I picked up my sword and Jarl walked me through the basics of grip and stance. Then we began to spar, with Jarl commenting on every move I made. By mid-morning I had stripped off my tunic. Sweat stood out all over my body and my hair was plastered to my forehead. My arms were so weary I could hardly lift the wooden training sword. I wondered how I'd ever do this with a real one. Again and again, Jarl repeated: counter, thrust, watch your opponent, force mistakes. At midday, we stopped.

"Go home now, son. But be back early tomorrow."

Every day for the next nine weeks I trained with Jarl. Denny had gotten his sword back after a couple of days and he and his brothers did their best to be paired with me during sparring. I, of course, did my best to avoid that. Nine weeks of training with a master left their mark and I was beginning to show signs of becoming a passable swordsman. It was clear to me, and probably to Jarl, that I was never going to be more than that. I was wondering how long it would be before he told my father.

One advantage of the situation was that boys who were in training were spared spending the afternoons in the fields. Dane, however, was not, so I found myself on my own in the afternoons and looking for ways to avoid Denny and his brothers. I began to spend my time in the forest around Cresswell, exploring for hours. I'd started out to the north of the village and worked my way around to the west and then to the south of the village. All I'd discovered to that point were trees and not much else.

Then one morning I had the misfortune to be paired with Denny's older brother, Clel. Jarl gave the order to begin, and Clel just smiled as we faced off, a slow, vicious smile that promised pain. At first, the sparring went normally, and I began to think Clel had just tried to unnerve me with that smile. Then Denny's younger brother hurt the boy he was sparring with, and Jarl went to deal with that. Immediately, Clel stepped up his attack on me. I held my own and kept him from landing a blow, but I was being forced back, step by step. Out of the corner of my eye I caught motion to my left and suddenly, intense pain flared in my lower back. My vision went gray, and I let go of my sword as I fell forward onto my hands and knees. I think I cried out in pain.

The next span of time is a blur. All I was really conscious of was the searing pain in my back, but I think I heard Jarl shouting and the sound of running feet. I slowly became aware that the pain was receding, was focused in my lower back on the left, and that I was lying face down in the dirt. There was a pebble sticking into my cheek where it pressed the ground. I heard Jarl explaining to my father what had happened. While Jarl had been distracted by the younger brother, Clel had driven me toward Denny, who jabbed me in the back with the tip of his training sword with all the strength he possessed. I heard footsteps coming my way.

"Lauren?" came my father's voice. "Lauren, can you hear me?"

I tried to say yes, but all that came out was a hoarse croak.

"Lauren, you've taken a blow to your kidney. I'm going to try and turn you over."

Strong hands pushed under my right side and lifted. I began to roll and tried to help, but pain pulled a whimper out of me. It hurt to move, but it helped to be on my back; I could breathe more easily. I saw more concern on my father's face at that moment than I'd ever seen there before.

"The healer's coming," he informed me. "Just lay still."

"I don't think I could do more than that," I managed to get out, my voice barely above a whisper.

It wasn't long before the healer arrived. She ran knowing hands over my back, asked me some questions, and then announced that I needed at least two weeks of rest from strenuous exertion. She left after telling me to let her know if the pain worsened or if I found blood in my urine. My father helped me to my feet and back to the house. I managed to sit up to eat lunch, but then laid down on my pallet and slept the afternoon away.

I woke late the next morning. The left side of my back was still very sore, and Keri said I had a huge bruise there. Still, I felt good enough to get up and break my fast. I felt good as I walked from my pallet to the table, so after I ate, I told Keri that I was going to go for a walk.

I decided to start exploring the forest to the east of the village. A low stone wall marked the edge of the village's pastures and fields. The wall was only about waist high but getting over it irritated my back, and I found myself wondering why no one had ever built a gate in the wall; villagers often searched the edges of the forest for medicinal and edible plants. As I moved into the forest, my left foot occasionally slipped on a loose rock and pain flared in my back. Each time, the pain was followed by a flash of anger at Denny and Harl's other sons. That quickly transformed into anger at my father for making me train and frustration that I couldn't study to be a minstrel. Then I reached the end of the fields cleared by the villagers and entered the forest.

I walked in silence under the trees. Slowly my anger drained away, and with it the gray, empty hurt that constricted my chest. The space they emptied was then filled with birdsong and quiet, and the cool, fresh scent of the trees. As I came out of myself, I began to notice the forest itself. Everything was amazingly clear and defined, the colors fresh and vibrant, the sounds distinct, as if the world had just been created, unstained, from someone's dreams. Music rang like joy in my heart, and I tried to sing it but, like a dream that fades just before it's told, the music died before it reached my lips. I walked in that joyful dream until the tinkling of water stopped me.

Suddenly thirsty, I looked around and noted that the sun had risen halfway to its zenith; I'd been walking for about an hour. I was standing on what looked like a game trail, but a broken arrow beside the path suggested that Cresswell's hunters sometimes came this way. The sound of water was off to my left.

I scrambled down a shallow slope toward the sound of the water. Off the path, the underbrush was thick and tangled. It took me a full five minutes to force my way through.

I found myself on an abandoned road. It was paved with stone slabs which had been cut and carefully fitted together to form a smooth surface. It was also quite ancient; trees had long ago taken root in the small cracks between the stones and were now grown to great size, cracking some stones and dislodging others. In other spots, grass and weeds had taken root, but overall the road was relatively well-preserved, given its obvious age. The road ran roughly north-south and I was facing south. The ground to my left sloped gently down to a stream. To my right, the ground sloped up to the path I had been on before.

The sound of water now came from ahead. As I walked, the ground to my right became steeper, finally forming a sheer face perhaps twice my height. Then I found the source of the water.

The ancient road builders had set a great slab of stone into the side of the embankment. From a crack in this, water welled to form a glistening sheet that filled a pool at the foot of the stone. A small trickling stream was the result of the overfill and passed under the road in a small culvert. It was not the spring that surprised me, however, but the object set in a carved niche above it. The figure set there, a woman in a long flowing gown, was one of the Dark Ones.

I crouched down beside the pool and recalled what I knew of the Dark Ones. In ages past, the world – including what was now the Federated Kingdoms – had been ruled by the Dark Ones, the greatest servants of the One Evil. In that time wars were rampant. Cities and nations fought amongst each other, set against one another by the Dark Ones. Desiring more power, the Dark Ones had raised the Elves to fight for dominion over Men. For many long rounds the Elves had feigned friendship with the Alomar, but when their true nature and aims became known, the Alomar went to war. In the midst of the battle the Keepers of the Alomar had expended their power and driven the Dark Ones, and their minions, the Elves, away. Worship of the Dark Ones was forbidden.

I squatted there for long moments as all this passed through my mind. I wondered if drinking the shrine's water would be considered worship. A small voice inside me said no, and I used my cupped hands to drink. The water was cold and refreshing. It tasted faintly of the fertile earth from which it sprang. The lingering ache in my heart, the pain of being forced to train, was eased. I reached up to wipe my mouth with my sleeve but froze at the sound of a voice from behind.

"It is a sign of respect to sprinkle a few drops at the foot of the statue, to thank her for sharing her water."

I turned, my hand darting to the hilt of my dagger, to see a man standing some ten feet away. In one hand the stranger held the reins of a large brown horse. The other was held outward in a gesture of peace. The bright blue sash at his waist marked him as a minstrel.

"Her name is *Tael*," the stranger said. "She is one of the greatest of the Old Ones. Hers are the dark, hidden springs, as are the rivers and lakes. All water is under her dominion."

The minstrel was tall, with long dark hair that hung loose on either side of a lean, handsome face. His face looked as though it was often smiling, but it now was cautious, perplexed, his brows furrowed over gray-blue eyes.

"She is one of the Dark Ones," I replied, alarmed and cautious. "How did you come to know her so well?"

The perplexed look on the man's face deepened.

"I believe the Old Ones were here before the Keepers of the Alomar, and that they will be here long after the Keepers are gone."

I was very aware of the change of phrase. I looked more closely at the minstrel. His hands were long and delicately fingered, his clothes made of fine cloth. He was obviously from a noble family. It was strange that such a one was a follower of the Dark Ones.

"Who are you?" I demanded.

At that, the minstrel looked even more puzzled. His reply was carefully worded.

"My name is Ryan. As you can see, I am a minstrel. Please, if you will, tell me how you came here."

I didn't think it would do any harm to answer.

"My name is Lauren, son of Dalach. I live in the village of Cresswell. Do you know it?" The minstrel nodded. "I was walking along the path, up there," I pointed, "and I heard the water trickling down here. I was thirsty so I climbed down. What's the matter? What's wrong?"

Ryan was staring at me, dumbfounded.

"You heard the water?"

"Yes, why?"

"Lauren, listen."

I fell silent. I could hear the occasional bird call, the droning buzz of cicadas, and Ryan's horse snorting. The water was still welling out of its crack, was still spilling over into the stream, but there was no sound. Confused, I looked at Ryan. He looked amazed as he answered my unspoken questions.

"Dark Ones, or Old Ones, as you will, Lauren, they are real, and they have power. No one hears the water of a spring guarded like this unless *Tael* calls him."

My blood ran cold.

"No!" my voice came out as little more than a hoarse whisper. "I don't want to be called by the Dark Ones. They're evil!"

I turned and ran. After a brief pause – probably to tie his horse – Ryan followed. One after the other, we ran down the road and then I crashed off into the underbrush.

"Lauren," Ryan called. "Lauren, come back. You don't understand. Lauren."

I soon outdistanced the minstrel and slowed to a walk. How close I'd come to giving in, to listening to the blasphemy. Certainly, the Dark Ones were powerful. Theirs was the Dark Magic that lured men from the true worship of the goddess Mar. I had spoken to one of their followers and I was afraid.

Deep inside, however, some part of me was curious. Worship of the Dark Ones may have been evil, but it was magic, and I was fascinated by magic. Once, when I was younger, a wizard had passed through Cresswell and had spent hours summoning animals and levitating objects to amuse the children while his horse was reshod. What had interested me most was the wizard's ability to call light from his staff. After the wizard rode away, I tried to make a stick light. After three unsuccessful days I threw the stick away. The *magenahr*, though it proved that I had no magic, had revived my interest. So, while my conscious mind ran from the Dark Ones, my deepest heart wanted to reach out and learn more.

Running from Ryan had strained my back, and I spent the afternoon resting at home and helping Keri with some light tasks around the house. I laid awake many hours after retiring that night. I kept picturing the shrine of *Tael* and reliving my conversation with the minstrel, Ryan. I twisted and turned and at last fell into uneasy sleep. My dreams were troubled by things I had never seen. Then everything changed, became somehow more real. I stood on a sandy patch of land with the endless waves of the sea crashing in on either hand. I was staring into ominous black clouds massing on the horizon in every direction. Grief and anguish washed over me like waves, forcing tears from my eyes. The sense of loss overwhelmed me.

"I lost her, Dane," I said. "I tried but I lost her."

I turned to find that it was not Dane beside me at all, but *Tael*, a mixed look of grief and joy on her face.

I woke in a cold sweat with tears streaming from my eyes. The iron colored, predawn light was just beginning to leak through the windows. With an effort I hauled myself off my pallet; my bones were weighted down with a sense of loss carried over from my dream. My neck was stiff, and I had a faint headache. As I stood, I felt the first stirrings of nausea. My body ached from the previous day's exertion.

Moving slowly, almost like an old man, I crossed the room and lifted the bar securing the door. The cool morning air was a relief; it washed away the sick feelings and steadied my shaking limbs. By the time I reached the wall behind our house I was feeling well enough to – careful of my back – climb up.

I sat on top of the wall and let my feet dangle. In the dim light, the fields below me were a dark sea, the forest beyond like gathering storm clouds. It was a cloudy morning, with light breezes that gently stirred my hair. As I sat watching the sky lighten, I replayed the dream in my mind. Unlike most dreams, which quickly fade, this dream stayed with me, the images as vivid as when I first saw them. The emotions that they stirred were fading, the monumental sense of loss now just a vague nagging uneasiness.

My thoughts were jumbled. I'd said something about losing her, but I had no idea who "she" was. Where was I? What was I dreaming about? The questions returned to my mind again and again. I tried to answer them but couldn't. I didn't understand why a dream seemed so important but sensed that it was. The sun had risen to become a silver ball in the clouds before I retreated from my questions and returned to the house.

Keri was up, stirring up the fire, when I entered. In answer to her unspoken question, I said, "I couldn't sleep. I had a bad dream, so I went for a walk."

"Ah," she replied. "I heard you call out in your sleep. Something about Dane. What were you dreaming of?"

"I'm not sure," I answered. I picked up a piece of bread from the day before and took a bite. "I was in a strange place by the sea," I continued brokenly as I chewed, "watching waves come in. I turned to say something to Dane only there was a..." Something told me not to mention *Tael*. "There was a monster in his place."

"That would be troubling," Keri quipped, "to find a monster instead of your best friend."

Still slightly shaken, I frowned at the gentle jest, and she said quickly, "Sit down, Lauren, and I'll make some farina for you."

I sat down at the table and stared into the fire. If I closed my eyes, I could clearly see the images from my dream. I felt empty inside, the crushing sense of loss gone, but I couldn't stop thinking about my dream and what it might mean. The house was quiet; there were small sounds from the hearth where Keri was preparing the farina, the crackle and pop of the fire, occasional drops of rain that fell hissing down the chimney.

This calm was shattered when my father burst into the house. Once again, he'd spent the night drinking at the inn.

"Morning," he nearly shouted. His voice was slurred.

Outside, there was a clap of thunder and rain began to pound on the roof.

I frowned and twisted to face my father. "Good morning," I replied.

My father seated himself at the head of the table. Keri placed a bowl of steaming hot farina in front of each of us and then went back to the hearth and returned with three stoneware mugs of tea.

I absently mixed butter and sugar into my farina. My gaze returned to the fire. I decided that I really wanted to talk to someone about my dream. I looked at Keri and my father. Keri was obviously lost in her own thoughts. My father was asleep where he sat. It couldn't be either of them. There was only one person I could think of who might understand.

By the time I finished breakfast the rain had stopped, and I set out to retrace my steps to *Tael's* spring. I crossed Cresswell's muddy fields, searching my memory for landmarks. Almost unconsciously my feet found the correct path. As I entered the forest a chorus of birdcalls and dripping leaves surrounded me. Within an hour I reached the hidden shrine.

I noticed a large tent of forest green set up a short distance away. The clear voice raised in song said that Ryan was still there. That thought was somehow reassuring.

Moved by an odd impulse, I knelt at the pool of water. I cupped my hands and drank deeply, sprinkling the last few drops at *Tael's* feet. Then I stood and walked toward the minstrel's tent.

"Ho, Ryan," I called. The singing stopped abruptly, and the singer stepped out of the tent door.

"Lauren?" he asked.

"Yes."

"You came back?" the singer asked guardedly.

"Yes."

The minstrel held the tent door open.

"Come in, please."

I felt a brief flash of fear. Stiffly I passed Ryan and entered the tent. Saddlebags and baggage were piled untidily in the rear. A couple of rumpled blankets were spread on the floor and a small candle burned against the gloom of the rainy afternoon. The minstrel's guitar lay in the corner.

"Please, sit down" Ryan invited as he moved around me to pick up his twelve-stringed instrument. "I'll not harm you. You must know that; you came back. Why?"

I sat cross-legged on the floor and Ryan seated himself on a folding chair.

"I don't know," I said. "I didn't know what else to do."

I grimaced. The emotions of my dream were building in me again; I wanted to know what the dream meant but was afraid to learn.

"Lauren, tell me," Ryan asked, his eyes full of concern. "Maybe I can help. Sometimes it helps just to talk."

"I," I started and then faltered. "I... Last night I dreamed about her."

"*Tael*?"

I nodded.

"Then I think I was right. You are called. For what I do not know, but you are called."

"But they're evil, Ryan. How can I serve the Dark Ones?"

"The Old Ones," Ryan corrected, but I was now agitated.

"Old Ones, Dark Ones, whatever! They are the enemies of Mar and the Keepers."

"Or," Ryan said calmly, "are Mar and the Keepers the true enemies?"

I fell silent. The question was disquieting and the answer it implied was heresy. I backed away from dangerous ground. Watching the older man finger his guitar brought to mind other questions.

"Ryan?"

"Yes?"

"Why are you here? Why stay out here and not at the inn in Cresswell?"

"I didn't come to visit Cresswell. Do you know where this road goes?"

I shook my head.

"A bit north of here is an ancient settlement, a walled village. It's one of perhaps half a dozen that we know of. They were here and long abandoned when the Elves came to these lands. We call the people who built them the Lost. I'm here to study what's left of the Lost settlement."

"I'd like to see that," I said. "I've lived here all my life, and no one has ever mentioned an abandoned settlement nearby."

Ryan smiled.

"Not surprising. The villagers probably explored it many rounds of the seasons ago and didn't find anything of value. We probably have time for a quick look. I'm assuming that you need to be home before the evening meal."

I nodded. After Ryan packed his guitar into its case, we started walking north along the ancient road. As we passed *Tael's* shrine, I broke the silence.

"Ryan, what's it like to be a minstrel?"

He glanced my way.

"It's freedom," he answered. "Being free to go when and where you chose, to learn whatever you choose. But there is a commitment, too. A commitment to learning and spreading knowledge. It never ends and I'll never give it up. I love it."

I smiled. That sounded very much like what I was longing for.

"I would like to be a minstrel," I said.

Ryan made no reply, and we walked in silence for a few moments.

"Lauren," he said suddenly. "You said your father's name is Dalach."

"Yes."

"I know of him. I imagine that he'd want you to follow him on the warrior's way. Why are you not in training?"

I didn't answer for a moment, and then the whole story came pouring out, from the trip to Amersford to my father's insistence that I begin training. I finished with my injury at Denny's hands. Ryan's face was suddenly serious and thoughtful.

"Would you like to go to Songhaven, to the minstrel's college?" he asked.

"Yes."

"Now?"

That surprised me and I panicked at the thought of just walking away from my home.

"I can't," I said, all my resolve gone.

"Why?"

"I just can't!" I cried. "I have to go now."

Ryan stopped and placed a quieting hand on my shoulder.

"Lauren, I'm not going to force you to go," he said. "I'll be here studying the Lost settlement for maybe a moon. I may even come to play in Cresswell. If you decide to leave, I just want you to know that you're welcome to come with me."

That calmed me down and I was grateful for the offer.

"My thanks to you," I said.

"Well, then, shall we go visit the settlement?"

I nodded and we resumed walking. In just a few moments, we rounded a bend in the road, and I stopped as I caught my first sight of the Lost settlement.

From where we stood, the road ran straight to what had once been a gate in a stone wall. The opening was empty now, whatever gate had once existed now long gone. The wall was made of mortared stone and stood perhaps three times the height of a man. The stone was gray and weathered, covered in some spots with lichen and in others with vines.

In several places I could see, trees had grown up right against the wall and cracked it and, in one place, caused the wall to crumble inwards.

We walked up to the gate and entered the settlement. The wall enclosed a circular area at least four times the size of my village. The road continued straight through to the wall on the far side.

"The road runs exactly north and south," Ryan said. "Exactly the same as every other Lost settlement but one. And like every other Lost settlement, the other major road in the settlement is aligned with the summer solstice sunrise."

I could see the intersection of the north-south road and the solstice road. There was something there.

"Ryan, at the intersection. Is that…"

"It's a standing stone," he explained. "Every Lost settlement has one in the same location. As far as we can tell, all but one came from the same source, but we've never been able to identify that source."

"And no one knows who they were?"

"No. The ruins were here before the Elves arrived in these lands. The Altierans settled south of the Gray Mountains long after the Elves arrived and the Alomar later still."

There were buildings lining the road, some crumbling, others looking remarkably sound, all weathered by uncounted rounds of abandonment. It seemed that most of the settlement was still standing. I wanted to explore it all. Reluctantly, I turned away.

"Ryan, I should head home. I didn't tell anyone that I'd be gone all day. I'd like to come back and help you explore this place, though. Would that be alright?"

"Of course. I'd appreciate another set of eyes. Meet me tomorrow morning?"

"Yes!" I confirmed. "And I'll bring lunch so I can stay most of the day."

For the next nine days I met Ryan at his camp each morning and we spent the day exploring the ruins of the Lost settlement. The buildings had all been constructed of the same mortared stone as the defensive wall, but all of them lacked a roof. From the notches in the tops of the wall we surmised that they had once had wooden roofs supported by large wooden beams and that the wood had long since rotted away. The interior walls were also of stone and nearly all of them had been painted at some point, most in various earth tones. At least one wall in each building, however, had been covered in a floor to ceiling mural. Though the paint was flaking off the walls, it was clear that the murals had all been stunningly lifelike when first painted. Most were simple landscapes, but many included animals and one or two included a dragon. Interestingly, in each of the murals with a dragon, the dragon was accompanied by a person wearing clothing the same color as the dragon. Neither of us could come up with a reason why the painters would do that.

As we explored the settlement, we talked. In retrospect, Ryan began my education at that time. We talked about the history of the Federated Kingdoms of Alomar. Ryan had been everywhere, it seemed, and his tales and songs of faraway places kept me spellbound for hours. He also began teaching me songs, and we were both surprised at how quickly I picked them up. I soaked up the knowledge Ryan offered thirstily, always asking for more. Several times I missed the evening meal.

When I returned to the village on that ninth day, Dane met me at the gate. As I entered, he grabbed me by the arm and dragged me behind his father's forge, a look of fear and concern on his face.

"Dane, what is it?" I asked.

"Denny followed you," he answered. "This morning. He followed you into the forest. He said that you've been out there worshiping at a shrine of one of the Dark Ones."

My blood ran cold. For reasons I didn't fully understand, I'd been sprinkling water at *Tael's* feet each time I drank from the spring. Denny must have seen that.

"I haven't been worshiping the Dark Ones," I explained. "There's a minstrel camping out there. He's been teaching me, and we've been exploring some ruins nearby."

"That doesn't matter," Dane said. "Denny says that he saw you worshiping the Dark Ones. It doesn't matter why you were really out there. Lauren, it's going to get around the village. What do you think will happen when your father hears?"

"He's going to be furious. He forbid me to spend time with minstrels."

"What are you going to do?"

"I don't know. But right now, I'd better get home."

Keri was the only one home when I arrived. I helped her finish preparing the evening meal and then we ate together. My father was out; when I asked Keri where he was, she just shrugged. I expected my father to storm in at any moment, but he was still out by the time that we went to bed. I lay in my pallet for a long time listening for my father's return and then fell into a fitful sleep.

When I woke the next morning, it was still dark. I rose and quietly gathered some odds and ends of food that I could carry with me for breakfast and then slipped out the door. I'm not sure why, but I grabbed my sword and sheath as I left and took them with me.

It was odd. I felt like I needed to be out of the house before Keri and my father heard about my visits with Ryan and the claims that I was giving worship to the Dark Ones. I still expected to meet with Ryan for the day and then return home. I don't know what I expected to happen then; I wasn't going to be in any less trouble with my father and I'd be gone, and he'd have the whole day to hear stories about me. Still, I felt the need to be away.

The sky was just beginning to lighten when I reached Ryan's camp. I was surprised to find him up, but he was squatting next to a small fire preparing tea. He was just as surprised to see me and noted the sword at my hip. I explained what happened and we discussed what I should do. It was fully light by the time he convinced me that I should go back to the village and talk to my father.

Just as I stepped out of the forest, Denny and two of his brothers ambushed me. Denny and Clel remained directly in front of me; the other brother circled around me to my left. All three held drawn swords.

"What do you want?" I demanded. I tried to sound defiant, but I was terrified. I had only trained against one opponent. Jarl had never even mentioned fighting more than one at a time.

"Should a man turn his face from Mar, he shall be destroyed," Denny quoted. "Should a man revere the Dark, he shall die, his very soul shall be forfeit. That's from the *Torun Mar*."

"If you finish that passage, Mar administers her own judgements," I answered. "And I don't revere the Dark Ones."

"I saw you," Denny said, and without another word, he attacked.

I drew my sword and just barely met his first rush. I swung at him, and he stepped back. He looked at Clel, who took a step away from Denny and then they both started moving toward me. I heard something behind me and risked a glance over my shoulder. Denny and Clel moved forward, both swinging. Denny's sword caught mine and knocked it from my grasp. I stepped back, but the point of Clel's sword caught my left shoulder and scored a line of fire diagonally across my chest. I could feel blood running down my chest. In a blind panic, I turned and bowled over the brother behind me and ran. I could hear Denny and Clel behind me, yelling for their brother to catch up.

Blind to all but my pain and the ground before me, I fled along the boundary of the forest.

"Lauren! No!" a man screamed.

Too late I saw the group of men felling a tree to make new timbers for the roof of the village barn. Suddenly, time slowed almost to a halt. In that instant I saw the men with axes and the enormous tree that was falling straight toward me.

Deep in my guts, something lurched. My skin felt as if thousands of ants were crawling all over me. Then it seemed as if something passed out of me, and I stood dazed with the lower part of the tree lying at my feet. The end facing me was sheared off as smooth as a tabletop.

I stood looking at it for a long count of minutes, my mind empty of everything except the image of the tree. Then, barely aware of the muttering crowd of men gathering around me, I turned and looked at the top part of the tree laying behind me. Just like the other part of the tree, it had been cleanly sheared off. A whole section of the tree had simply vanished.

"Look at him! I cut him; he was bleeding!" Clel screamed.

I looked at the people around me, then. Clel and Denny were yelling and pointing at me. I felt as if I was going to faint when I looked at my chest. My tunic was still soaked in my blood and was still slashed from my shoulder to my stomach, but the wound was gone, vanished without leaving a scar.

"Did you see that?" one man yelled. "A flash and 'poof', the tree's gone."

"It's Dark Magic!" cried another.

Too dazed to respond, I stood staring at the smooth end of the top of the tree as the men ran back to the village. I felt empty. What happened was simply too big to fit in my mind. There was no way that the villagers could ignore it and everything I knew was gone. I was sure that I couldn't go back to Cresswell.

Some time later, Keri found me there, still standing by the tree. Without a word she came up and stood beside me. She stared at what was left of the tree, looking as if a giant knife had sliced it cleanly in two, and then she looked at me. I could see fear in her eyes. Still, she spoke.

"Lauren, what happened?" she asked, her voice gentle.

"What do they say happened?"

Keri turned to face me, saw the tears running down my face. Raw emotions – fear, panic, loss – washed through me. I didn't know what she would say.

"They say that three of Harl's boys attacked you, wounded you. That you ran in front of a falling tree. That suddenly you were surrounded by gold fire and part of the tree just disappeared. And the wound, too."

"It's true," I said, my voice harsh with emotion.

"That you worship the Dark Ones," she said neutrally.

"No!" I screamed from the bottom of my soul. "I don't. They're evil. I'm not evil. I don't know what happened. I don't know."

My legs just wouldn't hold me anymore and I dropped to my knees, sobbing. Keri knelt beside me, trying to comfort me with her hands. She was afraid, I could tell, but she stayed with me. I don't know whether she believed that I was practicing Dark Magic, but if she did believe it, her love for me overcame the fear. I don't think I truly understood how much she loved me until just then.

I looked up at her at last. My heart felt like ashes, gray and dead.

"Yes, Lauren," Keri answered before I could ask. "I still love you, son of my heart."

"I love you too, Keri."

Together we stood and I went to retrieve my sword. Then, hand in hand, we began walking back across the fields.

"What has Father said?" I asked, my voice raw with emotion.

"He has refused to believe it. He's furious with Harl's sons for attacking you. He's angry at the men for saying what they did. Lauren, he'll force them to allow you to stay. But be careful, son. Don't do anything to force him into believing them. And watch them. They're scared of you." She paused for just a moment, and then continued. "Perhaps you should leave with that minstrel."

I stopped short, mouth agape with surprise.

"How do you know?"

"I talked to Dane when I noticed how much time you were spending out in the forest. You were going to see the minstrel, weren't you?"

"Yes."

"Not worshiping the Dark Ones?"

Visions of myself kneeling at the spring rose in my mind. I ignored them.

"No."

"He does?"

"Yes."

"I think maybe you should go with him, then, but do not accept his beliefs."

She turned and together we entered Cresswell, passed the stares of shocked and fearful neighbors, and headed home for supper.

My father was standing in the doorway when we got to the house. I could smell the ale on him as we got close. He was wearing his blood red warrior's sash. Keri and I stopped, and he began to advance on me, an enraged growl rumbling up from deep inside him. The look on Keri's face checked him, though, and he stepped back into the doorway, blocking the way into the house. Keri said quietly, "He was not going to the shrine, Dalach. A minstrel was camped nearby. He was going to see him."

She had put her arm around me and now she pulled me closer. Together we faced my father's rage. His face was distorted in anger and his fists were clenched so tightly that the muscles in his forearms stood out in bold relief.

"What about the tree? And his wound?" he snapped.

"I don't know. He doesn't either."

My father started to reply, then simply crossed his arms, and glared at me.

"Brother, what has happened? You were not so angry when I left."

For a moment, my father said nothing. Just as I began to think that he wouldn't answer, he spoke.

"Jarl came to see me. He was there, helping to fell the tree. He saw what happened. He came to tell me that he cannot train a practitioner of the Dark Magic, will not work with a follower of the Dark Ones. Boy, what have you done?"

I started to answer, but Keri stepped forward.

"Dalach, you cannot..." she started.

Without a word, my father backhanded her so hard that she fell back and hit the ground at my feet. Without thinking, I drew my sword and stepped between her and my father.

For a moment, he looked remorseful, then he turned his gaze on me. His face hardened and his eyes went flat. I'd seen that look before, on the road home from Amersford.

"You dare draw steel on me, boy?"

He reached behind him, pulled his sword off its hanger beside the door.

"Jarl won't train you, so I will. First lesson: never draw steel unless you intend to use it."

My father yelled – something between an inarticulate curse and a war cry – and swung his sword. It hissed past my face. He reversed his swing and brought his great two-handed broadsword flashing back. I finally reacted. I brought my own sword up and just barely stopped his attack. My father took a step forward and I stepped back. He swung again and I tried to block, but at the last moment he altered his swing, and my sword was ripped from my grasp and went spinning off to the side. Triumph flared in my father's eyes and as he raised his sword to strike, I saw my death there. I turned and ran straight toward the crowd that had gathered around us. They parted before me. No one tried to stop me as I fled from my father's killing rage.

I pelted through the village, not really hearing the cries that suddenly rose behind me. The sun had set, but there was still light, just enough for me to see, but my panic was blind. The sudden slope outside the gate was enough to pitch me headfirst down the hill. Uncontrollably, I tumbled down, my fear a whimper in my throat. I slid to a stop at the bottom of the hill, rolled and jumped up. Fear and panic were my masters then and they had but one command: flee!

I ran, stumbling on the uneven earth of the fields. My breath came in ragged gasps and my lungs burned like fire. A red mist drifted across my sight, then shattered in pain as I ran full speed into the wall of stones at the edge of the field.

For long moments I lay gasping for breath, hugging my throbbing legs to my chest, a broken heap of agony and fear. Then I saw in my mind the look in my father's eyes as he lifted his sword to strike, and the fear rose like bile in my throat. I climbed unsteadily to my feet, crawled over the wall, and shambled toward the forest.

I forced myself to a limping run. It was darker now. The moon was full but didn't penetrate the canopy of the forest. Branches leapt unseen from the darkness to smack me and tear at my clothes, but I crashed through them, unheedful of the pain. Fear kept me running long past the time my endurance should have ended.

Tinged with red, the night swirled around me. I no longer had any idea where I was. I stumbled, slipped, and fell face first into a shallow stream. Water filled my mouth and nose; I crawled forward, coughing, and spitting. Again, I climbed, whimpering, to my feet. I was past all seeing, panic blind to my surroundings, but some part of me must have recognized where I was. I wailed my last hope in misery.

"Ryan!"

The minstrel's name echoed into the depths of the suddenly silent forest. I dropped to my hands and knees, the last of my strength gone with my cry. I tried to crawl forward and collapsed, my face pressed into the rich loam of the forest floor.

CHAPTER THREE

I don't know how he found me, in the dark and with only that single cry to hint at my location. After I cried out, I just laid on the forest floor, too spent to move. I may have drifted in and out of consciousness. I remember hearing a breeze softly rustling the leaves and the gurgling sound of water flowing. There were periods of darkness, and then a footstep and torchlight. For a moment I thought my father had found me, and I tried to force myself up. Then Ryan said, "Lauren, peace. It's me."

I managed to get my eyes to focus and saw Ryan jam the end of his torch into the ground. Then he came to me.

"Lauren, are you hurt?"

I tried to answer, but only managed an inarticulate croak. Ryan took my arm and gently helped me turn over.

"*Mirdl,*" he exclaimed when he saw the state of my clothes.

I was beginning to come back to myself and struggled to sit up. He helped me.

"My thanks to you," I managed to get out.

"The blood. Is it..." he started.

"It's mine," I answered.

"We need to get you to my camp. I have bandages..."

"No," I said. "I don't need them. But I need to leave. I need to get out of here before he finds me."

Ryan didn't need to ask who "he" was. He stood, then offered me a hand up. Even with his help, it was a struggle to stand. I had to lean heavily on the minstrel to walk; he was stronger than I would have expected. I was closer to his camp than I would have guessed, but he hadn't lit a fire so I could easily have passed by without noticing. He eased me down onto a log and squatted down to examine me in the light of the torch.

"You have what looks like a sword cut in your tunic with a great deal of blood that you say is yours, but no wound. You've got scratches and bruises all over your face and arms. There are holes in both knees of your trousers..."

"I hit the wall at the edge of the fields at full speed," I informed him.

"Lauren, what happened?"

I didn't want to talk about it, but I had to convince him that we needed to leave.

"Denny and his brothers ambushed me when I went back," I said. "They disarmed me. Cut me. They'd told everyone in the village that I was worshiping the Dark Ones. Jarl told my father that he wouldn't train me anymore because of that. He tried to kill m..."

I choked on that, then went on.

"Ryan, we need to leave before he gets here. Denny knows the way. He'll bring him here."

Ryan locked his gaze onto mine, waited for me to go on. When I didn't, he stood.

"Lauren, you're not telling me everything. But, given the state that you're in, I do believe that I need to get you out of here. After our conversation this morning, I was thinking it might come to this, so I've already packed almost everything. Let me strike the tent and we can go."

In a short time, the tent was down and stored on his horse. He came back to me, handed me something.

"Here, chew this."

"What is it?"

"Willow bark. It will help with the pain. Can you stand?"

I nodded, and slowly stood. I ached all over. I started walking – hobbling actually - toward the horse, but Ryan stopped me, shaking his head.

"We'll never get away with you walking like that. Have you ever ridden a horse?"

"Not really."

"Well, you're going to have to tonight. All you'll really need to do is sit there. As long as you don't fall off, Dawnstar and I will do the rest."

"Dawnstar?"

"That's my horse's name. Did we never talk about that?"

"No, we always walked to the Lost settlement."

I stumbled over a root and bit back a cry. Only Ryan's support kept me from falling.

"I'll need to get a good look at you when it gets light," Ryan said. "You must have hit that wall fairly hard. I hope you didn't fracture anything."

"I've never broken a bone," I responded. "So, I don't know for sure how that feels, but I don't think I did. Ryan, we won't be following the road that leads out of Cresswell, will we?

"No. We'll follow the remains of the Lost's road. South of here, it continues to parallel Tolan Creek down to the Amersford-Durning Road just outside of Durning. About a mile south of here it really deteriorates and from that point on it isn't much more than a broad dirt track, but it's still passable. It's actually in better shape than the track out of Cresswell."

"That's good. I'm afraid that my father might have someone looking for me on the road."

By that point we'd reached the horse.

"True. Alright then, up you go."

With considerable help from Ryan, I got onto Dawnstar's back and we set off at a walking pace down the ancient road.

After an hour, I was starting to nod off. In the dark, there wasn't much to see, and it was difficult to converse with Ryan from horseback while he was leading out front with the reins. I was glad, then, when Ryan called a halt.

"This is where the paving ends," he said. "We should stop here for the night. I think that if someone were following us, we'd know by now."

With Ryan's help I got down from Dawnstar's back. Between the willow bark and an hour of resting on horseback, I felt a great deal better. I said so to Ryan.

"That's good," he replied. "Perhaps sleep will improve you even more. I don't think we should pitch the tent; we might need to leave in a hurry."

He pulled a couple of blankets out of his pack, and we settled in to sleep.

I couldn't see. I was in a dark place, and alone. Something was looking for me in the darkness, something huge and powerful and evil.

Suddenly, I found myself high on the tower of a ruined mountain city. Below me was a sheer drop of several hundred feet. Mountains stood below me, peak after peak to the east. Somehow, I could see past the mountains to the plains beyond. Dark clouds massed there, towering above the more distant of the mountains. Thunder rolled once, then again, and the mountains shook, as if in fear. There was a power building there on the plains, and

I could sense that it was seeking me urgently. Already it seemed aware of me, the black clouds swelling upward and then aiming at me. Then, from behind me, came a voice, clear and bell-like in its resonance. It said a word I knew from somewhere but did not understand.

It said, "*Endollin.*"

I started awake, shivering, to the quiet night sounds of the woodlands. Every one of my senses was alert, my body tense. I heard nothing, though I felt that some real sound had awakened me. There was just enough light to show me Ryan's sleeping form. Finally, I began to relax.

An owl cried from the tree above me, a strange, eerie cry that nearly made me jump out of my skin. Realizing what it was, I forced my clenched muscles to relax. The dream rushed into my consciousness then, bringing with it the conviction that it was somehow connected to the destruction of the tree.

For a long time, I lay awake, thinking on that dream, and all that had happened to me in the last day or so. Listening to the night sounds, the sounds of the world going on as normal, I at last drifted once again into sleep.

In the morning, I woke feeling strangely at peace. Tattered clouds of fog wandered among the trees, waist high, lending an unreal aspect to the forest. Tolan Creek sounded muted, distant, as if it lay under a thick blanket. I sat up, rubbing the sleep out of my eyes as I looked around. The ground had been sloping gently down as we travelled the night before and we were now just a few feet above the level of the water. To the north was the broken pavement of the Lost road and to the south, a broad dirt track. I wondered if someone had pulled up the paving stones and used them elsewhere or if the road to the south had never been paved. The forest between the road and the creek was more open than the forest to the north; there was hardly any underbrush, and I could see the creek. Suddenly thirsty, I rose and stumbled toward the stream.

My dream came back to me then, with a startling clarity that stopped me in my tracks, and I scanned the area with fearful eyes. For a moment I watched for any sign of danger, then began berating myself for such foolishness. It was only a dream. At the stream, I dropped to my knees and drank. Then I splashed cold water into my sleep logged face.

When I returned, Ryan was awake. The minstrel nodded wordlessly as I joined him.

"Sleep well?" the singer asked as he used a flint to start a small fire.

"Well enough," I answered. "Why the fire?"

"We need to heat some water to clean you up and I need to check you for serious injuries. How are you feeling?"

"Still sore, but better."

"Good. Given the way you were moving, I think you're right: you didn't fracture a leg bone."

He looked me up and down.

"One way or another, we're going to need to do something about your clothing. You look like you were on the losing side of a battle."

"Maybe because I was. Twice."

Ryan snorted a brief laugh.

"I guess you were."

Ryan set a pot of water near the fire to warm, then had me remove my tunic and trousers. I had cuts and scrapes all over my arms and – according to Ryan – my face from my headlong flight through the forest. My legs were the worst, though. Both knees were bruised and bloodied from my collision with the wall. There was a fairly deep gash over my left knee and Ryan gently swabbed that wound, cleaning away all the dried blood. I took the cloth after that and cleaned my arms and torso while Ryan went to his packs and retrieved a small, corked jar and a bandage. He unstopped the jar, dipped his fingers in, and smeared some of the contents on my left knee.

"That stings," I said accusingly. "What is it?"

Ryan smiled.

"A salve to help heal your cut. It's made from, among other things, extracts of oak bark and witch hazel. Sit still so I can finish."

I mutely endured the stinging as Ryan covered my wound with salve. Then the minstrel bound the fresh bandage around my knee. Finished, Ryan sat back, resting on his heels.

"I don't think I have much to fit you. I might be taller than you, but I'm also thinner, so my tunics are all going to be too small." He cocked his head thoughtfully. "Mayhap just a vest for now; it doesn't get too cool at this time in the round. I'm afraid you'll have to make do with your own trousers; mine would never fit." He began washing his hands in the bowl.

"Lauren?"

I was afraid that I knew what was coming.

"Yes?"

"If we're to travel together, I need to understand how it is that your tunic was sliced open from shoulder to gut and covered in what you said was your blood, but there's not a mark on you where a sword wound should be."

I was suddenly very aware of my heartbeat. I didn't want to answer. Part of me was afraid that if he knew the whole story, he'd leave me on my own. Part of me was afraid that he'd say that it was Dark Magic. If I didn't answer, though, he might abandon me.

"What I told you last night was true," I said haltingly. "But I left out a part. After Clel wounded me, I turned and ran. I was running blindly, and I ran in front of a tree that was falling. I felt strange and the people who were watching said that I was surrounded by gold fire. The part of the tree that would have hit me just disappeared. And my wound vanished like it had never happened."

Ryan rocked back on his heels, sat down with a thud, a look of complete surprise on his face.

"Ryan, do you know what happened to me?"

For a moment he just stared at me.

"No," he said finally. "No. I do not."

"The villagers said it was Dark Magic."

"Lauren, I have said that the Old Ones are powerful, and they are, but I have never heard a tale of them acting in such a way. I do not think they saved you." And then, a heartbeat later, almost in a whisper, as if to himself, "What are you?"

I had no answer to that. We sat in silence a moment. Ryan was staring at the ground. I was watching him, waiting for some sign as to how he felt. When I couldn't bear waiting anymore, I spoke.

"Ryan, what do I do now?"

At first, he didn't look up. His long black hair was hanging forward, hiding his face. For the first time, I noticed the silver highlights among the black.

"That is your choice, Lauren. What do you want to do?" For just a moment more, he stared at the ground. Then, at last, he met my gaze. I could see that he'd made some choice. I felt as if my heart stopped. Then he said, "My offer still stands."

Relief flooded my veins.

"To go with you? To Songhaven?"

"Certainly, Lauren. If that's what you want."

"It is. When can we go?"

"As soon as I find a vest for you and get these few things packed," Ryan answered as he rummaged through his packs. "Here," he said, tossing something at me. "Try this."

It was a vest of a soft, dark green material, large enough to be loose on Ryan. It fit snugly on me. I looked down at myself. I was wearing a vest with no tunic, leaving me bare-chested, torn and bloodied trousers, and the boots my father had gotten me from the trader. I felt like I looked ridiculous.

"How's this?" I asked uncertainly.

Ryan looked over from where he was fastening the packs on Dawnstar. He fought to suppress a smile.

"That'll have to do."

Clouds moved in while we broke our fast and repacked the few things we had used. Thunder rolled far off in the distance as we set off into the increasing heaviness of the morning. The forest was slowly falling still. Only the stream was unaffected; it continued to gurgle like an infant at play.

At last, the clouds cracked, and a light drizzle of rain filtered through the trees. Soon our hair was plastered to our heads, our clothing damp. We trudged along uncomfortably, in silence. Painful emotions flickered through me like lightning and not all the moisture on my face was rain.

"What are you thinking about?" Ryan asked.

"Last night," I replied, and hesitated. "My whole life. He always seemed so harsh, so bitter towards me. Keri said he loved me, but I'm not sure he ever did."

Ryan did not answer for a time. The rain got harder, beating a loud staccato path through the leaves.

"Do not judge him too harshly," he said abruptly. "You don't, I think, know your father well enough."

That surprised me.

"Your father," the minstrel continued, "was once at the very peak of the Federation. No one, saving the High King himself, was in a position of greater power. He was the High King's War Duke, general of the armies. He..."

"He never told me that," I broke in.

"Compassion," Ryan said enigmatically. He remained silent for several steps before continuing. "So, there he was, at the height of his career when, suddenly, uncontrollably to his mind, his life was wrenched out of its path. Your grandfather was chief of the village Cresswell, and he died. Then his wife died, leaving his infant son – you – alone. He had to return to Cresswell. Lauren, think of that. From the King's right hand to the leader of an obscure back country village. That must have been a bitter dreg to swallow."

"Ryan, except for his rank, I knew those things. Keri told me a while ago. I think I told you soon after we met. My father returned to lead the village. That says nothing about me."

Ryan stopped and put his hand on my arm, and I stopped, too. He looked frustrated.

"Lauren, if you're to be a minstrel, you must learn to think. Was your father Egan's only child?"

"No, Keri was his..." I broke off as Ryan's point hit me. He saw the understanding in my eyes and nodded.

"Your father could have left leadership of the village to Keri. There was only one reason he came back to Cresswell."

"I still don't understand, Ryan. If he loved me, why was he so hard on me?"

The minstrel paused for a moment, framing his reply, rain streaming down his thin, angular features.

"Perhaps," he responded, "he wanted for you what he could not have for himself. He could not have the honor and glory, but maybe his son, this son who resembled him so closely, could take up the sword and carry it in his place. Take no offense at this, but you must have disappointed him terribly."

He paused for a few steps, then continued.

"I cannot excuse his attack on you, Lauren. Even drunk, he should have known better. And I'm not suggesting that you go back. Your father is ill – dependence on alcohol is an illness – and until he is cured of it, you're in danger there. But he did give up a great deal for you. That has to count for something."

We walked in silence for a short while, and I thought about everything Ryan had said. It explained much of how my father treated me, how he had acted toward me. All the things

I had learned chipped away at the bitter core of resentment I'd felt toward my father, a hard lump of raw feeling that I hadn't realized was there. I was still hurt, and I still wanted to be away from him, but I finally felt like I understood my father.

"Ryan, do you know my father?" I asked, out of curiosity.

"I wouldn't say I know him," he answered. "Once when I was younger, I visited Badon. While I was there, I had the great honor of playing for High King Aerman Sorren and War Duke Dalach Egan-son."

"You never told me."

"It wasn't important until now."

We spent the night in the shelter of a group of pine trees that stood back away from the stream. The rain had let up and was now little more than a light mist, and the closely intertwined branches of the pines sufficed to keep us dry. We didn't bother with the tent.

After hobbling Dawnstar on a grassy sward by the stream, Ryan unpacked a bundle of dry wood and soon had a small blaze burning. I gathered wet wood and laid it near the fire to dry.

Darkness seeped into the glade as we ate our meal of dried meats and hard biscuits. Ryan tried several times to talk but I didn't feel like talking. The world had shifted around me. I felt like I was standing at a crossroads, on the threshold of change. One fork led to the past, the life I had known. The other path stretched on to eternity, leading to a shadowed and uncertain future. From this point, all I had to do was take one step down either path and I would never be able to turn back. The prospect was at once frightening and delightful.

After we ate, Ryan packed away the food and brought out his guitar. I watched the shifting shapes of the fire, and the leaping shadows it created. The minstrel's instrumental tunes were gentle, contemplative ones. They matched my mood exactly, as if he could read my thoughts.

After a time, Ryan's music became more purposeful. He played some introductory chords and sang:

How many rounds have passed,

Wearing at a love that cannot last?

Two people, alone in time
Till one shall pass to eternity.
Sparkling sands beneath their feet,
Wondering when, again, they'll meet.
Silently, with a bond of love
They sail away to sunset's shore.
Golden sunsets shine no more,
No splashing waves upon the shore.
Can one small soul stand all alone,
And lay a gentle heart to rest?

The last notes faded away, replaced by the crackling of the fire. Ryan looked up at me and he looked spent. We sat and regarded each other through the flames. Unspoken questions drifted between us.

"That fit," I said. "Almost as if the whole night revolved around that song. You sang how I felt. Will I ever be able to do that?"

The minstrel nodded.

"I think so," he replied. "That is what all minstrels hope to do, to capture a moment like that. I've only done it once or twice before. It leaves you feeling empty, peaceful. I think it's because there is no other song for that moment, and any other would spoil it."

He paused, rubbing his hand up and down the neck of his guitar.

"There will be no more songs tonight," he stated.

We reached the walled trading city of Durning just before sunset of the next day and spent the night in a crowded inn. Ryan earned our night's lodging with an evening of songs. I even earned a handful of iron coins for myself singing some simple tunes the minstrel had taught me that afternoon as we walked.

As Ryan's performance was coming to a close, he paused and spent a few moments retuning his guitar. It sounded to me like he was lowering the pitch on the lowest pair of strings. Then he began to play some introductory notes, but instead of pressing the strings down, he simply touched a pair of strings as he plucked them, yielding clear, bell-like tones. He transitioned into a more normal style of playing and sang:

> I hear the bells of Songhaven,
> As sweet as dreams in mornings light.
> They ring to greet the rising sun,
> And call me home before the night.

There were more lyrics, but I was fascinated by the fact that he'd made his guitar sound like bells. I wasn't the only one who appreciated his artistry; the applause lasted a long time.

The next morning, we joined several other early risers in the common room to break our fast. We were nearly done when a nondescript man in equally nondescript clothing entered the room. His eyes darted around the room, passed over us, then returned. He stood staring intently at Ryan until I nudged the minstrel and pointed him out.

"Finish your meal," Ryan instructed me, then rose and crossed the room to the man. They spoke quietly for several minutes, the minstrel's expression growing graver and graver with each word. Ryan appeared to thank the man, who then left. Ryan returned to our table.

"Who was that?" I asked. "What was that about?"

"Perhaps nothing," Ryan answered and paused to down the last of his tea. "We should go. We need to buy supplies."

He grabbed a biscuit and bit into it as we headed for the door.

At that hour, there was only one shop open, so that's where we purchased supplies. With my coins I bought a new tunic of sturdy, dark brown cloth and tan trousers of supple deer hide. I also bought a small shoulder pack, like Ryan's, with a small supply of dried foods to go in it. I saw a few other things that I would have liked, but those essential items exhausted my meager supply of money. Because it was late in the third moon of *Tymnacynn* and we were heading into the mountains, Ryan purchased a hooded cloak for me. Reprovisioned, we set off into the wilderness beyond Durning.

For two days we travelled through the foothills of the Breton Mountains. The land became rolling, studded with outcroppings of weathered rock. More and more trees appeared, first clustering together in small groups and then into woods. The sun shone brilliant in a blue crystal sky, untroubled by clouds.

It was a time of learning for me. As we walked, Ryan told me of the plants we saw: the pennyroyal, milkweed, and plantain. I was taught to find yarrow, an infusion of which is said to heal cuts, and the so-called healing herb, said to help knit broken bones. I learned to pitch the tent, and take it down, and how to choose a good campsite. Ryan poured information my way and, like a dry sponge, I soaked it up.

On the third day we began to climb in earnest. The slopes of the mountains were mantled in countless shades of green and we toiled upward in sunlight tinted emerald green by the trees. Ryan was quick to spot the almost invisible traces of the minstrels' trails and as a result we labored unencumbered by the thick underbrush.

The minstrel now pointed out the different trees and their uses, and I learned to identify the various kinds of oak and hickory, the chestnut, and the mountain laurel. Ryan also taught me how to read the signs that guided him through the wilderness. We talked endlessly as we walked, discussing everything around us. For the first time in my life, I was content.

As we pitched the tent on our first night in the mountains, I asked, "Ryan, you said you had something to show me in the meadow we just came through. Why not set our camp there instead of here among the trees?"

Ryan looked up over the work we were doing. Like mine, his face was grimed, and his hair sweat matted from our day's exertions.

"Because," he explained, "we are in the wilderness, away from the areas where the King holds the peace. A fire in the meadow could be seen for miles, a beacon to bring outlaws down on us."

I felt my mouth form a silent "O" of surprise. Then I answered, "There's so much to remember, out here, just to live. Things we didn't think about in Cresswell. I don't see that a warrior's life is any harder than this."

"It isn't," the minstrel stated. "We travel every bit as hard as a soldier on the march, and more in danger because we go unarmed. The minstrel who is considered soft is much maligned, Lauren. We are a hardy lot."

As evening fell, we walked back through the darkening forest to the meadow. After reaching it we stood, silent, in the waist high grass, gazing back down the mountainside.

Below us, the lands we had traversed in the last few days lay in darkness. A gentle breeze whispered through the small pines that dotted the clearing. I fancied that it was speaking a word, just beyond my comprehension. I spent long minutes trying to understand, then shook my head and turned to Ryan.

"What is it you wanted to show me?"

In reply, the minstrel simply gestured to the sky. My gaze travelled in the direction indicated and I gasped in wonder.

I had never seen the stars like this. From Cresswell they had seemed cold and remote, as untouchable as the air itself. But here, in the high, clear mountain air, they burned like countless fiery diamonds scattered across a field of the blackest velvet. All the night sky was ablaze with light. I was awestruck.

"I've never..." I stammered, then simply said, "They're beautiful."

"The Elves loved the stars," Ryan said quietly. "In fact, the word 'star' was used more than any other in the Elven language."

Momentarily annoyed, I snapped, "The Elves were evil. How could they appreciate such beauty?"

Ryan's shadowed face was still. He didn't look at me but continued to gaze into the heavens as he softly replied, "Perhaps that love should tell you something."

I tried to frame an angry reply, but the feelings that held me would allow no discord. As quickly as it had come, my anger left, wafted away by the gentle night breeze.

Ryan began to speak.

"The stars are our surest guide in the wilderness, Lauren. Trees may fall, rocks may crumble, all other landmarks pass away, but the stars will always be there. They've always been there. They saw the coming of Elf and Man to this land, the rise, and fall, of the Elven Kingdom and the rise of the Kings of Men at Badon." Something strange came into his voice. "They'll see the end of us all."

The minstrel pointed.

"See that grouping there?" he asked.

I nodded. "That's the Huntress."

"Dartem, the Huntress." Ryan confirmed. "Do you know her story?"

I shook my head.

"I'll need to teach you that. What others do you know?"

"The Hound." I pointed it out. "The Seven Sisters." I searched the sky to the east but couldn't find them. "They must be behind the mountains now."

"They are."

Ryan then went on to show me other constellations, slowly working around a great circle to the north.

"Even if you forget all else I've told you tonight," he said, "never forget this. See the star there, the bright, violet one?"

In the direction the minstrel indicated, I saw a great star, far above the northern horizon, burning with a steady, red-violet flame.

"That's the North Star," Ryan said. "It is the only star that does not move. If you can find it and you know what you are doing, it will guide you wherever you wish to go."

He paused for a moment, then continued.

"The Alomar call it the Keystone. It is said that it is the last piece of the world that the Creator put in place and that it holds the world together."

I nodded. I'd heard that.

"The Altierans call it Sendolen," Ryan continued. A chill ran down my back, but I wasn't sure why. The minstrel's voice took on the cadences of storytelling. "Their legends say that in the time before the world was complete, the Altierans were nomads, with no home of their own. In each new place they visited, they were reviled for their brown skins, their wandering, and their prosperity. Even then, they were consummate traders. Always they were driven out, forced to wander again. Then Sendolen became their leader, led them to the lands that they now call their own, gave them peace and stability. When he died, he became the North Star, the one constant in the sky, to remind them to live in peace and to avoid chaos. They also say that there will come a day when another great leader, another Sendolen, will appear wearing the star on his hand and that the fate of the world will be his to choose."

The minstrel's voice fell silent.

"I've never heard that story before," I said. "The minstrels who came to Cresswell never mentioned it."

"They are charged with teaching the history of the Alomar," Ryan answered. "It would be rare for them to mention it. As a minstrel, you'll learn much that is not taught in the villages."

I smiled in the darkness.

"I'm looking forward to that."

I was standing in a wide circle of pine trees. Within the circle there was light, diffuse and gentle, with no obvious source. Beyond the circle, though, there was nothing but an impenetrable blackness. There was no undergrowth, but the ground within the circle was dotted with outcroppings of lichen covered rock. Several shallow streams flowed through the circle, filling it with the merry sound of water flowing over rock. Before me stood a woman clothed only in her long golden hair. To her right stood a man with long white hair who was wearing a white robe and another woman clothed in red and black. To the golden woman's left another man sat on one of the outcroppings of rock. He was clad in a gray tunic with black trousers. To his right stood another woman, dressed in blue with green trim. No one spoke, but they were all smiling faintly, and I sensed that they were waiting for me. Despite the strangeness of the situation, all I felt was peace and contentment and a deep sense of rightness. Then I realized that I recognized the woman in blue. *Tael*.

I woke to find the sun barely risen and Ryan just beginning to stir. I built up the fire while he retrieved our food bag from where it hung over the branch of a tree. I was thinking about my dream and my realization from the night before that there was so much that I didn't know about the world.

"Ryan," I said as we sat down to break our fast.

"Yes?"

I told him about my dream, and he confirmed what I had already guessed. The people I saw in the circle of pines were the five greatest of the Old Ones: Earth, Time, Fire, Air, and Water.

"Tell me about them," I said.

On the Autumn Day of Passages, three days later, we were camped along a trail that ran southwards along the eastern ridge of the Breton Mountains. Before dawn we rose and climbed a nearby outcropping of granite.

We stood, I felt, on top of the world, facing east. Dark heights opened before our feet, making my head spin if I stepped too near the edge. The seemingly endless march of mountaintops below us was slowly becoming visible in the growing light. As the first edge of the rising sun climbed above the eastern mountains, Ryan raised his arms and began to chant:

> We open our hearts this day
> To give thanks to the Old Ones.

I answered:

> We give thanks for the earth and all upon it.

This was not the version sung in the churches of Mar and the Keepers, the version being sung in the towers and on all the high places of the Federation. This chant was older than that, it was a song of the Old Religion, sung only in isolated, private rituals such as this. Ryan continued:

> We give thanks to *Aenn*
> Who feeds us in her love.
> Thanks to she who makes the land fruitful.

I responded:

> Praise and thanks to *Aenn*.

> We give thanks to *Wyn*
> Who carries the hawk and the dove in his gen-
> tle hands.
> Thanks to he who fills us with the breath of
> life.

> Praise and thanks to *Wyn*.

> We give thanks to *Sar*

Who in her love is warmth.
Thanks to she who warms hearth and home.

Praise and thanks to *Sar*.

We give thanks to *Tael*
Loving giver of water.
Thanks to she who gives us lifegiving rain.

Praise and thanks to *Tael*.

We give thanks to *Ynes*,
Who counts the days and seasons.
Thanks to he who gives unending new begin-
nings.

Praise and thanks to *Ynes*.

As I chanted, the air around me seemed to shimmer and I felt a vague tingling on my skin. My hair seemed to move slightly, as if stirred by an otherwise unfelt breeze. For one brief instant I felt a part of the land; I was possessed of the slow, patient strength of the mountains, felt the warmth of the sun on outstretched leaves, drifted aimlessly as a butterfly. For an instant only I was all of those things, and more, then the song was over, and I was back in my own body. The sun now stood completely above the horizon.

I looked over at Ryan, saw a look of wonder on his face. Then he turned to climb down from the outcrop.

"Ryan," I asked as I followed. "Is it always like that?"

Ryan looked up at me, his face still wearing a bemused look.

"No, it is not always like that. This was the first time." Wonder crept into his voice. "Lauren, for a moment I felt like a part of the land. That has never happened before today."

I was silent as we completed our climb. The wonder I felt about what had happened was being replaced by guilt. The past few days, I had been learning about the forbidden Old Religion and had just participated in one of its rites. I had just violated everything I had been taught and committed blasphemy against the Goddess Mar. Ryan noticed my unease.

"What's troubling you, Lauren?" he queried.

"I've been taught my whole life that the Old Religion is wrong," I answered. "That what we did just now is blasphemy. But in all my life, none of Mar's worship songs ever felt like that. That song fit, Ryan, it was natural. I find myself asking how something that felt so natural can be wrong. If it's right, then everything I was taught is wrong. And if what I was taught is right, will not the Keepers sense my disbelief and hunt me down? Ryan, what is right?"

Ryan did not answer. We walked toward our camp, unspeaking, surrounded by the untamed songs of the birds and insects.

"Ryan," I insisted.

The minstrel stopped, spun to face me. The sun was behind him, and I could not see his face. When he spoke, his voice was curt and tinged with anger.

"There are none as sightless as those who blind themselves. Lauren, the answer lies all around you. You must find the courage to open your eyes and see it. More than that 1 will not say."

He turned and continued down the trail. I followed, puzzling over what the minstrel had said. By the time we reached their camp, the incident had been pushed aside.

"It is the Autumn Day of Passages," Ryan said. "A day for celebrating, not a day for anger."

"I agree," I answered. "Ryan, I came with you to learn. What you're telling me makes sense, but it's hard to go against what I've been taught. I'll try to do better."

Ryan smiled at me.

"My thanks to you, Lauren. And I'll try to remember that it is hard to overturn a lifetime of indoctrination. I'll also try to remember one of the first and most important lessons a minstrel learns."

When he didn't continue immediately, I asked, "What's that?"

"Question everything."

Our mood lightened as we broke our fast. We washed down our morning meal with some of the minstrel's hoarded wine in a toast to the autumn and to a bountiful harvest. By the time that camp was struck, we were talking as animatedly as we ever had.

Our trail now led along the heights of the eastern Breton Mountains. The oak, hickory, and chestnuts of the lower elevations had given way to spruce and fir, with occasional stands of yellow birch and mountain ash. In some places, the ground was covered in moss. In other places were rhododendron, blackberry, and huge ferns. We were heading south along a path so narrow that we had to go single file. Occasionally to the left I could see open space beyond the trees that suggested a valley. I asked Ryan about it when we paused for our midday meal.

"That's the Rillian Valley," he answered. "Songhaven is built into a mountain overlooking the valley. We'll be there in a day and a half, perhaps."

"Why is there no road leading to Songhaven?" I asked. "It's like a small city, isn't it?"

"I don't know," he replied. "No one really knows. Songhaven was one of the settlements built by the Lost. Why they didn't construct a road leading to it no one knows. When the Elves discovered it, they realized that the isolation and the beauty of the site made it an ideal place for study. They called it *Calyth*, Haven, and declined to ease access to the place. When the Alomar came, they also sent scholars to study at *Calyth*. Over time, scholarship became more and more the province of the minstrels, and the name of the city became Songhaven. Now Songhaven is part of the Federated Kingdoms and the Alomar Kings have also chosen not to link the city to the others with a road. Doing so would be a massive and costly undertaking."

We set up camp early that evening. We were running out of water and Ryan knew of a spring about half a mile down a side trail where we could replenish our supply. When we woke the next morning, clouds had moved in. The air was cool and moist and the trees on either side were vague shadows. By midday, the clouds had burned off, but the day was still cool. I began to see clearings off the trail to our right and Ryan explained that those were fields where the residents of Songhaven grew their food.

After we paused to eat our midday meal the trail widened until it was broad enough for us to walk side by side.

"We'll make one more stop this afternoon," Ryan said. "There is something I want to show you. Then, when we reach Songhaven, we'll find you a room for the night. Tomorrow morning I'll present you to Ambrose."

"Ambrose!" I exclaimed, startled at the mention of that legendary name.

"He is the Master of the college," Ryan reminded me.

"I know," I replied. "But..." I abruptly changed tack. "How long ago did you study there, Ryan?"

"About twenty-four rounds ago. I was about your age, then. Mylor was Master then. Ambrose was then wandering with his master, a minstrel named Colin. Imagine our surprise when we heard that a minstrel had used prophecy to find Aerman Sorren and to secure the throne for him. Some among the minstrels actually urged Mylor to proclaim Ambrose no longer a minstrel." Ryan paused to laugh. "Instead, when Ambrose returned, the old man resigned and made him Master of the college."

Ryan stopped and tied Dawnstar's lead to a tree.

"We want to go down this side trail," he explained, "and it's too narrow for the horse."

The track we took was almost overgrown. I felt that I was wading through a waist-high sea of bright green fern. Ahead of me, Ryan stopped in a clear space. I could see open sky beyond him and guessed that I was coming to a cliff.

This proved to be true. I joined Ryan at its edge. Below us lay a valley, covered in a deep green forest. Winding among the trees was a river, its exposed portions glinting silver in the afternoon sun.

Without a word, Ryan pointed to the right. My gaze crossed a mile wide void and saw, on a rocky out-thrust of the mountain, the seven, tiered walls of Songhaven, the city of the minstrels.

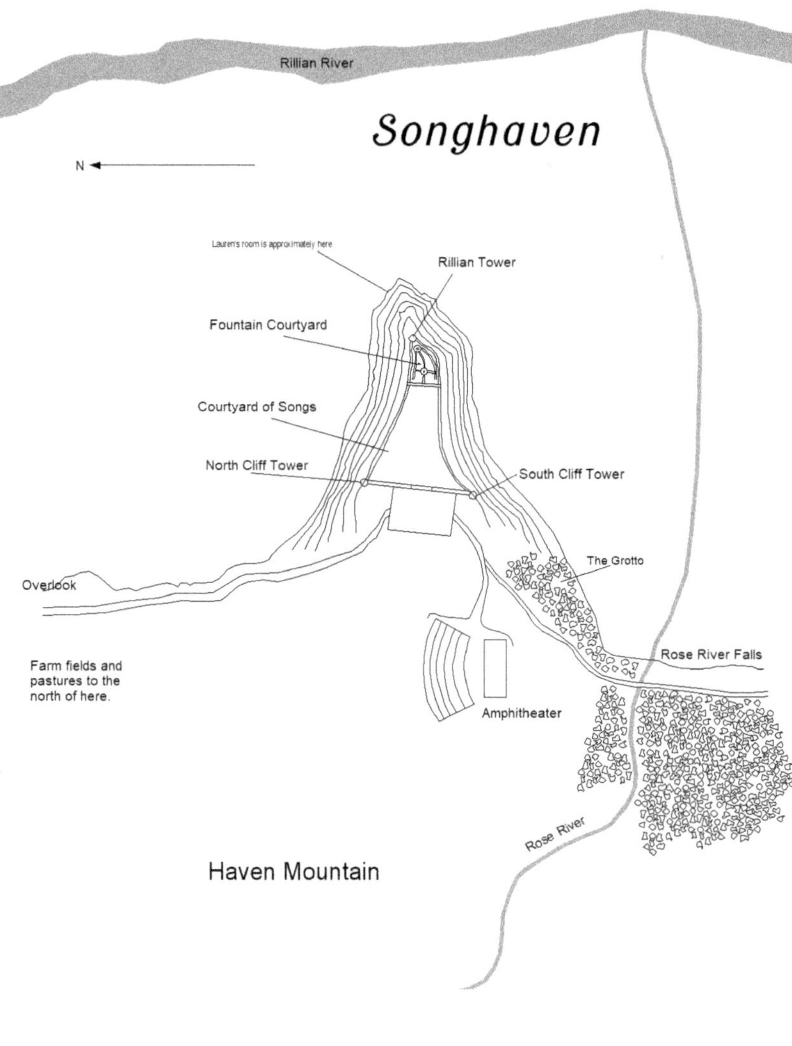

Rillian River
Songhaven
N
Lauren's room is approximately here
Rillian Tower
Fountain Courtyard
Courtyard of Songs
North Cliff Tower
South Cliff Tower
The Grotto
Overlook
Rose River Falls
Farm fields and
pastures to the
north of here.
Amphitheater
Rose River
Haven Mountain

CHAPTER FOUR

I can't describe how I felt in that moment when I first saw the city of the minstrels. Amazement was certainly part of it. The seven natural tiers of storm gray granite had been smoothed by the mysterious people known as the Lost and walls of glittering tan fieldstone erected along the outer edges. A tower of the same stone rose from the farthest outreach of the top tier, and two more like it stood where the walls faded into the mountain.

Reverence was part of it, too. I was seeing something that I had only heard about, something no one else I knew had ever seen. I felt as if I had stepped into a story sung by a minstrel. Some part of me felt that the moment was sacred. Faintly, I could hear the bells of Songhaven chiming the third hour past midday. The sound drifted across the void through the still summer air. Almost, it seemed, they were calling to me, calling me home. Behind me, Ryan softly sang:

> I hear the bells of Songhaven,
> As sweet as dreams in mornings light.
> They ring to greet the rising sun,
> And call me home before the night.

I spun to face the minstrel, excitement welling up in my chest. I could feel myself smiling widely.

"Your song is all this," I exclaimed. "The sound of the bells and everything."

"This place is special," Ryan replied. "There is no other place in the world like it. I tried to capture that in my song."

We were silent a moment, just listening to the breeze whispering its secrets among the trees. I shaded my eyes and looked out across the sunlit valley. It stretched away to the north and south as far as I could see. Something about the forest down there looked ancient, undisturbed.

Curious, I asked, "Does anyone ever go down there?"

"Not much, anymore," Ryan answered. "The Elves used to, long ago. They had a small settlement down there, somewhere near the river. The histories say that the Elven settlement was abandoned shortly after they built it. They claimed that there was something unchancy about the forest down there. In terms of getting down into the valley, there's simply no easy way down within tens of miles of Songhaven. It would require rappelling down cliffs to reach the valley floor. That's actually fortunate."

"Why do you say that?"

"The southern end of the valley opens on the Kelmar Empire. I have no doubt that if they could get to it, they would raid Songhaven. For over a thousand rounds of the seasons, the Kelmar have opted to raid into the Federation through the easier passes to the north. It's also possible that the forest offers some protection."

The minstrel let me take in the view for a few moments longer, then said, "We should go."

Mutely, I nodded and turned back to the trail. As we walked through the sun dappled forest, I was lost in my own thoughts. I was wondering what I would see in the city, where I would sleep, and what I would eat. What if I failed in my lessons? I was suddenly nervous about nearly everything and I felt as if there were a chunk of ice in my gut. Still, I was also excited, and my heart was racing. As we were near to the end of our journey, we quickened our pace.

As we neared Songhaven the path broadened even more until it became a small, gravel-covered road. The forest gave way to a broad grassy meadow. As we exited the forest we paused, and I took in the view. To the left was an unobstructed view of the valley and the prominence that housed Songhaven. The road ran along the cliff's edge to a broad paved area in front of the city gates. Almost straight ahead I could make out some sort of structure beyond the meadow. When I asked, Ryan told me that it was an amphitheater. To the right, the bulk of Haven Mountain rose into the clear blue sky.

Then we were before the gates. I leaned back to take in the entire sixty-foot height of the bell towers. Between them stretched a wall three times the height of a man. The gates themselves were of oak, bound with iron and carved with images of the mountains. They stood open and I could see people moving about within. There were no guards.

Ryan's face was lit with a smile. He gestured toward the open gates.

"Shall we enter, young Lauren?" he asked.

I took a step forward and froze. For an instant the world faded into gray, lightless mists. The walls of the city became insubstantial. From deep within the ghost of Songhaven shone a violet-colored star. Deep in my mind a voice spoke, clear and resonant. It said, *"Endollin."* Then the moment passed, and I stumbled forward.

"Lauren, what is it?" the minstrel asked, his voice full of sudden concern.

I shook my head and passed my hand in front of my eyes. For a fleeting instant, I felt that something similar had happened to me before, but before I could focus on that thought, it was gone, and I found myself reluctant to talk about it. In another heartbeat, I wasn't sure what had just happened.

"Nothing," I said. "I think maybe I'm just over excited. Can we go in now?"

Puzzled, Ryan just looked at me, as if he wasn't sure he believed me. All at once a soft wind sprang up from the valley, came hissing through the trees and swirling around the towers. From far above came a shimmering echo from the bells. Ryan looked up at the towers, then back at me. He looked as if he was about to say something but stopped. With a puzzled look still on his face, he turned and walked through the gates. I followed him.

We entered a large courtyard full of people. Together we stopped and looked around, me with curiosity, Ryan with the satisfied look of a man who has come home. I could now see that a walkway ran along the top of the walls. This was reached by twin sets of stairways located on either side of the far wall, straight ahead. Built into that wall were stables and doors that, I guessed, allowed access to the rest of the city. On either side of the courtyard, shops, inns, and stalls were built against the walls. From behind the far wall, its base out of sight, the third bell tower rose into the clear, blue sky. In the center of the courtyard was a communal well, surrounded by benches, many of them occupied.

The people caught my attention then. A minstrel sat alone on one of the benches, quietly playing her guitar. To my left, a group of people that I assumed to be students sat on the ground around their instructor. Most of the people, though, seemed to be ordinary people who were performing the mundane tasks of supporting the city.

"Ryan, hardly anyone is wearing a sash," I noted with surprise.

Ryan chuckled.

"Of course not, Lauren," he replied. "Do you think everyone here is a minstrel?" He opened his arms to include everyone in the courtyard. "Some of the residents of Songhaven came here to be minstrels. Most don't make it through the training though. Actually, very few do. Many of those who don't earn the blue stay on, crafting instruments or teaching those at lower levels. Many others were born here, grew up here, and chose to stay here, just like any city"

"Lauren," he continued. "Songhaven is both the College of Minstrels and a city. It's a very small city, to be sure, but it's still a city. Some of the people here are minstrels or students training to be minstrels, but most are simply residents of the city. And like the residents of any city, they need farmers to grow their food, they need tailors and healers and smiths and merchants and all the other crafters and tradespeople that any city needs."

"I guess I never thought of that," I answered. "In my mind I always just thought of Songhaven as the College."

"Many people do," Ryan said, smiling, his gray-blue eyes sparkling. He clasped my shoulder in a firm, friendly grasp. "Welcome to Songhaven, Lauren, son of Dalach."

"It's an honor to be here," I replied.

"Ho! Ryan. Welcome home," a loud voice called from the crowd.

It was an exuberant voice, one that matched its owner. The man who hurried toward us resembled nothing more than a colt prancing across a field.

"Cadal," Ryan called back. "How've you been?"

"Right fine, Master Ryan, right fine," He turned this attention to the horse. "Dawnstar, good to have you back. I'll take him now, Master Ryan. His stall has been freshly cleaned, with new hay and all. It'd be a pity to keep him from it."

"Hold a moment, Cadal," Ryan said. "Dawnstar has brought a new student; Lauren, son of Dalach, of the village Cresswell."

Briefly, Cadal ripped his attention away from the horse and regarded me.

"Welcome to Songhaven, young Lauren. I'm Cadal, Master of the Stables, though the horses are the only ones to accord me my title." He grinned. "Don't you be forgetting it on me though, or I'll just send you out on the meanest horse in the Federated Kingdoms."

I could barely contain my laughter.

"I won't forget, Cadal," I promise.

"See you don't," the stable master warned and turned to Ryan. "Shall I have your things sent to your room?" he asked.

"Yes, please, Cadal. I would appreciate that."

The stable master nodded and then led Dawnstar away.

"Ryan, who was that?" I asked, amused.

"Exactly who he claimed to be," Ryan answered. "He tends the stables here. Some say Cadal loves his horses more than any person and I'm inclined to agree. But come, we've got to find the Warder of the City and get you a room. Then I've got to arrange your meeting with Ambrose."

Following Ryan, I entered one of the doors I had seen and started down a wide, well-lit stairway. A huge rocky prominence that thrust out from the side of Haven Mountain had been shaped by wind and weather into seven natural tiers. The Lost had tunneled into the living granite of the mountain and created a warren of residential rooms, storage rooms, passageways, and workshops. According to Ryan, the inner chambers, the ones without windows, were mostly used as workshops, storage rooms, or businesses. The rooms cut into the face of the cliff, the ones that opened onto one of the wide terraces, were all residences. I tried to keep track of where we were going as I listened to Ryan, but I was completely confused by the time we found the Warder of the City in one of the storage rooms. The man was taking inventory of the supplies there. The Warder was an elderly man, withered from long, worried rounds of running the city. His feelings, though, hadn't withered with his body and his greeting was warm and sincere.

"Ryan!" he exclaimed. "What a pleasure. Good to have you back, and with a new friend, I see."

Ryan stepped forward and clasped the Warder's hand.

"It's good to be back, Kayne, for a while at least. This is Lauren, son of Dalach of the village Cresswell. He's soon to be a student here. If you've got a moment to spare, I'd like to get him a room."

Kayne chuckled and sat on a barrel.

"I've always a moment to spare for new folks, Ryan." The Warder turned to me. "He knows that, Lauren. I hate to see new people wandering about with no idea of where to go. It just so happens that I know right off of a room for the young man. It's down on the Tier of Time, right next to Pegara of Han. She's in room 6. Lauren will be in 5. You know where that is, do you not, Ryan?"

Kayne's words were delivered in such a rush that I wondered if the man ever took a breath. My head was already spinning with confusion, but Ryan nodded, smiling.

"Kayne, you always seem to put people where they'll be happiest. I think Lauren will be just fine there."

Once again, I followed Ryan into the maze of passages, determined, this time, to learn my way.

"Ryan," I said. "Please tell me where I'm going."

The minstrel slowed his pace, his expression contrite.

"My apologies," he said. "I tend to forget that when someone first comes here, they don't know where they are."

"The city," he explained, "is divided into seven levels. The highest level is considered the seventh and is known as the Tier of Songs. That's where we came in. The first, or bottom, level is the Tier of Time. In between are the Tiers of Notes, Melody, Chords, Harmony, and Lyrics. Roughly, the names correspond to the elements of music."

"I see," I replied. "But how do I find my way around?"

"The stairway we started on is called the Central Stairway. It joins the seven levels. Sooner or later, all passageways lead back to it. Learn that and the rest is easy."

"You are lucky," the minstrel continued. "The rooms on the Tier of Time have an unobstructed view of the valley. You should enjoy it."

The passageway we followed soon joined the Central Stairway in a circular chamber some 30 feet in diameter. Six passageways opened off the chamber. To our right, the Central Stairway went up. Beyond that were two passageways to other places on our level. The fourth passage, directly across the circle from the first, opened onto the Central Staircase heading down. The last passageway, directly to our left, also led to other destinations on this level. Lamps burned on shelves between each opening and, below each of the lamps, the number 4 was painted on the wall.

"So," I said. "We're on the fourth level?"

Ryan nodded and headed for the stairs to the lower levels. As we descended the minstrel spoke again.

"I'm going to leave you at your room," he said. "Then I'll find Ambrose and arrange for you to meet him. I'll send someone, though, to take you to the evening meal and show you around."

At the stairway's end we stepped into sunshine. The granite had been smoothed into a wide terrace and paved over with flagstones. A fieldstone wall, about waist high to me and as thick as it was tall, ran along the edge. My heart fluttered; the view was as beautiful as Ryan had promised.

After a moment of savoring the scenery, we turned left and passed four doors. At the fifth we stopped and entered.

"This is it, Lauren," the minstrel said. "Make yourself at home. I'll send someone back for you, but now I must speak to Ambrose."

Ryan left, leaving me alone and speechless. I couldn't understand the minstrel's sudden rush. I stood in the doorway and watched as the singer strode away. Then I turned, set my pack down beside the door, and examined my room.

It was deeper than it was wide, with walls of unpainted granite, mostly a light gray, but with specks of black and streaked with white. In the far-right corner of the room stood a bed of carved oak, bare of bed linens. Wooden shelves had been fitted into an opening cut into the wall opposite the bed. In the back wall was a fireplace and, to go with it, in the far-left corner was a box for firewood. The room was fully as large as the main room of my father's house in Cresswell and it was mine, alone.

I dragged one of the chairs away from the table in the middle of the room and sat down at the window beside the door. I couldn't see into the valley from where I sat but, across the valley, I could make out a hazy blue line of distant mountains.

I could hear snatches of conversation as people walked by and a distant voice raised in song, but they made no impression on me. I sat just watching the distant mountains grow darker as the sun set behind me. It seemed to me that I had reached an end point, a resting place. The peace of Songhaven leeched away my cares. I no longer wondered why Ryan had been so rushed, felt no worry about my coming interview with Ambrose, ceased to feel the pain that had driven me from home. No, not from home. From Cresswell. This was now home.

It felt like hours that I sat, not feeling, not caring, only distantly awed as the stars appeared in the deep indigo sky. My silent contemplation of the twilight sky was broken by a soft voice calling my name. I felt as though I had just wakened from a deep sleep, somewhat confused and not sure I'd really heard anything.

"Lauren?"

This time it was a question, followed by the soft rustle of clothing and the metallic squeak of the shield being drawn back from an oil lamp. Flickering amber light filled the room, revealing a young woman holding the lamp.

"Lauren, are you feeling well?" she asked.

With a start, I returned to myself.

"Yes," I stammered as I quickly stood. "Fine. My thanks to you."

In the flickering light, I could see that she was just a few inches shorter than me. Her golden brown hair was rough cut, a little shorter than shoulder length, and fell freely about her face. I've always struggled to describe Peg. She always looked very young to me, almost baby faced, except for her eyes. They were brown with just a hint of green and there was a wisdom in her gaze, a compassion and warmth that seemed out of place in such a young-looking face. The first swell of womanhood was just beginning to strain her simple clothes, a kirtle of red wool over a chemise of white linen.

"I am Pegara of Han," she said. She had the lilting, musical accent of the people of Han. "People just call me Peg, though."

"Peg, I am Lauren, son of Dalach," I replied. "I'm pleased to meet you."

It surprised me to realize just how much I meant that.

"Ryan sent me to find you. He didn't remember to do it until after the evening meal, but I think we can still get you something to eat."

At her mention of food, I realized that I was hungry.

"I am hungry, my thanks to you."

Peg smiled and gestured toward the door.

"Follow me, then, and we'll fix that. We'll also need to get you some bed linens. Then I'll give you the starlight tour of Songhaven."

She paused and set the lamp on the table.

"I'll leave this here," she said. "The city is lit well enough, and you seem to need it. It's not good to sit alone in the dark; it withers the heart. Are you sure that you feel well? You didn't even hear me come in."

"The last few weeks have been so full of doing," I explained. "I think I just needed some time to stop and not do anything at all. I'm fine and I'd love to see Songhaven with you."

Peg smiled shyly and brushed past me on her way to the door. As she passed, I noticed that she wore the delicate scent of lilacs. I stood for a moment, wondering why I should notice such a thing, then Peg called from the doorway.

"Are you coming, Lauren?"

I nodded and followed her, embarrassed, but I didn't know why.

Peg led the way first to a supply room for bed linens and then to the city's refectory and she made me repeat the directions to each as we walked. We stopped at the refectory only long enough to get a basket of bread, cheese, and fruit which I ate as we walked.

We started our tour by returning to the courtyard that Ryan and I had first entered. It was nearly empty now, but there were still groups of people talking or singing. Oil lamps hung from all the walls.

"This is the Courtyard of Songs," Peg said. "In a more normal city, this would be the central square. When the weather is fair, many of the instructors hold their meetings here. The stables are built into that wall."

"That I know," I told her.

"You've met Cadal, then?"

I smiled.

"Yes."

We laughed together for a moment, then Peg reached into my basket and grabbed a piece of cheese. She nibbled on it as she continued.

"Beyond the wall is the Fountain Courtyard. That is probably where you'll meet Ambrose tomorrow. The entrance to the Rillian Tower is there. The two towers behind us are the North Cliff Tower and the South Cliff Tower, respectively."

We continued through the city, level by level, and I hung on her every word. When we reached the Tier of Time, Peg stopped and turned toward me. It suddenly occurred to me that I thought she was beautiful.

"There's one more place I want to show you," she said. "If we're lucky, some people I want you to meet will be there."

We stopped briefly at my room to drop off my new bed linens, and then she led me to where the terrace wall faded into the mountain. There was a gate built into the wall there. Peg unlatched it and stepped through. I followed her onto a gravel path. We walked side by side through a grassy field and into the woods. The moonlight and the trees cast eerie shadows, then gave way as we entered a cleared hollow surrounded by massive spruce trees. Several people were there before us and were seated on benches or on the ground itself.

"This the Grotto," Peg said quietly. "It's not really a grotto, but for some reason some long ago students called it that and it stuck. We get together here quite often, just to talk or practice. The Masters almost never come here."

She turned away and softly called, "Avery?"

"We're over here," a voice replied, just as quietly.

In the silver light of the full moon, I saw a figure in a dark tunic rise from a bench on the far side of the clearing.

"Come, Lauren," Peg said. "I want you to meet my friends."

She walked toward the group around Avery, with me close behind her. My first impression of Avery was height. The youth was so tall that my head came only to his shoulders. His long hair was blonde, bound in a long braid down his back, his thin face pale in the moonlight.

"Who is that with you?" he asked Peg.

"Avery of Canim, this is a new student, Lauren of village Cresswell," she replied. She pointed out the others in the pale argent light. "On the other bench are Denys and Rachel. They sing the most beautiful duets you've ever heard. The one on the ground is Tavis."

At the mention of his name, Tavis rose. His skin was dark, and his black hair was close cropped and tightly curled, clearly marking him as an Altieran, the first I'd ever met. His voice was deep and resonant, his speech almost melodic.

"It is an honor to meet you, Lauren of Cresswell," he said with a smile.

"And an honor to meet you, Tavis. It is an honor to meet all of you," I replied.

"Is Lauren going to join us tonight, Peg?" Denys asked.

"As I said before," Peg said to me, "we like to come out here and talk. Sometimes we just socialize. Other times we discuss the things we are taught," Peg explained to me. "Would you like to join us tonight?"

"I'd like to stay," I said. "If no one minds."

"Then pull up some grass," Avery invited. "And jump in when you have something to say."

Peg sat down on the grass where she was and patted the ground beside her. Feeling suddenly clumsy and oafish, I joined her on the ground. Avery resumed a story that he had been telling when we arrived, something about how that day's guitar lesson had gone completely awry when a sparrow had landed on the neck of the instructor's guitar and couldn't be chased off. The others jumped in with events from their own days. I just sat and listened and observed the others. Avery seemed to be the unofficial leader of the group. He'd been at Songhaven almost a full round of the seasons, longer than anyone else in the group, most of whom had arrived just a few moons before me. He clearly had a forceful personality, open and gregarious. Tavis was the oldest of us. It had taken quite a bit of convincing to get his parents to allow him to travel to the Federated Kingdoms to study with the minstrels. He seldom spoke, but when he did his comments displayed a remarkable insight and quick wit. Denys and Rachel had grown up together in Landfall and it was simply taken for granted that they would eventually marry and travel together.

My gaze, though, kept returning to Peg and several times when I looked her way, I found her watching me. When that happened, she quickly looked away, but then our eyes met, and she leaned toward me just a little and smiled. She looked as if she were about to say something, but Avery spoke up, forestalling whatever she was going to say.

"May I ask you all something serious now?" he asked. A couple of the others nodded their consent. "My Master has told me time and again that minstrels may not carry weapons. I do not understand why not. Do we not have the right to protect ourselves from outlaws and Kelmar raiders?"

There was a moment of silence and then Denys spoke up.

"My Master told me that there is no actual legal prohibition against minstrels carrying weapons. He said that it started out as a custom that has, over time, gained the force of law."

"Maybe so, but some laws are unjust," Avery countered.

"Be practical, if nothing else," Tavis said. "Imagine trying to carry a pack, a guitar and a sword."

"Practicality has nothing to do with it," Avery scoffed. "If it were permitted us, I'm sure it could be done."

"But should it be permitted?" Rachel asked.

"We need to protect ourselves," Avery insisted.

Peg spoke up then.

"Why would we need protection, Avery? All the world knows that minstrels carry little money and that we go unarmed. When was the last time you heard of a minstrel being attacked?"

"Still..." Avery started.

The memory of terrible fear and confusion, the smell of ale, and the flash of naked steel rose in my mind.

"There's something you are all missing," I said softly. They all turned to me. I couldn't look at them and say what I felt I needed to, so I just stared down at the ground as I spoke. "I think that what we need protection from," I went on, my voice tight with pain, "is our own emotions. Have you ever looked into the face of someone who meant to kill you? There's a look in a man's eyes when he kills. I don't believe that a minstrel should ever have that look. I would hate to hear the song that had such feelings at its heart."

The group fell silent, considering what I had said. Some of them looked to have understood. I leaned back and stared at the night sky. The stars seemed so far away, up above the tops of the trees. Then I turned and found Peg watching me, her face full of questions.

"What things have you seen, Lauren, that none of us ever has?" she asked.

I didn't answer. I had been sitting with my legs straight out in front of me, but now I drew them in and hugged my knees to my chest. I struggled to find a way to answer her but couldn't find the words.

"Peg, I'd like to go back to my room now," I said instead.

She was silent a moment, then answered softly.

"I think I understand. Let's go."

We stood and brushed the grass from our clothes. As we turned to go, I remembered courtesy and hesitated.

"I enjoyed meeting you all. I hope I see you again," I said awkwardly.

"Good night, Lauren," Tavis replied. "And welcome to Songhaven."

When we reached my room, we stopped at the door. I felt awkward, started to speak, and then stopped, not sure what I wanted to say. I studied Peg's face and our gazes met. I wanted to say something or to have her say something, I just didn't know what. I opened my mouth to speak without knowing what I would say, but she cut me off.

"Sleep well, Lauren. If you need anything, I'm right next door. I hope I see you tomorrow."

She turned and walked to her room. I stared after her, feeling empty and helpless. I was hoping that she'd look my way before she went into her room, but she simply opened the door and disappeared inside. Feeling disappointed, I entered my room and blew out the lamp. I flung myself down on the bed feeling frustrated. I tossed and turned for a time and then noticed, just before I dropped off to sleep, that the fragile scent of lilacs still hung in the air of my room.

The day dawned bright, with a sky like clear azure crystal. I broke my fast with the leftovers in the basket from the previous night and was leaning on the terrace wall outside my room when Ryan came to find me. The minstrel's expression was grave.

"Have you eaten?" he asked.

I nodded.

"Ryan," I asked, "what is to happen?"

"You are going to meet Ambrose, Master of the Minstrel's College and Avatar of Minstrels. If he sees the minstrel in you as clearly as I, you will be assigned to a Master and begin training. If not, you will, in all probability, be a farmer here. Now come, he's waiting."

He turned and started toward the Central Stairway.

"Ryan, wait," I said. "Something is bothering you. You've been so different since we arrived. What is it?"

The minstrel's dark, angular face looked troubled and, almost, embarrassed. He stopped and turned to face me.

"I didn't know how to tell you and, until we got here, I wasn't sure."

Ryan hesitated and the break in his composure worried me.

"I have to leave tomorrow," Ryan explained finally. "Remember the man I spoke to that morning in Durning?"

I nodded.

"He passed word to me that there's trouble in Meren. I shared that news with Ambrose last night and he agrees that I must go see what is happening there. I didn't know how to tell you."

I was vaguely disappointed. I had assumed that Ryan was going to be there to begin my training.

"Ryan, if you're leaving, does that mean you won't be my Master? I was hoping that maybe you would be."

"I was hoping so, too. Just because I have to go out in the world for a time doesn't mean that you won't be assigned to me, but that decision is up to Ambrose. I had really hoped to stay and get you settled here, but..."

He gestured that we should go. We began climbing the Central Stairway in silence.

"Ryan," I said finally, "I admit that I will miss you. I met someone...um...some people last night, though, who I'm sure will help me get settled in."

"Pegara of Han," he said with a knowing smile.

Quickly, we climbed the Central Stairway and passed through the Courtyard of Songs to the Fountain Courtyard. The Fountain Courtyard was roughly triangular in shape, and we entered in the center of its base. Straight ahead at the point of the triangle was the Rillian Tower, rising high into the limitless sky. The Fountain Courtyard was a garden, where neatly trimmed bushes and trees grew behind carefully built walls of fieldstone. Flowers of all types were in bloom, a well-ordered profusion of color. A neatly manicured gravel pathway led straight into the gardens. Some twenty paces in the pathway entered a large gravel paved circle. On the far side of the circle the pathway continued deeper into the gardens toward the Rillian Tower. To the left and right, smaller pathways wound their ways through the gardens.

What captured my attention, however, was the standing stone. It was a near twin to the one in the center of the Lost settlement near Cresswell. The stone was twice as tall as a man and was obviously unworked. It was dark gray mottled with lighter and darker grays. In places there was a light film of gray-green over the gray, perhaps some kind of lichen. It may have just been my imagination, but the air around the stone seemed cooler than elsewhere and the gray seemed to drink in the bright fall sunlight.

"You told me that the Lost built Songhaven," I said to Ryan as we walked around the circle. "But coming on the stone still surprised me. This courtyard isn't laid out like the other Lost settlements, though."

"It may have originally been," Ryan answered. "The Elves found Songhaven long before they found most of the other settlements. The only other one they had ever seen was *Aennsrhyd*. As with that city, they chose to leave the stone itself but built a garden over whatever was here when they first arrived. If they kept any records of what the courtyard originally looked like, they were lost long, long ago."

As we left the circle, I was sure the air felt warmer. After a short walk, we entered another circle. At the center of this circle was the Fountain. Ambrose was seated on the edge of the Fountain basin, watching the splashing water run down the smooth marble shapes. My first impression of the legendary minstrel was disappointing. Ambrose appeared to be no more than a thin, middle-aged man in a nondescript gray robe. It seemed to me that only his bright blue sash gave him any color at all.

Then Ryan spoke, calling out respectfully.

"Master Ambrose."

The Master looked up and gestured for us to come closer. I took two steps forward and faltered, my first impression of Ambrose shaken to its foundation. Indeed, Ambrose was a middle-aged man, his long once brown hair now mostly gray. His face was lined by rounds of toil and brown with the sun, but his eyes were smoky green, flecked with gold, and they contained such raw power that even I could see it. Those eyes had looked deeply into places most men would have feared to look and had seen there the path that guided the High King to his throne. I stood, awestruck, and waited for someone to speak.

Ryan broke the silence.

"Ambrose, I present to you Lauren, son of Dalach Egan-son, of the village Cresswell."

"So," Ambrose said. "Ryan, leave us please."

I heard Ryan quietly leave but dared not tear my eyes from the Master's smoky gaze. For long moments I stood, not moving, scarcely daring to breathe, waiting for Ambrose to speak. The bells of the city chimed the noon hour. My sense of awe and fear were fading. I shifted my weight slightly. Ambrose raised one bushy gray eyebrow and spoke.

"You grow impatient," he said. "Perhaps you have not the patience to be a minstrel."

I froze, my heart pounding with renewed anxiety.

"You chose not to dress up in finery," Ambrose noted, then cut off my reply with one strong, knobby-fingered hand. "I know, you were going to tell me that it is all you own. Still, I can see that you are one who appreciates simplicity. That is good. Now, tell me, son of War Duke Dalach Egan-son, why are you here?"

For a moment, I did not realize that I had been asked to speak.

"You don't answer," Ambrose said and stood. He was taller than I expected and thin to the extreme. "Curious. Did you fail out of a warrior's training and come here because you felt you had no other choice?"

"Master," I answered, finally finding my voice. "I am here because I wish to learn more than what the Elders of the village teach. I want to sing. I want to visit all the cities of the Federated Kingdoms."

"You do not need to be a minstrel to do those things. A tinker or wandering merchant could do the same."

"You don't understand," I said, surprised by my own temerity. "I didn't fail out of warrior's training. I never wanted to be a warrior. My father forced me to train, and I hated every moment of it. The time I spent with Ryan exploring the Lost settlement, the things I learned from him as we travelled here, those have been the best things in my life."

I paused for just a breath.

"Master Ambrose, please. Being a minstrel is all I've ever wanted to do."

Ambrose nodded. His solemn face suddenly broke open in a joyful grin and his eyes sparkled with mirth.

"That, young Lauren, is all that I needed to hear. Ryan," he called. "Join us."

As Ryan returned, Ambrose extended his hand to me and said, "Be welcome in Songhaven, Lauren, son of Dalach. I do see the minstrel in you."

As our hands met, Ambrose screamed. The Master fell back away from me, clutching frantically at his chest, his weathered face contorted by searing agony. He fell hard against the base of the Fountain, his breath coming in ragged gasps. He gave one more strangled cry, then fainted.

Ryan and I reached him at the same time. Together we bent over the fallen minstrel. I could only watch as Ryan felt the Master's limp wrist for a pulse.

"Fear not, Lauren," he said. "The Master still lives."

At that, Ambrose's eyes fluttered open, their pupils wide. He looked straight at me.

"You," he breathed. He sat up, his alarming gold-flecked gaze still on me. "Is it you?"

I didn't know how to respond to that. Ryan rocked back on his heels, shock showing on his features. Ambrose struggled to stand. Ryan quickly stood and helped him up. Belatedly I stood as well.

"Are you ill?" Ryan asked.

"Only shaken," Ambrose replied. One hand still gripped the front of his ash gray robe.

"But Master..." Ryan persisted.

"Ryan, leave it be," Ambrose commanded. Anger kindled the gold flecks in his eyes. He brushed himself off and straightened his robe before sitting once again on the edge of the Fountain.

"Lauren, have you submitted to the *magenahr*?" he asked.

I glanced quickly at Ryan, who looked surprised, then answered, "Yes, Master Ambrose."

"And what was the result?"

"They told me that I have no magic, that I'm not a wizard."

Ambrose didn't answer, but simply stared at me as if looking for signs that I was lying.

"Where were you tested?"

"In Amersford."

"It was Master Crom who examined you?"

"Yes, sir."

"Did someone go with you to Amersford?"

"My father did."

"And he could verify what you were told?"

"Yes, sir."

Ambrose turned his attention to Ryan.

"Ryan, to your knowledge, has anything unusual ever happened that involved this boy?"

For an instant, I felt the sting of being referred to as a boy, then an ice-cold clot of fear formed in my heart, and I felt the chill spread out through my body. Did Ambrose somehow know what had happened with the tree?

"No, Master," Ryan answered. "Nothing other than his father's attack which I told you about when we first arrived. Master, what is wrong?"

Again, Ambrose did not reply immediately, but sat searching my face. I was sure that he saw my shock and dismay. I didn't understand what was happening and was suddenly afraid that he was going to send me away.

"Ryan, take Lauren to the Master Crafter and get him an instrument." The look of suspicion remained on his face, but his tone softened somewhat. "I cannot explain to you what has happened, but I am well. Lauren, Ryan is to be your Master, but know that I will be watching your progress. Now, both of you go, you've got things to do."

I was feeling relief and confusion in equal measure as we turned and walked away. When we were back in the circle with the stone and out of Ambrose's hearing, Ryan stopped and shook his head.

"Lauren, that was the most incredible thing I have ever seen. I have never seen Ambrose behave so toward a new student. Truth be told, I've never seen him act that way with anyone. What happened between you two while I was out of earshot?"

I quickly described my conversation with Ambrose, trying to gauge Ryan's reaction to what I was reporting. When I finished, he simply shook his head again.

"He was fine until he fell?" he asked.

"Yes. He was like a different person afterward."

"Lauren, I simply do not understand. At least I'm to be your Master. I need to get you an instrument and get your lessons arranged, then I need to prepare for my trip."

Ryan led the way to the workshop of the Master Crafter, deep within the mountain on the Tier of Chords. The Master was a man of my height, with thick, black hair that was tied back to keep it out of his face. His nose was rather too large and looked as if it had been broken long ago. His arms were thin, with wiry muscles, and tended to accent his over large, but nimble, hands. When we entered the workshop, he was shaping a guitar neck from a rough block of wood.

"Taran?" Ryan interrupted.

The Master looked up from his work with soft brown eyes.

"Yes, Ryan?"

"I would like you to meet Lauren. He's just become a student here and Ambrose has sent us to get him a guitar."

The Crafter stood, put aside his work, and wiped one big hand clean of wood dust. He extended it to me.

"Welcome, Lauren, welcome."

I took the Master's hand and felt the first stirring of excitement. I was about to get my guitar. For the first time I realized that it was truly happening; I was to begin training as a minstrel.

"Ryan," Taran asked, "shall I give him his first lesson now? I've time if you want."

"That would be a help to me," the minstrel admitted. "I have to prepare for a trip to Meren. Lauren, can you find your way back to your room from here?"

I nodded; I'd been watching as we came in.

"The Central Stairway is nearby, isn't it?" I asked.

"Yes," Taran replied. "That settles it. Even for such a short time, it was good to have you in my shop again Ryan. Have a good trip and may Garth guide your footsteps and put you on the path back to Mar."

I glanced at Ryan to watch his reaction to Taran's blessing, but the minstrel kept his face neutral.

"Ryan, fare you well," I said. "May your steps be guided."

"My thanks to you, Lauren," Ryan replied. "Step outside with me a moment. I'd like to have a word before I go."

We stepped into the passageway outside the workshop.

"Lauren," Ryan said softly, his blue-gray eyes full of concern. "I do not understand Ambrose's reactions toward you, but it was clear that he was still feeling somewhat hostile toward you when we left him. I wish I could stay and investigate, but the situation in Meren will not wait. While I am gone, do what you are asked and do it well."

"I will," I promised.

"And Lauren, don't do anything unusual."

I looked at Ryan in alarm, but he just smiled. Suddenly I understood why he had answered Ambrose as he had. Though we had never spoken about it but that once, what had happened with the tree was our secret. I smiled back.

"Safe travels, Master," I said.

Ryan nodded and hurried off. I returned to the workshop.

Master Taran guided me to a room behind the shop, where guitars hung in neat rows on specially built hooks.

"Lauren, have you ever played guitar before?"

I shook my head.

"Well, just take a look around and see if any of the instruments catch your eye."

I tentatively stepped forward.

"Is there anything special that I should look for?" I asked.

"Nothing in particular. Look for one that speaks to you. If you see one that appeals to you, I'll check it to make sure that it is sound."

I was just a little overwhelmed. I had never in my life been offered such a choice. There were, perhaps, one hundred instruments hanging in the storeroom. I wandered, looking briefly at each one. The tops varied from a very pale beige to a warm dark tan. Some had a bit of yellow in them. The backs varied as well, some were a reddish brown, others a dark brown, some were a very light brown. The headstocks of some were quite plain, others were inlaid with intricate designs, a few had gemstones embedded in them. The room was silent; we were deep inside the mountain and Taran had left me on my own. To me, all of the guitars were beautiful, but no one stood out from the others.

I was standing in the very farthest reaches of the room scanning the guitars there, but I wasn't really seeing them. I was wrapped up in my own mind, wondering how I would ever choose. As my eyes passed over one instrument, though, it seemed that I could hear the faintest of notes from it, as if some errant breeze had set the strings to humming. But there was no breeze.

That snapped me out of my reverie. The guitar was one of the plainer ones. The top was a dark golden brown, the back medium brown. The headstock was unadorned. The flickering light of the oil lamps reflected from the silver strings and tuning pegs like tiny stars. I was entranced. I wasn't sure if that's what Taran meant when he told me to look for an instrument that spoke to me, but I wanted this one. I reached up and took it from its hanger.

"That is a fine instrument," Taran said when I brought it into the workshop. He took it from me. "See, there are no gaps at any of the joints and the neck is arrow straight. And look here, see the top?"

I nodded.

"That is spruce, young Lauren, and it gets darker with age. See how dark this is, compared, say, to that one over there?" He gestured toward a guitar on one of the workbenches. "This is an old guitar, very old. But it frets true and the older an instrument gets, the better it sounds. You've made a good choice, young Lauren, a very good choice indeed. Now, I'll fit you for a strap and tell you a bit about guitars and how they're made."

Taran went to one of the workbenches and placed my guitar in a stand. He seated himself and gestured for me to do the same.

"As I said," the craftsman continued, "the top of the body is made of spruce. The back of the body, and the neck, on your guitar are mahogany, but other woods are also used. Usually, the back of the body is stained."

"Mine is spruce and mahogany," I repeated.

"A very hard wood is needed for the fingerboard," Taran explained. "We use rosewood for that. This," he said, indicating a piece of white material holding the strings above the fingerboard. "This is called the nut. It, along with the bridge and bridge pins, are made of bone."

Curious, I asked, "Master, why do I need to know all this?"

"Your guitar is a friend to you," the Master Crafter patiently explained. "True, you do not need to know how a man's bones are put together to be his friend, but some knowledge of healing is always helpful."

"I still don't understand."

"On the road," the Master tried again, "should the major parts of your guitar somehow be damaged, there would be little you could do. But, if all you needed was a new bridge or nut, some knowledge of how they are made would be helpful. That, with a bit of bone and a knife, would have you playing again in a short time."

"Now, I see," I said. "Please, show me more."

Eyes alight with the joy of his work, Taran picked up one of his tools. The afternoon passed quickly and wore into evening before I realized it. We ate the evening meal together in the shop. Late that night, when neither of us could work any longer, I returned to my room with my guitar. I also had a guitar stand and a case and strap, both of leather. I was tired, but happy, and I sat for an hour or so, just holding my guitar before I blew out the lamp and went to bed.

When I woke the next morning, I suddenly realized that I had no idea where I was supposed to go or what I was supposed to do. Moments later, however, there was a knock at my door, and I opened it to find both Ryan and Peg waiting for me.

"Well," Ryan said, a smile on his face. "Your first day as my student and you're late getting up."

I wasn't sure what to say and it occurred to me that I was finding myself in that state quite a bit. An answer popped into my head.

"My apologies," I answered. "My teacher left me in the middle of the city yesterday with no clear instructions except to work hard."

Ryan turned to Peg.

"Pretty mouthy for a new student, wouldn't you say."

"Very."

"Well," I said. "Is one of you going to tell me where I need to go, or do I need to wander the city calling out for someone to tell me where to go?"

Ryan answered.

"I've arranged for you to join Peg's cohort, so she can take you around to your classes today. However, I received word this morning that Ambrose wishes to see you again. He'll be waiting for you at the Fountain at midday."

"Do you know why?" I asked.

"No."

"Should I take my guitar?"

"I don't know. You probably should, in case you need it. Lauren, I must go now. Remember what I told you yesterday."

"Safe travels, Master," Peg and I said together as Ryan turned and strode away.

That left us there alone. We looked at each other shyly.

"Peg, I..." I started.

"I missed you yesterday," she said at the same time.

"Me, too. I was in the workshop with Master Taran until late last night and before that was my meeting with Master Ambrose."

"Tell me about that," she said. "How did it go?"

As we walked to breakfast, I described my first full day at Songhaven to her. After that, we attended a class on the history of the Federation and then my first guitar lesson. I was behind the rest of the class, but I showed an aptitude for the guitar and the instructor said that, with some extra practice each day, I could most likely catch up to the other students.

By the time the lesson was done, the fingers of my left hand were sore, and it was nearly midday. After promising to meet Peg in the refectory for the midday meal, I left to meet with Master Ambrose.

I entered the circle around the Fountain just as the bells tolled midday. Ambrose was there before me, seated once again on the base of the Fountain. The minstrel was bent over his guitar, his knobby fingers dancing over the silver strings. As I approached, he looked up and the music ceased. Carefully, Ambrose leaned his guitar against the Fountain and stood.

"Lauren, good day to you. I see that you brought your guitar. May I see it?"

"Good day, Master Ambrose," I answered as I handed over my guitar. I watched mutely as Ambrose sighted down the neck. Then the minstrel tapped the body in several spots and played a few notes. Then he leaned the instrument against the Fountain next to his.

"That is a fine instrument," he pronounced. "You chose well. Now, let us walk."

I followed alongside Ambrose as we strolled silently through the gardens.

"Lauren," he said finally. "I behaved very badly toward you yesterday. For that, I apologize."

I was taken aback. Ambrose was apologizing to me?

"I cannot tell you now why I acted as I did. Someday, perhaps, but not now. I will be following your training, but I do not mean that as a threat. I am certain that it sounded that way yesterday."

He fell silent again for a few moments. We continued walking; Ambrose gazing at the flowers as we passed, me watching him.

"You intrigue me," he admitted when he spoke again. "I would like to meet with you occasionally to talk. I may even have some things to teach you."

"I would like that, Master Ambrose," I replied.

The minstrel stopped to examine a flowering bush.

"What will you be teaching me?" I asked.

Ambrose straightened and turned to regard me.

"Without looking, what color are the flowers on the bush behind you?" he asked.

I frowned and said, "I don't understand."

"The bush behind you. You must have seen it as we walked up. What color are its flowers?"

I shook my head.

"I don't know, Master."

"Lauren, a minstrel is more than just a singer," Ambrose explained. "One of the other things that a minstrel is, both spoken and in song is a storyteller. To be a good teller, you must have an eye for detail. You must always be aware of what is around you. Do not just see. Observe. Take in all the life around you. Do you understand?"

"I think so," I replied.

The Master resumed walking. Before following, I checked the bush. It was a lilac, and the flowers were purple.

"As advisors to kings, minstrels must also know the history of the Federated Kingdoms, as well as its laws," Ambrose continued. "To survive in the wilderness, the lore of the plants and animals must be yours. All these things, and more, Ryan and the others will teach you. I, as you might imagine, have a somewhat unique insight into the politics of the Federation. That I can share."

We walked in silence for several paces and reentered the circle around the Fountain.

"There is more to learn, though," he went on. "The things I mentioned before are mere facts. They, of themselves, are not enough. You must also learn that which will allow you to use what you know for the greatest good."

"What do you mean?"

"Consider a warrior, for example," the prophet answered. "He possesses the knowledge of warfare, of killing and destruction. By itself, that knowledge is neither good nor evil. If the warrior uses it to destroy those he simply does not like, or to further his own selfish ends, that is evil. However, if he uses it to maintain his position against a usurper, or to support his rightful king, that is good."

"I think I see," I said. I was silent a while, pondering what Ambrose had told me. The minstrel stopped and sat on a bench.

"We will speak more of these things later," he said. "Now, I am sure that you have afternoon lessons. Go and enjoy the midday meal."

CHAPTER FIVE

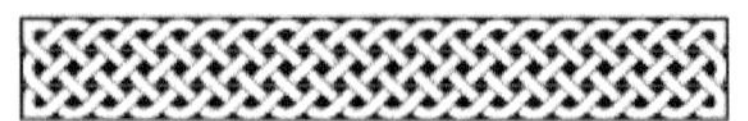

The next rounds of the seasons passed quickly. About a round after I arrived in Songhaven, word reached me that my father had placed Cresswell in Keri's capable hands and returned to his position leading the High King's army. Strange tales of animals born misshapen or behaving in bizarre ways continued to come in from across the Federation as did reports of blighted crops and livestock, but none of that happened near Songhaven. Kelmar raids into Federation territory increased in frequency and ruthlessness. Rumors of unrest in Meren persisted, sometimes including Canim, sometimes not, constant whispers of treachery, but their kings were always overtly supportive of High King Aerman Sorren. Most troubling of all was that more and more we heard that the preaching of the Repentant was beginning to include subtle hints that the troubles plaguing the Federated Kingdoms were due to the failings of the kings, the High King most of all.

My friendship with Peg strengthened and deepened and, when not at our lessons, we were almost as inseparable as Denys and Rachel. I also grew close to the others: Avery, Denys and Rachel, and Tavis. Our mornings were spent studying with the minstrels of Songhaven, committing to memory a vast repertoire of teaching songs, historical ballads, seasonal songs of thanksgiving, and popular songs for entertainment. We also studied the history and laws of the Federated Kingdoms. For those of us who could not read and write before coming to Songhaven – me and Tavis – we were taught those skills.

Afternoons were spent with our individual Masters, studying whatever they chose to teach us. My lessons with Ryan tended to occur outside the walls of Songhaven, up on the slopes of Haven Mountain or in the forest to the south of the city. Ryan was often away, however, on trips to one or another of the cities of the Federation, though several people mentioned to me that he was often seen heading south from Songhaven when he left. I found that odd, because there was nothing but wilderness south of the city, but the few times that I asked about those trips Ryan simply avoided answering.

A moon or so after I arrived, Ryan returned from Meren. The next day, we hiked into the woods south of the amphitheater to the Rose River. We followed the river upstream to where the ground began to slope up toward the summit of Haven Mountain. There, hidden in an outcropping of granite boulders overlooking a small waterfall, was a shrine to *Tael*.

Ryan stooped down, scooped up a handful of water, drank most of it, and then spilled the rest at *Tael's* feet. I followed suit, but then asked a question that I had been thinking about for some time.

"Ryan, why do you worship the Old Ones?"

He turned to look at me, a puzzled look on his face.

"I don't worship them," he responded. "Why do you think that I do?"

"The thanksgiving song you taught me. It called for praise of them."

He smiled.

"Now I understand," he said. "You were raised to worship Mar and the Repentant always use the word praise to mean worship. Praise, though, also means to express approval or commendation."

"But..." I started, but he cut me off.

"Lauren, sit. We should talk."

I sat on a large rock on the bank of the river. Ryan sat on a tree that had fallen across two rocks. For a moment, we listened to the sound of the falling water.

"The Old Ones are not gods," he said. "If you think back on everything I've ever said about them, I've never said that they were. I know not what kind of being they are, but they are not gods. They do not demand worship, as does Mar. They are powerful and they are ancient and they are living beings. As such, they deserve the same respect that we owe to any living being. I pour water for *Tael* not as a form of worship, but as a form of respect."

"But what about Mar?" I asked. "If she is a god and she created the whole world and everything in it, why don't you worship her?"

"You just came close to quoting the *Torun Mar*. What do those scriptures say about the creation of the world?"

"The *Torun Mar* says that Mar created the world out of the nothingness of the Void. There is nothing in the world that Mar did not create and, therefore, the whole world owes Mar love and worship."

"So, Mar created everything in the world?"

"Yes."

"And Mar is all powerful?"

"That is what the *Torun Mar* says. It was dictated by Mar herself."

"Yes, it was. So, if Mar is all powerful, would it be reasonable to assume that the world is just exactly the way she intended it to be?"

"Yes?" I answered hesitantly. I suddenly wasn't so sure of myself. It was clear that Ryan was building to something.

"The Old Ones are in the world. If Mar created the world and it's just the way that she intended, then if the Old Ones are evil, Mar must have intentionally created evil."

"But..." I started and fell silent. My mind was racing. Everything that Ryan had said about Mar was directly from the *Torun Mar*, but the Old Ones were never mentioned in the scriptures. What Ryan had just said, though, was perfectly logical, but a benevolent god – as Mar was said to be – would never intentionally create evil.

"Lauren," Ryan said softly. "I just shook your world to its foundations. This will not be the last time, either. You have been taught one very narrow view of the world. My intent is to make you examine that point of view, to think things through to their logical conclusions. I'm going to ask you to question what you think you know, to learn more about everything you think you know, and to learn about things that you don't even know exist. I'm going to push you well beyond the simple recitation of facts and the singing of songs."

He fell silent and we simply listened to the falls for a brief while. When he spoke again, he didn't look at me.

"If you don't think you can do that, you can go to Ambrose and request another Master. Do you want to do that?"

I didn't hesitate.

"No. I want to learn from you, Master Ryan."

About once each moon, I also met with Ambrose. His interest in me still puzzled me, but I enjoyed our lessons, which focused on the politics of the Federated Kingdoms. One afternoon in my second round, we were meeting, as usual, in the Fountain Courtyard. We were seated on the base of the Fountain, one of Ambrose's favorite places. Peg's Master, Katryn, had been sent out to Meren, for new rumors had come in that trouble was brewing there, so Meren was on my mind that day.

"Master Ambrose, why is Meren so problematic?" I asked. "Since I've been here, four minstrels have been sent out because of trouble there."

Ambrose turned his gaze on me. I still found his smokey green eyes with their flecks of gold unnerving.

"Why do you think?"

I thought for a moment on all I knew of the kingdom of Meren.

"I know that in 553 Meren was made a principality after their king had High King Aran murdered. But that was nearly 460 rounds of the seasons ago. Could they still be angry over that, even though their king was restored in 647?"

Ambrose smiled an indulgent smile.

"That may be part of it, perhaps the part that most of their people remember. Think, though. Their king had Aran killed. Do happy liegemen kill their kings?"

"No," I had to admit.

Ambrose dipped his fingers into the water, a faint smile on his lips.

"Thirty-five rounds after Sorren was made High King by the Keepers, Meren rebelled. The killing of Aran was the fifth time that they attempted to overthrow the High King's line. The people of Meren are a fiercely proud and independent lot, convinced of their own importance and superiority over others. Their relationship with the Federation has always been a somewhat tenuous one. They resent anyone ruling over them and deep down they believe that they would be better off on their own."

"Then why are they still part of the Federation?"

"Because they also know, deep down, that they need the rest of us."

Ambrose stood.

"Come," he said. "I have several books in my room that discuss this issue. I think you will find them interesting. I would be willing to lend them to you if you would like."

"I would like that, Master. My thanks to you."

It was not long after that that I sang with Peg for the first time. I was in the Courtyard of Songs, practicing the change from a G chord to a modified B minor in a song that Ryan was teaching me. After several successful attempts, I decided to just play something and I chose *The Highland Skies*, an uplifting song about a shepherd from the Highlands who left the simple life there for the excitement of life in Badon, but who was drawn back by the Highland's rugged beauty. As I was beginning the second verse Peg, who had quietly come up behind me, put her hand on my shoulder and joined in, singing a harmony part that made the song soar. Smiling, she stepped around and joined me on the bench. I found myself smiling in return and subtly altering my vocal to fit better with the part she was singing. In that moment, there was no one else in the world but us two, weaving our voices together as one. I had never experienced anything so intimate. As we went into the second repetition of the chorus at the end of the song, I went for the high note that I usually didn't even attempt, but with Peg's support, I hit it solidly. As the final chords died away, we sat staring into each other's eyes. I knew in that moment that I loved her.

"Are you two alright?" Tavis asked, breaking the spell.

It was only then that we became aware of the applause and cheers of the crowd who had gathered to listen to us.

One spring day during my third round, we were all gathered around Master Elissa in the Courtyard of Songs. Her passion was history, and she was telling us about the uprising in Marsden Forge in 881. High King Roth had raised taxes to fund repairs of the Great South Road between Badon and Amersford. The people of Marsden Forge felt that they shouldn't have to pay for a road they didn't use and revolted. Roth died trying to put down the uprising. Suddenly, Elissa changed the subject.

"What," she asked us, "is the main role of a minstrel?"

We all looked at one another, not sure how to answer. Elissa was known for asking questions that had no easy answers.

"I've always had the impression from my Master that a minstrel's main role is communication," Rachel answered.

"But if that is all it is," Avery asked, "wouldn't a simple messenger do, without having to go through rounds of study?"

"It is the rounds of study that make us better than a messenger," Peg answered.

"So, we've practiced," Avery retorted, "and can repeat the message after only one hearing."

Peg shook her head and pushed her golden-brown hair from her face with delicate, tapered fingers.

"You are missing the point, Avery," she explained. "No one gives a minstrel a message to carry. We listen, gather information, and pass on only what is important. Our rounds of study help us to judge what is important."

"Is that really necessary, Peg? Wouldn't an efficient network of messengers replace us?"

"No!" I said, before Peg could answer. "A messenger will simply pass on the message, nothing more and nothing less. For example, the message may be that Amersford intends to raise its grain prices. Useful, perhaps, to a merchant, but not to a troubled king. A minstrel, however, would see all the ramifications of the price increase and be able to advise the king."

"So, we're more advisers than messengers?" Avery asked.

"Yes," Peg and I both agreed.

"But don't kings have other advisors?" Elissa interjected, "If a minstrel is nothing more than an advisor, why are there minstrels?"

Tavis spoke up then.

"Minstrels do many things, Master Elissa. We are, indeed, advisors. But we also teach, especially in the smaller villages where no teaching would otherwise occur. We also seek new knowledge, such as Master Ryan's recent treatise on the Lost settlements. We also entertain. Is it possible that there is no one main role for a minstrel?"

Elissa stood, a broad smile on her face.

"I think, Tavis, that it is not only possible, but highly probable. We are done for the day. I will see you all tomorrow."

As she left, we all stood.

"I have to meet with the Master Crafter," Avery said. "I need new strings for my guitar. I'll see you all later."

One by one, the others left too. Soon, Peg and I were the only ones left.

"Master Ryan is away, so I have no commitments this afternoon," I said.

"Master Katryn is also away," Peg responded. "So, I'm free as well."

In my eyes, Pegara had grown more beautiful with the rounds. The pale-yellow gown she wore was cut to accent the soft swell of her breasts and clung to the gentle curve of her hips. We joined hands and I felt a trembling deep inside. There was a tension building between us. I looked into her deep brown eyes and saw my feelings mirrored there.

"Let's take a walk," I said, my throat suddenly dry.

Hand in hand, we left the Courtyard of Songs through the main gates and turned south past the amphitheater. We crossed the wooden bridge over the Rose River and left the road to wander through the green shaded woods. Neither one of us spoke.

The woods opened onto a large field. The grass came to our knees and was dotted yellow and violet with sunflowers and thistle. The cloudless azure sky arced far above us, with only a single hawk lazily drifting in all its vast expanse. The sun burned hot.

In the middle of the field, we stopped and faced each other, still holding hands. The sunlight brought out golden highlights in Peg's hair, suffused her with a golden glow that made her beauty radiant. I was confused, overwhelmed by feelings I didn't understand.

Peg simply said, "I love you, Lauren."

"And I love you, Peg."

We melted together in a kiss that seemed to go on forever. When it ended, we stepped back slightly. Peg's gown slipped to the ground between us. Within my chest, my heart ached, and I gathered her to me, felt her yielding softness against me. For a long while, all I was aware of was the warmth of the sun on my skin, the smell of the crushed grass mingled with Peg's scent of lilacs, and the joy as our bodies moved together. When finally we were finished and lay side by side in the grass, I raised myself up on one arm to gaze at Peg. She was flat on her back, her eyes closed, a slight smile on her face. I still cannot find the words to describe how I felt in that moment, but the image of Peg lying amid the grass and the wildflowers with the sunlight dancing over her naked body is with me still.

In the fall of that same round, I was in the forest along the upper end of the Rose River with Ryan during one of our afternoon meetings. Though it was late in the season, the day was unusually warm, and we were enjoying a ramble through the woods without heavy cloaks.

"Lauren," the minstrel said. "See this plant?"

He held up a saw-toothed leaf for me to examine.

"This is jewelweed," he continued. "It is not very remarkable in appearance, but the sap of jewelweed relieves the itch of poison ivy and other skin irritations."

I stepped away from Ryan, intending to go around the plant for a better look. A dry rattle stopped me in my tracks; a timber rattlesnake lay coiled at my feet.

"Lauren, back away quickly but carefully," Ryan hissed.

I jumped backwards just as the snake struck. Fortune was on my side; the snake's fangs closed on empty space. Leaving the snake and the jewelweed to themselves, we hurried away through the forest and came to rest on a large rock overlooking a deep pool in the river. My fear was subsiding, replaced with anger.

"Ryan, we should have taken a rock and killed that snake," I said.

"Why?"

"Because snakes are evil."

"No, Lauren," Ryan corrected me. "Some snakes are dangerous, but none of them are evil."

"But Master..." I started, but Ryan cut me off.

"No, Lauren, listen," he said firmly. "You have heard me speak of the Song of the Seasons, correct?"

I nodded; he had mentioned it several times in the past.

"The Song," the minstrel continued in a softer voice, "is the music our world makes as it moves in its path. All living things, trees, animals, people, even snakes, all are notes in the harmony of the Song of the Seasons. Each is singing the note that nature meant for it to sing. Thus, a snake may be dangerous, but it is not evil. It is only acting according to its nature."

"Then you are saying that there is no such thing as evil?" I asked, my curiosity aroused.

"No. People can be evil, for only to people is it given to choose the note they sing. If someone chooses to sing in consonance, that person is good, that person is acting according to nature. If, however, a person chooses to sing in dissonance, that is evil, for the person is acting against all of nature."

I fell silent, pondering what I had heard. Though the day was warm, the rock we sat on retained the fall chill and I could feel the bite of it through my clothes. A scarlet leaf dropped from the tree overhead and drifted into the lake. I watched and wondered if death, too, was a part of the Song.

"Ryan?"

"Yes, Lauren?"

"How does death fit into the Song of the Seasons?"

"As the notes in our music sound only for a given length of time, so too the notes of the Great Song."

We let the quiet sounds of the fall day drift over us. I lay back on our rock and studied the multicolored roof of the forest. This time it was Ryan who broke the silence.

"Lauren, the Autumn Day of Passages is next week. Since the summer, your performances have been excellent. You may not know this, but you've come to be known throughout the city. The Warder and Ambrose asked me to see if you would sing at the celebration. Would you?"

Excitement and pride swelled my chest, but I stayed lying down.

"Do you think they would mind if it was a duet?" I asked.

A puzzled frown touched Ryan's face.

"Whom did you have in mind?"

"Pegara of Han."

"Ah, I see," he said with a smile. "I have heard that you and Houl's daughter have grown quite close."

I sat up quickly. I couldn't believe what I'd just heard.

"What?" I demanded. Shock and disbelief washed over me.

Ryan looked puzzled.

"I said that you and Pegara had become close."

"You said," I cried, "that Peg is the Princess of Han."

"Yes. She is."

Sudden understanding hit Ryan.

"You didn't know?" he asked.

"She never told me," I acknowledged. "She never told me."

"Lauren, you've known her for three rounds of the seasons. How could you not know?"

"I knew that she was *a* Pegara of Han. I didn't know that she was *the* Pegara of Han. None of my lessons ever mentioned that the Princess of Han was training to be a minstrel. Why would a princess train to be a minstrel?"

"She has three older brothers. That makes her fourth in line for the throne. The odds that she will be called on to take the throne of Han are relatively small."

I just looked at him, dismay growing in my chest.

The flickering amber light of the lamp filled the room, making the shadows dance. I sat at the table in my room, my twelve-stringed guitar in my lap. Idly I strummed gentle, melancholy chords that echoed the tears welling up in my eyes. I didn't answer when someone knocked softly on my door.

The knock was repeated; still, I didn't answer. The door opened and Pegara stepped in, wrapped in a gray shawl against the autumn chill. She wore a gown of sky blue.

I looked up and a single tear slid down my cheek. Peg's greeting died on her lips and, instead, she simply said my name, "Lauren?"

I said nothing and hung my head to look at my guitar. Then I gently picked some opening notes and sang:

> How do you talk to a princess?
> Say I love you to a queen?
> Is it my place to do so,
> Or should I not be heard but seen?
> I'm just a lowly minstrel,
> Wandering through the night.
> Should I say I love you,
> Or turn my head and cry?

I fell silent. The last chord hung in the air, then died away. Peg lowered her gaze.

"So," she said softly. "You know."

"I do," I answered and paused. "Now."

Peg took off her shawl, hung it over the back of my other chair, and sat down. She refused to meet my gaze.

"Why didn't you tell me?" I demanded, my voice soft, but strained.

Peg looked up. Tears filled her brown eyes.

"I knew it would create a distance between us. From the night we met, I knew you could be special to me, and I didn't want that distance to be there. Would you have spoken to me if you had known?"

"But your father is the King of Han," I cried.

"And you are nothing but a farm boy," Peg said.

"Right," I painfully agreed, completely missing the sarcasm in her tone.

"No! You are the son of War-Duke Dalach Egan-son. Lauren, your father commands mine in battle."

"Your father remains a king. Mine is now a farmer."

"Was a farmer," she corrected me.

Peg reached across the table and laid one soft hand on my arm. She smiled, though her eyes were still full of tears.

"Lauren, my father inherited his title. It is his, whether he deserves it or not. Your father earned his. That has to mean something. Besides," she added, "what does it matter what our fathers are. We are both minstrels and, therefore, equals."

"There is that," I admitted.

I leaned my guitar against the table and spent several minutes studying the tuners. Then I looked at Peg.

"Why did you come here tonight?"

"I came here, you fool," she said, with no mockery in her voice, "to share your bed."

We never noticed, late that night, when the lamp gave one final flicker and went out.

I woke the next morning with Peg's arm draped over my chest. Gently, so as not to wake her, I moved it and left the bed. The autumn chill had seeped into my room, and I quickly searched for something to wear. As I pulled on my trousers, I noticed that sometime during the night, Peg had slipped on my dark brown tunic.

The tunic left her shapely legs bare, and the cold quickly raised little goosebumps all along them. As I looked down at her, I felt the strange mixture of protectiveness, possessiveness, and affection that I called love. Asleep, her hair in disarray, Peg looked small and vulnerable. Gently, I pulled the blanket over her and tucked it down. She stirred softly and I kissed her cheek.

"It's all right," I whispered. "Sleep on my love."

As quietly as I could, I crossed the room to the wood box. Soon, I had started a small blaze in the fireplace. After warming myself for a few moments, I selected a book from the shelves, sat down at the table and unrolled it to study.

An hour later, when Peg woke, the room was warm. She pushed off the blanket and sat up.

"Good morning, my love," she said in a drowsy voice.

I turned. Seeing her in nothing but my tunic, her golden-brown hair disheveled, made me want to take her in my arms and never share her with the world. I smiled.

"What?" Peg asked.

"You dressed like that is a sight more beautiful than the mountains," I answered.

Peg laughed. In her bare feet, she padded across the floor and flung herself into my lap. She planted a kiss on my mouth.

"What shall we do today?" she asked.

"Can we just stay here for a while?" I asked. "Until my midday meeting with Ambrose, I have no place to go."

"Nor do I," Peg replied as she got up and flounced back across the room to the bed. "But I don't know if I'll stay. You just want to keep me here and stare at my legs."

I laughed as I stood to follow her.

"You might be right," I said. "But I'll never admit it."

At that, Peg dropped onto the bed, letting the tunic rise to reveal all of her legs, and a good bit more. I flung myself down beside her and took her in my arms.

"You're a terribly saucy wench for a princess," I noted.

Peg laughed.

"Only when I'm with farm boys," she said.

I arched my eyebrows in mock surprise.

"And how many farm boys have you been with?"

"I'll never tell."

"Oh, I think you will," I cried and began tickling her. Laughing, Peg tried to tickle me back, and we wrestled around. Trying to escape her jabbing fingers, I scooted back and fell out of the bed.

"I win," Peg said between laughs. "You got out of the bed."

"The fire is going out," I noted. "I just got out to build it up."

"Sure you did."

I added several logs to the dwindling blaze and returned to my seat at the table.

"We never did decide what to do today," I noted.

"I thought I was going to stay here and let you stare at my legs."

"You are a shameless wench," I replied. "But I love you anyway."

Peg laughed again and sat up, cross-legged, in the middle of the bed.

"Lauren?" she asked in a serious tone.

"Yes, love?"

"What do you and Master Hair do during your meetings? I rarely see you take your guitar."

"Master Hair?" I asked. "Who's that?"

"You haven't heard? Some of the new students have started calling Master Ryan that because his hair is always loose and all over the place."

I just shook my head. Ryan seemed to pay little attention to his hair. Peg asked again, "So, what do you do in your meetings?"

I pushed the unrolled book into the middle of the table and propped my legs up.

"We talk," I answered. "He tells me about different things and questions me about previous lessons."

Peg's brown eyes shone with interest.

"What do you talk about?" she insisted.

"Anything, everything," I replied. "How to use plants for medicine. History. Philosophy. Yesterday we talked of the Song of the Seasons."

"What is that?"

"You've not heard of the Song?" I asked.

"No," Peg admitted.

I was surprised, and it suddenly occurred to me that I was, perhaps, receiving a very different education at Ryan's hands. We hadn't discussed the Old Ones often since my arrival in Songhaven, but he had taken me to the hidden shrine to *Tael* along the Rose River and the ruins of a shrine to *Wyn* at the summit of Haven Mountain. I wondered if telling Peg about the Song would betray Ryan's secret beliefs. She was looking at me expectantly, eagerly, her love shining in her eyes, and I knew that I couldn't lie to her or hide things from her.

Briefly, I explained the Song to her as Ryan had to me. Peg listened with rapt attention.

"Not once has Master Katryn mentioned such a thing to me.," she said, shaking her head. "All we do is review my guitar and history lessons. Does Ryan not teach you guitar at all?"

"Sometimes," I answered. "But he says that playing guitar is only part of being a minstrel and maybe not the most important part."

For a moment, Peg was silent. The look on her face was strange.

"I cannot explain it," she said. "But I feel that someday, Lauren, you may be more important than Ambrose himself."

A sudden cold draft swept through the room, making me shiver. We both turned to the corner in surprise for, as Peg spoke, the draft had set my guitar's strings humming, a faint, discordant sound.

"Lauren," she appealed as the ghostly sound died away. "Lauren, come here and hold me."

I went to the bed and took her in my arms. Inexplicably, I was scared.

"I know that someday you'll leave Songhaven," she said. "Promise me," she pleaded. "Promise me that, when you do, you'll always come back to me."

"I promise," I said, hoping it was true. "I promise."

"I'll never get this," I exclaimed. I set my guitar aside in disgust, almost slamming it against the table. The strings rang discordantly. I felt a momentary pang of regret, and then my frustration overwhelmed it. "You would think," I continued, as I stalked around Ryan's room, "that after five rounds I could learn to play a simple passage after an hour's practice."

"But it's not a simple passage," Ryan replied calmly. "Let it rest for a while and we'll come back to it."

I did not reply. I stood staring out the window, watching a distant bird circling. Ryan, like most of the Masters of the minstrel's college, had a room high in the Rillian Tower and the window looked out over the valley. The late afternoon sun was behind us, and the valley floor was in darkness. An undefined anger with myself gripped me and I spun to face my Master.

"Why am I here?" I demanded. "Why do you keep me around?"

Ryan looked taken aback by the sudden outburst. I didn't usually behave this way, but I felt so incompetent.

"Lauren, I don't understand," he answered. "What's wrong? If it's this passage, don't worry. It took me weeks to get it down. Master Sean says that you are rounds ahead of where you should be."

"I should be better," I insisted.

For a moment, I just glowered at my Master, then turned back to the window. After a moment, Ryan came to join me.

"Lauren, I've known you now for five rounds and I think I'm beginning to understand you. For some reason, you are not sure of your own ability. To compensate, you work much too hard. You were moons behind your friends when you first arrived, and you couldn't even read or write. You not only caught up to them within a few moons, you've now surpassed some of them. You should be proud of yourself, not complaining about your lack of progress."

The sun had set, and the first faint stars were visible. A soft breeze wafted in the window, bringing with it a faint smell of pine.

"Did I do the right thing in coming here?" I asked quietly. "I love it here, but maybe I should have been a warrior as my father wanted."

Ryan put a hand on my shoulder.

"You are singing your proper note in the Song of the Seasons," he answered. "You were meant to be a minstrel."

The spring day was heavy with the weight of the impending storm. Massive black clouds were crowded in the sky and thunder rumbled in the distance. I was with Ambrose in the Master's study, at the very top of the Rillian Tower. He had begun starting each of our meetings by asking me to answer questions about some topic that had come up in passing in our previous meeting. That day, he had asked me about High Queen Adelene, the granddaughter of Sorren Stronghand. She had been the third of Sorren's line to rule. Sorren and his son Dreden had spent their time as High King repelling Kelmar attacks and overseeing the construction of the city of Badon. It was Adelene who had established the basic structure of the Federation's government. She had founded the High King's Council and with their help had put in place a system of taxation to fund projects that would benefit all the Federated Kingdoms. The first of those was construction of the beacon towers between Han and Badon.

I had been at Songhaven for six rounds of the seasons. I stood beside the unglazed window and watched the approach of the storm. I turned to find Ambrose watching me.

"That was an excellent answer," he said when I finished, his voice as melodious as ever. "Now, tell me what you know of the Great War."

I turned from the window, my brow furrowed in concentration.

"It was begun by the Elves in an attempt to gain dominion over men," I answered. "At first, they were successful, because the Alomar kingdoms were independent of one another, and each fought as a separate unit. Under Sorren Stronghand they united, and the Elves were beaten back to the Lellarin Plains, all the way to the gates of the city of *Elsgard*. There, the Elves rallied, and the battle raged for days, neither side able to gain the advantage. Then the Keepers, seeing the plight of their servants, took on the forms of men and came to Sorren's aid. With their power, the Elves were driven back and defeated, and the kingdoms of the Alomar saved."

Ambrose nodded and stroked his new beard. The Master was as vigorous as ever, but his hair had now gone completely gray.

"Very good," the older man said, "as far as it goes. There is more to the story than most people know."

That piqued my curiosity. I moved away from the window and sat down in a chair near my teacher.

"What I am about to tell you must remain secret," Ambrose continued. "Other than the kings, only one or two people know of it in each generation. I had it from my Master, Colin, as he lay dying of a brigand's wounds. It is a most dangerous secret, but I believe you are the one to have it from me."

I was on fire to learn what Ambrose was speaking of but forced myself to wait patiently as the minstrel got up and poured himself a goblet of wine. I declined an offer of wine for myself and leaned forward, intent and eager, as Ambrose reseated himself.

"The last Elven King was named Lorrestian," the prophet said. "Like me, he was a prophet, the only one of that accursed race to be so blessed. He saw, as the war began that it would fail. In desperation, he looked farther ahead in time, saw a thing that brought joy to his black heart."

Ambrose paused for a sip of wine. He set aside his goblet and leaned toward me. The tension of the approaching storm filled the room, made the air feel like lead and muted the minstrel's voice. My neck and shoulders were tense, and my head began to ache.

"He saw the coming of a man so powerful," Ambrose continued, "that he could challenge the rule of Mar and the Keepers and destroy the world. He named this abominable servant of evil the Lawbreaker and forged a ring and a sword that would answer to his power. It is said that they will wake when the Lawbreaker comes into the world."

The minstrel fell silent. I was amazed for I had never heard even a rumor of the tale Ambrose was telling.

"Where are the ring and sword?" I asked. My heart was racing and the ache in my head intensified.

Ambrose hung his head and hesitated before answering.

"I know not," he said. Something told me that he was holding something back.

The tension in the room was near its breaking point. I stood and paced fretfully back to the window, stretching my shoulders to try and ease the pain in my head.

"Then how are we to know when this doom is upon us?" I asked.

A wasp skidded in from the wind and managed to gain a precarious hold on the windowsill in front of me. Startled, I stepped back, and my head reeled, for the world changed around me.

I was alone in darkness. Power, huge and malignant, beat me down, crashed over me in overbearing waves from the being in the shape of the wasp. Terror wrung my soul, sent a dagger of ice deep into my chest. I gave one terrified, wordless cry and felt myself falling as the darkness overtook my mind.

I woke, aroused by a bitter smelling herb that Ambrose held under my nose. I coughed once and sat up, forcing the herb away as I did so. Rain lashed the outer walls, and an occasional drop slipped through the window to land on us.

"What happened?" I asked.

The prophet's smoky gaze was thoughtful, his face troubled.

"You staggered back from the window and screamed. Then you collapsed in a faint. You've been out just a few moments. Lauren, what did you see?"

"A wasp..." I started, then hesitated, unsure of how to explain what I'd experienced.

"A wasp?" Ambrose said wryly, glancing at the window. "Well, it's gone now."

"Ambrose, do not jest," I pleaded. "I saw a wasp land on the sill. Then, suddenly, it seemed as if it was not a wasp, but some powerful being that somehow at the same time had the shape of a wasp. It beat me down, held me down with a boot on my neck, and threatened to inject poison at the base of my skull to kill me. Then nothing, until you thrust that weed under my nose."

Ambrose stood and crossed the room to a series of shelves full of jars. He placed his herb into one, sealed it, and turned back to me, his gaze suddenly piercing.

"Lauren," he asked, his tone intense, "do you dream true dreams? Are you, too, a prophet?"

"No," I answered as I shakily climbed to my feet. "Not that I have ever remembered. And I failed at the *magenahr*."

I sat down in one of the chairs and cradled my head in my hands.

"I think I'd like a glass of wine now, Master," I said.

As Ambrose was pouring, I returned to my question.

"Master, how will we know when this doom is upon us?"

Ambrose set the empty goblet down and turned to face me. For the first time, I noticed the lines of care etched deeply into the Master's face. The prophet's voice trembled as he spoke.

"I fear," he said, "that somehow that doom is already upon us."

Another round passed. Ambrose and I did not speak of the Lawbreaker and the doom of the Federated Kingdoms again during that time. Shortly after his revelation I tried several times to bring it up, but each time he changed the subject without answering. Moons passed, life went on much as it had, and it began to feel almost as if I had dreamed that conversation. My friends and I completed our training and spent a moon preparing for our final examination before the assembled Masters of the College of Minstrels. Each of us spent two days before the Masters, with nothing but our guitars, and any Master could ask us anything: to play a particular teaching song, to debate some point of law, recount some bit of history, recite the steps for making a particular medicine, or to simply entertain them with a popular song. It was a long, grueling experience, but at the end of it all of us were judged worthy to wear the blue sash of a minstrel.

We were to receive our sashes on the Summer Day of Passages. Peg and I spent the evening before in the Grotto with our friends, chatting about a lot of nothing, all of us too excited about the next day to want to sleep. Long past sunset, Peg and I made our way to her room. We undressed and Peg slipped into bed. I blew out the lamp, felt my way across the room, and joined her. She snuggled up against me and put her head on my left shoulder and laid her arm across my chest. I put my arms around her and pulled her just a little bit closer.

"Goodnight, love," she whispered.

"Goodnight."

For a long while I just laid there with Peg in my arms, reveling in her closeness, the feel of her skin against mine. I wondered how long it would be before we could be with each other again after the next day. We had talked about our plans, but nothing had been definite the last time we had spoken. My consciousness began to drift between enjoying the feel of holding Peg, concerns about where I would go after being awarded my sash, and wondering whether Peg had firmed up her plans.

"Are you awake?" she whispered.

"Yes."

"I can't sleep," she said.

"Me neither. I was wondering if you've decided what you'll do after you get your sash tomorrow."

"What will you do?"

"I'm pretty sure," I answered, "that I'll be going out for a time. I'm not sure where or for how long, but both Ryan and Ambrose have hinted that I should. What about you? Do you want to come with me?"

"I've been discussing going out with Master Katryn. She thinks that it might be difficult for me to do some of the things a minstrel would do. As Houl's daughter, there might be concerns about my objectivity when I give advice."

"I can see the point," I said. "But it doesn't seem fair. You're a minstrel just like the rest of us. We've been trained to be impartial. So, what will you do?"

"You seem awfully concerned about what I plan to do. Are you trying to ask me to marry you?"

I could hear just a hint of teasing in her voice, but just a hint. I hadn't been trying to ask her to marry me just then, but I had been thinking about it. In one of my favorite daydreams, we'd hike to the summit of Haven Mountain. It was beautiful up there, with unobstructed views in all directions. Up there, seemingly on top of the world, I'd ask her to marry me. So, I hadn't been intending to ask her right then, but I had been thinking of it. I wasn't sure, though, how to respond in that moment. I decided to mimic her tone.

"A princess can't marry a farm boy," I said, trying to put just a hint of teasing in my voice as well.

She snuggled just a bit closer.

"But we're both minstrels," she reminded me.

I paused just a moment, held her just a little tighter.

"Will you marry me, Peg?"

"Ask me again when you get back. I promise that I'll say yes."

Well before dawn we rose, washed up, and donned our black hooded robes. We met the others at the foot of the Central Stairway and together climbed the six levels up to the Courtyard of Songs. None of us spoke. We exited the city to find nearly all the inhabitants of Songhaven gathered in the wide meadow beyond the gates. They stood in a huge circle, in places five or six rows deep, all facing to the northeast, waiting for the summer sun to appear above the distant mountains. No one spoke to us as we joined the back of the circle. Moments later, two couples who were to be married joined us.

The eastern sky lightened, the mountain tops outlined by a faint hint of red-orange light and then the first bright yellow sliver of the sun appeared. I heard someone sing the opening bars of the Summer Song of Thanks and recognized the voice as Ambrose's. Then the other Masters joined in. As the second verse began, all the rest of us joined in, a thousand voices giving thanks for our lives.

Then the song was done, and we watched as more and more of the sun rose clear of the mountains. Just before the last sliver cleared the mountaintops, the people before us moved to the side, opening a passageway into the center of the circle. All of us – students and betrothed couples – removed our robes and stood naked, ready for the transition to a new phase of our lives. I felt a brief flash of jealousy that my friends were seeing Peg naked, but then the people of Songhaven called out as one, "The Alomar are met. Are there any to come before us?"

One of the couples joined hands and entered the circle. I heard them announce their names and then the crowd called out, "We are the Alomar. We hear you. What would you have of us?"

I lost track of the rite, then. It suddenly hit me that the life I had always wanted was about to become reality: I was about to become a minstrel. My heart was racing, and my breathing had gone shallow. I wasn't sure whether I was excited or nervous or some combination of the two. I glanced at the others, and they looked like they were feeling the same thing. Rachel's gaze met mine and she gave me a small, lopsided smile.

The crowd called out, "We are the Alomar. We say they are husband and wife!"

There was a brief pause and then the crowd spoke again, "Are there any others to come before us?"

The other couple joined hands and entered the circle, and the rite was repeated. Again, there was a brief pause and then, "Are there any others to come before us?"

Avery led the way into the circle followed by Tavis, Denys, Rachel, Peg, and then me. In the center, we lined up side by side, facing Kayne, the Warder of the City. One by one we announced ourselves.

"I am Avery, son of Ronan and Brianna."

"I am Tavis, son of Matio and Valeria."

"I am Denys, son of Alen and Enid."

"I am Rachel, daughter of Con and Tara."

"I am Pegara, daughter of Houl and Reilynn."

"I am Lauren, son of Dalach and Elinore."

"We are the Alomar. We hear you. What would you have of us?"

As one, we replied, "We have completed the training and ask to be made Minstrels of Alomar."

Kayne nodded and spoke, "Is there anyone here who can speak to the qualifications of these students? Are they worthy to wear the blue?"

Together, the Masters of the College answered.

"We can speak. We have examined these students and found them worthy. We ask that you name them Minstrels of Alomar."

There was the briefest of pauses, just long enough for doubt to rise, and then the crowd spoke.

"We are the Alomar. We say that these students are students no longer. They are now Minstrels of Alomar."

Our individual Masters stepped forward then and handed each of us a sleeveless, knee-length tunic. I slipped mine on and then Ryan tied my bright blue sash around my waist.

"This is well deserved, Lauren," he said quietly, a wide smile on his face. "Go, celebrate, enjoy the rest of the day."

We spent the rest of the day celebrating with the rest of the city. By the time the sun had set, the six of us had found our way to the Grotto. Peg had just announced that she was going to stay on at Songhaven as an instructor, at least for a time, when we noticed someone bearing a torch heading toward us through the trees. The man stepped into the clearing and raised his torch high to spread the light. I was surprised to see that it was Ryan, his face grim.

"Lauren, I dislike interrupting your celebration, but you and I have been summoned. Ambrose's gift of prophecy has stirred. There is trouble coming and he is leaving for Amersford. We are to go with him, so we need to go make preparations. We leave at first light."

The news overwhelmed me. I didn't know what to say; I thought I would have more time before I left. I looked at Peg helplessly. She simply smiled sadly and took my hand.

"Go, love. But come back so I can say yes."

Part Two
The Prophet

The minstrel boy will understand
He holds the promise in his hands
He talks of better days ahead
And by his word your fortune's read

- from The Minstrel of the Dawn
- Gordon Lightfoot

CHAPTER SIX

The three of us rode out of Songhaven the next morning before the sun appeared above the mountains to the east. In the dull predawn light, colors were muted, and the city still slept. The only person we saw was Cadal, who led our horses out of the stables and handed them off to us. My mount was a dun-colored gelding named Windsfoal. We'd first been paired when I started learning to ride in my second round. Windsfoal was just three when we were paired, so in a way we had grown up together. We had gone on many day trips around Songhaven, but this was going to be our first long trip. Ryan was riding Starchild, a bay mare. Like her dam Dawnstar, she had a white star on her face. Ambrose was mounted on Realmstrider, a big palomino gelding. Cadal patted each of the horses on the nose, and then disappeared back into the stables before we were mounted.

I had hoped Peg would come to see me off, but as we rode through the gates, I realized that the previous night had been our goodbye. I didn't know how long it would be before I saw her again and sorrow dampened my mood. We passed by the trail that led off to the north, the one that Ryan and I had followed to the city seven rounds of the seasons before. Ambrose had chosen to head due east through the mountains, so we worked our way across the northern slopes of Haven Mountain. We didn't speak much; the bones of the mountain were close to the surface on the northern and western slopes, and we had to pick our way single file through the jumbled boulder fields. By midday we had worked our way off the western slopes onto a ridgeline running west and the way became much easier. We ate a light midday meal on horseback.

Late in the afternoon, the ridgeline we'd been following turned south, and we left it to follow a stream that headed a bit north of west into a hollow. We camped that night in a stand of pine trees near the stream. The sun set as we worked our way down the hollow and we set up camp quickly before the light faded. We were well off any regularly traveled routes through the mountains, so the risk of building a fire seemed small and the reward of a warm meal after a long day's travel seemed great. After we ate, I took our dishes to the stream to clean them. As I returned, I heard Ryan speak.

"Master, will you tell us now what you saw? What has prompted this journey?"

After a brief pause, Ambrose answered.

"It was nothing clear," he said. "In the vision, I was alone in total darkness, and I felt a growing sense of dread. I sensed some huge, malignant power searching desperately for something or, maybe, someone. In my mind a hoarse voice whispered the word, 'Amersford.' It would pause, sometimes for a short time, sometimes for longer, and then it would whisper again, 'Amersford.' I lay there, trapped in the vision, unable to move and seeing nothing but blackness, feeling nothing but fear, and hearing that voice whispering. Then the darkness shattered, and the dread fled, the voice fell silent. I saw the three of us, riding toward *Aennsrhyd* from the south. I woke from the vision then, with the conviction that we need to reach Amersford as quickly as possible, but we need to approach from the south."

I looked at Ryan and then we both looked back to Ambrose.

"What does it mean?" I asked.

"I do not know," he answered. "I cannot be sure, but I believe that there is, or soon will be, something wrong in Amersford."

The wood of the fire settled, and the flames leapt high, painting our faces in pastel shades of orange on a canvas of black.

"I've planned to leave Songhaven for some time now," Ambrose continued. "I've been grooming Elissa to take over the college. I grew a beard so that I could travel without being recognized. That may be useful now."

"How so?" Ryan asked.

"When we reach Amersford, I don't want to announce that I am there. I want to enter just as a group of minstrels traveling together. We can lay low, perhaps entertain in some of the inns, and listen for the news. Once we understand the situation we can go to the King's mansion and meet with Marc."

Ryan nodded.

"That sounds reasonable," he said. He looked at me. "Lauren, this will be your first time playing for audiences outside the college. Are you ready?"

In answer, I went to my things and retrieved my guitar.

I spent a moment checking the tuning and then picked out a light air, a simple dancing song from the northern city of Meren. Ryan and Ambrose listened until I finished and, as I started another song, Ryan retrieved his own guitar. A moment later, Ambrose fetched his.

Together we played for hours, beat back the dark loneliness of the wilderness and the gloom of Ambrose's vision with the light of our music. We played songs from all over the Federated Kingdoms, and I was surprised how easily I kept pace with the Masters. Then Ryan modulated and began an improvisation. I listened, entranced, as Ryan seemed to spin the darkness, and the stars, and the night sounds of the forest into music. For a moment I listened. Then I lowered my head and joined in.

Ambrose looked up in surprise as I began to play. I turned my attention to Ryan, and we focused on each other and the music we were making. We wove our melodies together and, when we knew the time had come, we stopped.

"Lauren, I can see how you earned your reputation," Ambrose said. "Your counter-melody brightened Ryan's musical stars, deepened the shadows, created night creatures dancing amid the trees. Ryan made a forest; you made it magic."

I just nodded and ran a hand through my long hair. I never knew how to deal with praise.

"I think I'd like to sleep now," I said and stood up.

"Probably a good idea," Ambrose replied. "We have another long day ahead of us tomorrow."

I woke the next morning to the gurgling of the stream and a fine layer of dew over everything. There was barely enough light to see by. Somewhere nearby an early rising cardinal sang, "whoit, whoit, tew, tew, tew." I rolled onto my back and sat up to find Ambrose sitting by the cold remains of our fire.

He was hunched over as if he were in pain, his face gray and haggard, his eyes bleary with lack of sleep. I quickly stood and approached him.

"Ambrose," I said gently. "Master. Are you well?"

Though I was speaking quietly, Ryan must have heard; in an instant he was standing beside me. He squatted down and put a hand on Ambrose's shoulder.

"Master," he said softly.

Ambrose looked up then, his eyes brimming with unshed tears and devastation.

"Master," Ryan repeated. "What is it? Are you well?"

Ambrose looked up.

"Ryan," he said. Then he looked at me. "Lauren. I…"

His voice was hoarse, and he broke off in the middle of whatever he intended to say. He wiped his eyes with the back of one hand and seemed to gather strength as he did so.

"Was it another vision?" Ryan asked.

"No," Ambrose replied, but then he closed his eyes and fell silent for a long moment. "Maybe." He opened his eyes and shook his head slightly. "I woke mortally afraid several hours ago, from a particularly bad dream or, perhaps, a vision. I have tried, but all I can remember is a single word."

Ryan and I waited for him to continue. When he didn't, I asked, "What word, Master?"

When he looked at me, the fear in his eyes was clear.

"Apocalypse," he answered.

I looked at Ryan. He looked as stunned as I felt. Ambrose suddenly stood.

"Come," he said, visibly making an effort to pull himself together. "Let us break our fast and get on our way. We have far to go and if we are to forestall whatever it is that is haunting me, we must get to Amersford quickly."

We ate as we broke camp. Before the sun was up, we were on our way. So, our days went. We were in the saddle before the sun rose and only stopped when it became too dark to find our way. Thus, in the midmorning of our seventh day out of Songhaven, we rode down the westernmost slope of the Breton Mountains and into the wide rolling grasslands between the Corun Hills and the great Amer River.

Our way was now easier, and we travelled further each day. The grasslands were verdant and fertile, and well-watered with countless small streams that flowed down out of the Corun Hills. Scattered stands of trees dotted the landscape. I found myself wondering why such fertile lands were unsettled. When I asked Ryan and Ambrose, neither had an answer or even a plausible theory. The sun was sinking toward the western horizon on our tenth day out of Songhaven, painting the sky in a multitude of reds and oranges, when we reached the Great South Road.

We set up camp behind a small hill, relatively hidden from anyone on the road. Since the fall of the Elven Kingdom, there was no regular travel on the Great South Road, but hunters often used it as an easy way to get to the Corun Hills. We lit no fire and so had a cold meal, but the night was warm and the sky clear. I sought out the Keystone, the North

Star, and found it, its red-violet light standing out from its white and yellow neighbors. It seemed especially bright that night.

"It will take us most of tomorrow to reach *Aennsrhyd*," Ambrose said when we'd finished eating. "I've been thinking of how we should approach Amersford. I am convinced that something is wrong there."

"Do you have any idea what that might be?" Ryan asked.

"No," Ambrose replied. "But I think we need to be careful. I saw us riding to *Aennsrhyd* together and that seemed to dispel the darkness, so I think we need to go that far together. But the more I think about it, three minstrels entering Amersford from the south at the same time will seem odd and might draw attention. Ryan, when we reach *Aennsrhyd*, I think you should go on ahead by yourself and enter Amersford on your own. Quietly poke around and see what you can find out."

"What will we do?" I asked.

"We will find somewhere in *Aennsrhyd* to shelter for the night and then enter Amersford the following day. If we're lucky, a boat from Landfall will be docking and we can try to appear as if we arrived on it. Ryan, you know the Minstrel's Haven?"

"Indeed, I do. It's possibly the best inn in Amersford."

"Let's plan on meeting there after Lauren and I enter."

Ambrose paused.

"I still want to enter the city incognito. We need to know what's going on, if anything, before I announce that I am there."

We spent the evening in quiet conversation and slept with no interruptions. We woke the next morning at first light. Ambrose's sense of urgency seemed greatly reduced now that we were close to our destination and caution was taking its place. We took our time breaking our fast and didn't set out until the sun was fully risen. The ride north was pleasant and by late afternoon the walls of *Aennsrhyd* were in sight.

Aennsrhyd was, in every way that I could see, the twin of Amersford. The walls were built of the same opalescent stone and the south wall, which we were quickly approaching, was an exact copy of the walls of Amersford that I had seen rounds before. In the center of the wall, the road entered the city through a pair of gates flanked by towers. The gates were open, and no guards warded them. *Aennsrhyd* had been abandoned after the War. Some said it was haunted by the spirits of the Elves. King Marc kept a small garrison in the city and some of the townhouses in the residential areas had been taken over by wealthy families who wanted privacy. No doubt, there were also some residents who wished to conduct their business out of the easy sight of the authorities, but the city was otherwise empty.

Just inside the gates, Ryan signaled that we should stop. His face looked concerned as we dismounted. There were several iron rings mounted on the wall to either side of the gate and Ryan and Ambrose each tied their horse to one. I followed suit and then the three of us gathered together.

"Something feels off," Ryan said. "This place is mostly empty, but there are soldiers stationed here and there are a few people living on the northern end of the residential district. Usually, there would be smoke from cookfires visible from here."

"I agree," Ambrose replied. "I don't believe Marc would abandon the garrison and if they were still in the city, we would see some evidence of them."

"Lauren," Ryan said. "Why don't you and I go ahead on foot, at least to the center of the city, and see what can be seen. Master Ambrose, would you mind the horses?"

"I will. Be cautious, you two."

Ryan and I headed into the city. As in Amersford, the Great South Road ran through the city from the southern gates to the northern gates. The area to the west of the road was the residential district while the area to the east housed commercial buildings. All of them were long deserted, doors hanging ajar or missing entirely, windows opening onto blank interiors. Though the cities had once been identical, there was now one major difference between Amersford and *Aennsrhyd*. In Amersford, the Great South Road ran straight through the city, but in *Aennsrhyd* it split to run in a broad circle around the center of the city. Inside that circle was a park – now run wild – but in Amersford some long ago King had run the road straight through the park and converted the land to the west of it into an estate with the King's mansion in the center.

The day was hot; the sun hung in the west of the cloudless sky. Heat radiated off the paving stones of the road, so it was a relief to get in amongst the trees and other greenery in the overgrown park. Though it was nice to get out of the direct sun, it was sad to see what must have once been a beautiful place now fallen into such ruin and decay. The plants had long ago encroached on the paved walkways and we had to pick our way carefully. At one point we encountered the largest patch of poison ivy I've ever seen; it completely blocked the way forward and we had to retrace our steps and find another way through. Periodically we stopped and listened for the sounds of the garrison. There was no breeze and each time all we heard was our own breathing. I could tell that Ryan was growing increasingly concerned. Then we entered the center of the park.

The paved pathway broadened out to form a circle surrounding a standing stone. I knew in that first glance that all the other stones erected by the Lost were imitations of this one. Like the others, it was twice the height of a man and mottled in shades of gray, but there was no lichen on this one. No plant grew within 20 feet of it. Unlike the other standing stones, there was a palpable presence about this one, as if some power or energy were radiating from it, but that power felt muffled, like a light glimpsed through a thick curtain.

"Ryan," I said quietly, "what is that stone?"

"I don't know. But I've seen admonitions in very old books to avoid touching it. I've always felt like that was a good idea."

I just nodded. Ryan gestured that I should continue past the stone. I took two steps forward to go straight across the circle past the stone...

I think I heard Ryan call out my name. Far overhead there was a crack of thunder that rolled endlessly through the cloudless sky. The world went dark, the ground seemed to tilt and spin beneath me, and I could sense some huge, black power searching frantically through the darkness for me. I might have screamed then. But just as suddenly as it tilted, the world righted, and I found myself leaning back against Ryan's chest. He had my arms in an iron grip that was all that kept me from falling. I got my feet under me, and Ryan let go.

"Lauren, what happened?" he asked.

I looked back at the stone. It appeared the same as it had, as if nothing had happened.

"I started to go on past the stone. But then I heard thunder, and everything went black. Something was looking for me in the darkness. Then everything was normal, and you were holding me up."

"I heard the thunder," Ryan said. "But I didn't see any of the rest of what you saw. I saw you step forward and then you fell back, almost as if you'd hit a wall. I just barely caught you before you fell."

"Does what happened to me make any sense to you?" I asked.

"In a way. As I said, I've seen warnings against touching the stone in ancient books. They never said exactly what happened to people who did, but the implication was that it was bad."

"Ryan, I didn't touch it. I was just walking by."

"I know," he replied. "I'm puzzled by that. It's possible, I guess, that something else set it off and you got caught in the reaction. We should talk about it with Ambrose. Now, though, we should get to the north end of the park and see what we can see and then get back to Ambrose." He paused. "How do you feel? Can you go on?"

"Yes, I can," I said as we started circling the stone to head north. I stayed as far away from it as I could.

It took us another twenty minutes to work our way up the overgrown path to the north end of the park, half of that crawling through the underbrush near the northern edge to avoid being seen. When we finally reached a place where we could see the road heading north, Ryan gave a short, ironic laugh and stood up.

"Ryan?" I asked.

"There's clearly no one here," he answered. I stood up beside him. "See that large white building with the blue trim."

I nodded.

"That's the garrison. If the soldiers were here, Marc's banner would be flying out front. They're not here."

He stepped out of the greenery, kicking his leg a bit to free himself from a clinging vine.

"At least now we can use the road. Let's get back to Ambrose."

The walk back to South Gate was eerie. *Aennsrhyd* was so like Amersford that it brought memories of my visit there to the surface and overlaid the emptiness around me with visions of the bright vibrant crowds I'd seen. I found myself feeling sad, wondering if the people who had lived here truly deserved the fate they had been dealt.

When we reached South Gate, Ambrose and the horses were nowhere in sight. A moment after we arrived, he hailed us from the door of what looked as if it could have once been an inn.

"Welcome to the Prophet's Rest," Ambrose said as we approached, a broad smile on his face.

"Catchy name," Ryan replied.

"I thought it had a nice ring to it. Perhaps I'll have a sign made." His tone became matter of fact. "While you were gone, I took a look around to see if I could find us some shelter. I'm fairly sure this place used to be an inn. It's reasonably well preserved, and the stables are mostly intact. I think we can spend the night here."

He led us into what had probably been the common room of the inn. There was a massive fireplace in the far wall. There was no furniture of any kind, but the rotting remains of a wooden bar stood along the lefthand wall. The end of one of the beams supporting the ceiling had rotted through and rested on the floor in front of the bar. Bits of wood – perhaps the remains of the furniture – lay scattered around the floor and a thick layer of dust covered everything.

Ambrose had gathered bits of wood from other nearby buildings and started a small fire in the fireplace in the inn's common room. We quickly prepared an evening meal and sat in a circle on the floor to talk as we ate.

"What did you find?" Ambrose asked.

"There doesn't appear to be anyone in the city," Ryan replied. "The garrison was empty. We never heard any indication that anyone else was around."

"That's odd," Ambrose said. "I've never known Marc to leave the south end of the bridge untended. What is going on here?"

"I'm not sure," Ryan replied. "I think I should ride into Amersford tonight as planned. If I leave soon, I can be there before they close the gates. I can do a little digging overnight and see what I can learn before you come tomorrow."

"I agree," Ambrose said. "When you go, I'd like you to take all three horses with you. Lauren and I will cross the bridge tomorrow before it's light and lay low near the wharves. If we're lucky, a ship will put in and we can act as if we came with it. That will be more plausible without horses."

Ryan looked at me and nodded.

"Master Ambrose, there is one other thing," I said.

Ambrose shot a glance at Ryan, then looked back at me.

"Go ahead."

"You know of the standing stone in the center of the city?"

He nodded.

"As we were passing it this afternoon, something happened. I was walking past the stone when suddenly everything went black. I felt like the world was tilting and turning under me. In the darkness, I sensed something searching for me. Then, just as suddenly, everything was normal again."

Ambrose's look of surprise and shock would have been amusing in other circumstances. I had never seen the Master look like that before. After a moment, he composed himself and turned to Ryan.

"And what did you experience?"

"Master, we had stopped for a moment when we entered the circle around the stone. Lauren started to cross the circle, walking normally, and it was if he hit an invisible wall and fell back. At the same moment, there was a peal of thunder. He recovered quickly and we finished our scouting."

"I heard that thunder," Ambrose said slowly. "Lauren, did you touch the stone?"

"No," I replied.

"He never got close enough to touch it," Ryan confirmed.

Ambrose looked thoughtful.

"I do not know what to make of this. We may need to visit the wizards when we are in Amersford. They may have some idea about what happened."

He stood and began brushing the dust from the floor from his clothing.

"As I've said, I do not wish to enter Amersford as Ambrose of the Minstrels. If I were to do so, word would get around and I would immediately be summoned to the King's mansion. I would have no chance to learn what, if anything, is wrong in the city. Do either of you know Ambor?"

We both nodded. Ambor was the oldest of the minstrels. He hadn't gone out in some five rounds or so; gout had claimed his feet and then his knees, and he could no longer sit a horse. Some days he could barely walk. He'd retired and spent his days reading and teaching the young children of Songhaven. Occasionally, he'd perform with the other minstrels. I learned my first Altieran story song from him.

"He hasn't gone out in several rounds," Ambrose said. "We are somewhat similar in appearance, and he always wore a beard. I believe that I can pass as him so long as we don't encounter anyone who knew him well. Now, Ryan, you had best be on your way. We will see you at the Minstrel's Haven tomorrow afternoon."

"Very well, Ambor," Ryan said. "I'm off."

Ambrose and I followed Ryan to the door and stood just outside it as Ryan disappeared in the direction of the stable. A short time later, he rode by on Starchild with Windsfoal and Realmstrider following behind on long leads. We watched until Ryan was out of sight, then Ambrose spoke.

"Lauren, do you remember when we spoke of the Lawbreaker?"

"I do," I replied and turned to face him.

"I wonder if perhaps he had something to do with what happened at the stone. It has an evil reputation; perhaps the Lawbreaker is trying to use it for something. Do you think the dark thing that was looking for you could be him?"

I could feel my heart begin to pound.

"I don't know. Why would you think that?"

"Do you remember the day that I told you about the Lawbreaker? That day you said that you felt some malignant power seeking you. That sounds too much like this to be a coincidence."

"But why would the Lawbreaker be looking for me? I'm nobody important."

Ambrose didn't answer. He put his hand behind his head and massaged his neck, a thoughtful look on his face as he stared into the distance. Then the answer to my question occurred to me. It occurred to Ambrose at the same time. I could see it in his eyes as he refocused on me.

"Not you," he said. "Not for yourself. But your father leads the Federation's army. Your betrothed is the Princess of Han."

"Yes," I said. "But how would that help him?"

"I am not sure but he may believe that capturing you might give him some sway over your father or the king of Han. We must keep you safe. If he wants you, it cannot be for the good of the Federated Kingdoms."

My head was reeling, my heart was pounding, and my breath was coming in quick, shallow gasps.

"Lauren, do not panic," Ambrose cautioned. "Calm yourself. Breathe."

"Breathe?" I just barely managed to get out. "Breathe? The doom of the Federated Kingdoms of Alomar is looking for me and I'm just supposed to breathe?"

Ambrose cocked his head.

"It is better than the alternative," he observed wryly.

The absurdity of it hit me then and I began to laugh uncontrollably. By the time I got myself under control, the panic had receded a little, and I could think again.

"Ambrose, what do I do?"

He looked around. The sun had sunk below the city wall some time ago and sunset was near. The western sky was painted in shades of pink and violet, with hints of gold on the edges of the scattered clouds.

"It's going to be dark soon. I think we should prepare our bedding. We'll need to douse the fire; there may not be anyone in the city, but if there is someone here, they are probably here for no good reason. No need to call attention to ourselves."

"And then?"

"Then we go on as we planned."

It didn't take us long to clear a space on the floor out of sight of the open doorway and spread our blankets. Then we sat outside and watched the stars come out, each of us lost in our own thoughts. I looked for the North Star, but I couldn't find it. The sky seemed to be clouding over. After a time, we went back inside. I thought that it would be hard to sleep given everything that had happened, but I quickly dropped into a deep, dreamless sleep.

When I woke the next morning, the air in the old inn was chilled. I rose and walked to the door. Outside, a thick fog hung in the air and fine droplets of water clung to every surface. The buildings across the way were hidden. I shivered though it was the middle of the first moon of *Tymnacynn*, the height of summer. I reentered the inn and went to my things. I was just pulling a light cloak out of my pack when Ambrose stirred, rolled over, and then sat up.

"Why is it so cold?" he muttered.

"There's a thick fog over the city," I answered.

"Mere fog wouldn't explain this chill."

Ambrose rose and dug his own cloak out of his pack. We decided to risk a small fire to boil water for tea; the warmth would be welcome. After a quick breakfast, we packed the few belongings that we'd used and set out for the north end of the city and the Amersford Bridge.

The buildings on either side of the road were merely vague shapes dimly perceived through the fog. As we walked, it felt to me as if the air was growing colder, the fog thicker. A sense of uneasiness was growing in me, a shapeless fear gnawing at my gut, as if I could see some disaster coming but couldn't stop it. As we neared the park in the center of the city, Ambrose stopped.

"Do you feel it?" he asked in a near whisper.

"That the heart of all of this is just in front of us?" I asked in return.

"Yes," Ambrose replied. "I think we know what we will find if we go to the center of the park, but I also believe that we have to go look."

I didn't want to go, but I nodded my assent.

The going was easier than it had been the day before; Ambrose and I were able to follow the trail that Ryan and I had forced through. Sooner than I liked, we were in the circle around the stone. The air was cold enough that I could see my breath. The fog was so thick, though, that I could barely make out Ambrose standing next to me. As we stood there, I began to sense something in the fog, a presence whose focus was all on the stone. I felt as if I could, with just a little more concentration, make out a whispering voice. Something about it told me I didn't want to hear what it was saying.

"Do you feel it," Ambrose asked again.

I nodded.

"There is intent here," Ambrose said. "I cannot say what its purpose is, but there is intent here. This is no natural weather. We must leave this place. We must leave now."

We quickly retraced our steps and then followed the road around the park and then on to the North Gate. Though it must have been midmorning at that point, we couldn't see the sun. The dim half-light made it difficult to judge time, but we soon reached the south end of the Amersford Bridge.

We paused there and I took a few steps off the road and peered into the fog trying to make out the north end of the Bridge. The shining opalescence of that great stone arch was dulled by the gray day. Faint gurgling sounds rose from the river, sounding nearer in the clinging mists.

"The city is about a quarter mile north of the Bridge," Ambrose said. "We could reach the South Gate in about half an hour. I do want to try and wait, though, to see if a ship puts in. In this fog, it will be easy to mix in with a group of passengers. Remember, Lauren, that for now, I'm Ambor."

"I'll remember," I replied.

"There is one more thing. You've seen the pouch that I carry?"

"Yes, I have."

"At the High King's coronation, I was given tokens of friendship by each of the petty kings. They are in the pouch. If I am in some way incapacitated, you may need them to ensure our safety. Marc's token is the only ring in the pouch."

"You believe that we go into danger, then?"

"I hope not, but perhaps."

We started forward and began to climb the southern arc of the Bridge. As we climbed, the faint dark shadow of the river fell away. The milky white of the Bridge faded into the mist and it appeared to me that we were walking on air in the heart of a cloud. A mild vertigo tugged at my head. We paused for a few moments when we reached the apex of the bridge; there were no sounds from the river below. It didn't take us long to reach the north end of the bridge and we left the Great South Road and walked a short distance down the road that led to the wharves. Then we sat down by the side of the road to take our midday meal and to wait.

The afternoon passed slowly. It was cold and damp and we were just sitting, which did nothing to keep us warm. By late afternoon, we were ready to give up waiting for a boat, but then we heard a call from out on the river.

"Ahoy the wharf."

"Holloa!" came the answer.

"This is the *Amer Maiden* out of Landfall. Can you guide us in?"

Ambrose and I scrambled to our feet and began gathering our things.

"Just a moment *Amer Maiden*. I'll kindle a guide fire."

A moment later we could barely make out a spot of light in the direction of the riverbank.

"There you go *Amer Maiden*," called the wharfman. "Can you see the light?"

"Aye. We're heading in."

Not long after, a group of five people climbed up from the wharves to the road. The adults in the group barely noticed us, but one little girl waved shyly. When I waved back, she smiled. Ambrose paused and unslung his guitar from his back.

"Just give me a moment," he said quietly and began removing something that was tied to the outside of his guitar's case. It was a cane. He returned his guitar to his back, leaned on the cane, and then smiled at me.

"Now I'm a more convincing Ambor," he said. Then he turned and began to hobble up the road toward the gates of the city. In moments, the city walls loomed above us, seeming to lose their shape in the mist. Before the gates stood two warriors in the white and blue livery of Amersford. They crossed their spears, barring the Gate.

"Who would enter the City of Marc, and why would he do so?" challenged one guard, his old voice thin and wavery.

"I am Lauren of the Minstrels," I replied. "With me is Ambor of the Minstrels. We seek but a meal and a night's lodging."

The guard seemed unusually old for someone on active duty. I shot a quick glance at Ambrose; it was clear that he'd noticed, too.

"Did you just come in on the *Amer Maiden*?" the guard asked.

Ambrose cut in then. "The cold and damp are causing my gout to flare. I'd appreciate it if we could get indoors and next to a good fire."

The guard looked at Ambrose as if he was seeing him for the first time. I could see empathy in his expression.

"Your purpose is good," he stated. He raised his spear with a thin arm and motioned for his companion to do the same. "Enter in peace."

As we entered Amersford, I was immediately struck by the absence of people. On my last visit to the city, I had been overwhelmed by the vast numbers of them, and not even the fog or the unseasonal chill would have kept those bustling traders from their business. Now most of the shops were closed, the doors barred, and the windows shuttered. Fog and shadows ruled the streets of Amersford. I strained to see through the gloom, trying to spot the light that would mean an inn.

"Take the third turn to the right," Ambrose instructed quietly. "The Minstrel's Haven is on that street."

I nodded to myself, still struggling to see. Dimly, I made out what I thought was the shape of a man, wrapped tightly in a cloak, darting across our path. The buildings of the city loomed above us on either side, dark giants in the cold mist.

"Ambor?" I asked, my voice sounding loud in the stillness. "Where is everyone?"

"I do not know. At this time of day, the streets should be full of people. Watch closely now, our turn should be coming up."

Without answering, I moved toward the dimly perceived side street. Ambrose followed. The street opened into a wide, torch-lit courtyard, surrounded on three sides by a tall, three-story structure. The ground floor of one wing, to the right, was obviously a stable. Straight ahead, a door stood open, ablaze with light. I could barely see the sign above it that proclaimed, in bright blue letters, that this was the Minstrel's Haven.

"This is the place to stay in Amersford," Ambrose said quietly as he came up beside me.

"It looks homey," I answered, as I noted the many, brightly lit windows and the sounds of music from within.

Together, we crossed the threshold into a blaze of light. The common room of the Minstrel's Haven was huge. Against the far-left wall, on a raised stage, a minstrel played. It was no one I knew, but he nodded at us as we entered, and I raised a hand in greeting. The rest of the room was filled with tables, each large enough for four or five people. Near the fireplace in the wall opposite the door, many of the tables were filled. I saw some fellow minstrels, a few warriors and, mostly, townspeople. The mingled scents of roasting meat and baking bread wafted out from the kitchens to the right.

I leaned toward Ambrose. "Why don't you sit down, Ambor?" I asked. "I'll try to find the proprietor."

"Good thought, lad," he answered, and hobbled off toward the tables nearest the stage. If I hadn't known better, I would have believed that he really suffered from gout.

I shifted my bags to a more comfortable position and turned toward the kitchen. My mouth watered and my stomach rumbled.

"Lauren!" a lyrical voice called from behind me. "Lauren, wait."

I turned to find Ryan striding toward me.

"Lauren, I didn't think to see you here. How are you, my friend?" I understood from his look that I should follow his lead.

"Ryan!" I cried and, setting my pack on the floor, embraced him. "I'm doing well. And how are you?"

"I am doing well. I see you've taken the blue. Congratulations. Come, join me at my table for some ale."

"Later, perhaps. I must find the innkeeper."

"I can help you, then. I know the innkeeper. Come, have a drink with me and I'll call Kaitrin over."

"I'm traveling with Ambor. Let me get him. Where's your table?"

He pointed it out and a few moments later, Ambrose and I joined him there.

"Ambor," Ryan exclaimed. "I haven't seen you in several rounds. How are you?"

"Fine, young Ryan, I'm fine. You seem as though you're doing well."

"I am," Ryan replied. "I'll call Kaitrin."

He twisted in his seat, eyes darting around the room. He obviously spotted her and stood.

"I'll be right back."

A few moments later, he returned with the largest woman I'd ever seen. In fact, Kaitrin was one of the largest people I'd ever seen. She could easily have put her chin on the top of Ryan's head, and he was tall. Her long blonde hair was tied back in a ponytail that showed off a rather plain face with wide set brown eyes and a nose that looked as if it had been broken and badly set. She wore a sleeveless tunic that showed off extremely well-muscled arms. Her left bicep was decorated with a tattoo of a golden eagle.

"You were in the High King's Guard," I said in surprise.

"Aye, young minstrel, I was." Her voice was rough and loud. She turned to Ryan. "What are you needing, Ryan?"

Ryan grinned up at her. "Kaitrin," he said, motioning towards me, "I would like you to meet some friends of mine. This young man is Lauren, and this is Ambor. They'll need lodgings for the night."

"The main room is quite busy tonight, but that's mostly locals. So, I've got plenty of rooms," the innkeeper replied. She turned her attention to Ambrose and a thoughtful look passed over her face.

"Ambor, you say. I feel like I know you, sir."

"I don't believe we've met, mistress," Ambrose replied.

She stood looking at Ambrose a moment. I was beginning to worry that she had recognized him for who he was.

"That your cane?" she asked, nodding toward it.

"Aye, mistress. My gout's so bad I can barely walk without it. This will probably be the last time I go out."

Kaitrin just stared at Ambrose for a moment more and then shook her head slightly and turned back to me.

"It will be three crowns for the room and thirteen irons for each meal. Call it four crowns for the night."

I retrieved the required coins from my pouch and handed them to her.

"My thanks, Lauren," Kaitrin said. "I'll be back in a moment with your meals and a key."

As Kaitrin walked away, Ryan turned to Ambrose.

"Ambor," he said. "It is good to see you out. How are you this evening, sir?"

Ambrose snorted and shot a blistering look at me.

"As fine as can be with this one forcing me to walk up from the boat in this cursed fog," he grumbled. "And me with my gout flaring. And what about you, Ryan? How have you been?"

Ryan smiled widely.

"Just fine, Ambor. I..." He stopped abruptly.

Once again Kaitrin loomed above us, her cheerful immensity crashing down upon us.

"Here are your meals, Lauren, and your key. Number twenty-three, on the second floor."

She set steaming bowls of stew in front of me and Ambrose, and a warm loaf of bread with honey butter.

"Is there anything else you'll be needing?" she asked.

"No. My thanks to you," I answered.

"Good rest to you, then," Kaitrin said and turned away.

Ambrose and I began eating. Ryan leaned forward and spoke so that only we could hear.

"There aren't many people willing to talk," he said. "The few who were would only say that trouble is brewing in Meren again. Serious, this time. People are leaving Meren, and some have even come this far. It's whispered that Larsen may close the roads through the forest."

I dunked a slice of buttered bread into my stew, then bit off a section. With the back of my hand, I wiped away a dribble as I chewed, then asked, "Is anyone saying what kind of trouble?"

"No, but Larsen is conscripting men into Meren's army."

"The Destroyer take them," Ambrose exclaimed in a fierce whisper. "They're not planning to rise against the High King again, are they?"

"I can't say," Ryan answered.

"What news from here in Amersford?" Ambrose asked.

Ryan shrugged.

"No one will say anything about what's going on here," he replied. "I almost got thrown out of one place for even asking. Something is definitely wrong though. Did you notice the guards at the gates?"

"Old men," I commented between mouthfuls.

"Yes. And I've seen none of Marc's regular troops around the city."

"Odd," Ambrose noted.

"No one's talking, though," Ryan said. "There's much fear in Amersford and, I think, danger for those who ask too much. Most of the shops are closed and no one goes out unless they must."

"Why?" Ambrose asked.

"I couldn't find out why. I've not found one person who will talk. My contacts in Amersford were all in Marc's regular troops and, as I said, none of them are to be found."

We finished our meal in silence except for the clink of spoons against our bowls. I thought about all that Ryan had said, trying to piece together the puzzle.

"Ambor," I asked suddenly. "Could it be that Marc's troops have gone to Meren?"

Ambrose's eyes started wide, then narrowed in thoughtful concentration. "It would explain all the facts we have," he answered. "Meren planning an uprising is no real surprise, but I would have sworn a thousand oaths that Marc was loyal to the High King."

The prophet glanced sharply around the room and lowered his voice further. "If what Lauren suggests is true, you may be in danger, Ryan. You've been asking the wrong sorts of questions. When we finish here, come to our room with me. Lauren, I want you to go out and visit the taverns. Ask no questions but keep your ears open. And here, take this."

Ambrose held out Marc's ring.

"If there is a problem, show them this."

My heart pounded and I felt cold and shaky. I felt danger crowding in around me like vultures around a wounded animal.

"What about you?" I asked. "What if you are stopped?"

"I'm not going out," Ambrose responded. "I'm going to our room and clean up. I may even shave my beard."

"Why?" I asked in surprise.

"So that I'm recognized. I've changed my mind; we're going to see the King."

A strange sensation flooded over me, then, a feeling that I stood on the brink of events I could not stop, that control of my life was being wrenched away from me. I felt as though I was drifting, listening, as if from miles away, to myself asking again, "Why?"

"Marc and I are old friends. If he plans to betray Aerman, I will know."

Ambrose put a hand on my shoulder and the drifting sensation faded.

"Go now and ask no questions. Listen, learn what you can and return here no later than midnight. When you return, we'll send word to Marc that I am here."

As I handed our key to Ambrose, I asked, "Where should I go?"

"Try the Sword and the Sash," Ryan answered. It's a favorite gathering place for the city garrison."

"How do I get there?"

"Return to the Great South Road. Go north and take the second right turning. After that, take the first left and you're there." Ryan's face grew somber. "Tread softly, Lauren. The city is full of danger tonight."

I nodded, swallowing a sudden lump in my throat. "I can feel it, Ryan."

I broke off, not knowing what else to say. With no further words, I turned and left the inn.

Though sunset was still somewhat more than an hour away, it was nearly dark as I stepped out onto the streets. A gentle breeze had sprung up, herding the fog down the street in great, billowing masses. A random swirl twisted around me, and music sounded in my mind. I'd heard it before, the day that I met Ryan. Caution was suddenly replaced by exhilaration, and I let the music take me.

It led me north, following Ryan's directions. But instead of turning into the Sword and the Sash, it took me farther. The music died away in front of a rundown, unpainted building, leaving me empty and confused, wondering if I'd really heard it and why it would bring me to that place. I shrugged and examined the building.

Greasy, unwashed windows all but blocked the yellow light from inside. I could hear the loud buzz of voices from inside, an occasional shout signaling some drunken argument. A sign beside the door read, in faded yellow lettering, the Black Dragon. I pushed aside the door curtain and entered.

The air in the tavern was close and stank of rancid ale and too many unwashed bodies. Despite its disreputable state, the tavern was packed. The chimney was bad and the acrid smell of burning meat drifted with the smoke around the room. I carefully picked my way between the tavern's patrons, my head reeling from the reeking air. I found a table whose occupant did not look too threatening and sat down.

The man was old, with close cropped white hair and fierce, bushy eyebrows. His crooked nose was large, forming a great mountain between his ale hazed eyes. He reached out a warrior's sword-scarred arm and laid a hand on my arm.

"Buy me a drink," he commanded with a ring of broken authority in his voice. Something about him reminded me of my father.

I motioned a serving girl closer and ordered a pot of the tavern's best ale.

"It's coming, oldtimer," I said. "While we wait, why not tell me how a proud warrior came to be in such a state?"

The warrior turned suddenly glittering eyes on me.

"Damned minstrels always could see right through me," he complained. He paused to glance around the room. "So, I might as well tell the truth. My name is Aldus. I used to be the Captain of the King's Guard. But not anymore. Not since the new magician kicked me out."

I fought to control my surprise. Aldus paused as the girl brought the ale. Her golden-brown hair caught a gleam of firelight and for a moment I thought of Peg. Then she was gone, and I returned my attention to Aldus.

"A magician?" I asked. "Not a wizard?"

"Aye, lad. First we heard was some wild man had come in from the wilderness to the south. Claimed he was a magician who could see the future. 'I have sensed a doom falling on this city,' he proclaimed in all the marketplaces and town squares. People thought he was strange."

"What did the wizards say about him?" I asked.

"That's the strangest part, young minstrel."

"Lauren."

"Ah, Lauren then. That's the strangest thing. The wizards locked themselves up and never answered him. No one's seen them since he came to town."

I poured us each a mug of ale and handed one to Aldus. The warrior accepted the mug and took several drinks from it while I tried my best to force down one swallow of the vile stuff.

"How did it come about that he forced you from the King's service?" I prodded.

"Like I said," Aldus answered. "At first no one paid him much mind. Then the King fell ill, started wasting away, and no one of the Healers could cure him. This went on for weeks and then the magician began to say that only he could cure the King, that he had the Keeper's favor and could save us from the coming doom."

"And someone listened to him?"

"Aye. The King himself heard what the man had said and had him sent for. The magician arrived at court, more horrid and ragged than the filthiest of beggars, and started raving about spells and the Keeper's anger and such. But he gave the King a potion that seemed to make the pain subside and he was invited to stay."

My head ached and the rancid air was pressing close.

"Aldus, let's go out and walk. The air in here is too thick."

The warrior raised his mug to his lips but stopped before drinking. A look of disgust filled his face, and he set the mug down.

"Why I came into this pit I'll never know. But you've woke me up, lad, and that walk sounds good."

We left the remainder of the ale and threaded our way to the door. I pulled my cloak close as we stepped out into the clinging fog. The breeze had died away.

"What happened once the magician moved in?" I asked.

"Lauren, you could get yourself into grave trouble asking about this man," Aldus warned, "What is your interest in it?"

"I have a friend who may be able to help."

"I'm beginning to doubt that it would help if Ambrose himself were to come down out of the mountains."

That startled me, but I said nothing.

"The King grew fonder of Phelan, that's the magician's name, he grew fonder of him every day. He gave the bloody fool royal authority, so his every whim is a royal command."

"No," I said, horrified.

"Yes," Aldus replied. "Lauren, he sent away nearly the whole army to find the last ingredient for his potion. The one he said would make it work and heal the King."

"What ingredient?"

"A unicorn's horn. He sent the army to the Lellarin Plains to bring back a unicorn's horn."

I stopped, struck still by amazement.

"A unicorn's horn," I exclaimed. "Unicorns don't exist. Is the man crazy?"

Aldus looked around warily, trying to pierce the fog with his gaze.

"Quietly, Lauren, quietly. This fog is unchancy and there could be many ears listening." He paused. "I protested also and was relieved of my command. Fifteen rounds of the seasons at Marc's side and I was ordered away by a crazy fool. Is it any wonder that I ended up in my cups?"

"No, you were greatly wronged, Aldus. But now I must leave you. My friend will be greatly interested in what you have told me. Luck must have guided me to your table."

Aldus spat.

"I'll never get that foul taste out of my mouth. Luck, you say. If so, you brought it with you, for there's no luck left in Amersford. Tread softly here, Lauren, and fare well. May the Keepers watch over you."

"And you also, friend Aldus. I believe we'll meet again soon."

I watched as the warrior strode away into the fog. I was relieved to find that it was not treason hanging thick in the air of Amersford, but the insanity in its place scared me. A raving madman had his hands on the reins of Marc's kingdom and was well on the way to tearing it apart.

Quickly, with a purposeful stride, I returned to the Minstrel's Haven. There was a new performer on the stage and just a few more patrons. They paid little attention to me as I passed through and climbed the stairs to the second floor.

Impatient and bursting with news, I searched for our room and found it at the end of the hall. I knocked quietly and waited. I heard from within the sounds of the door being unbarred. It opened an inch or two to reveal Ryan's anxious face.

"Lauren!" The door was thrown wide. "You're back."

"I am, Master Ryan, and I have news."

Ambrose turned from a basin filled with soap-scummed water. He was wiping the last traces of soap from his newly shaved face with a cloth.

"There is no treason in Amersford," I said tersely. Quickly, I related what Aldus had told me. Ambrose's face grew sterner each moment, the gold flecks in his eyes flaring dangerously.

"We must get to Marc as quickly as possible," the prophet said as I finished. "If this goes unchecked, it could rob Aerman of his strongest ally when Meren strikes. Lauren, give the ring to Ryan."

As I complied, Ambrose turned to Ryan.

"Take the ring to the guards at the gate to the King's mansion. Tell them it must go to the King. Make sure they know where to find me. Have you any money?" Ryan nodded. "Good. Bribe them if you must. Then return here."

A moment of anxiety for my teacher and my friend touched me as I gave the ring to Ryan.

"Go carefully, Master," I said quietly.

"I will."

I barred the door after Ryan and turned to face Ambrose. Beardless, the prophet looked much as he had when I first met him. Skeletally thin, Ambrose was almost colorless in an ash- gray robe trimmed with sable at the cuffs and throat. I shuddered. The prophet's smoky green eyes still held power.

"You should change," Ambrose commented.

"And then?"

"We wait for the King's summons."

After stripping off my travel-stained tunic, I tossed the soapy contents of the basin out the window. I refilled it from a large stoneware pitcher and scrubbed away the dust and grime of travel. I had just donned a pair of supple deer-hide trousers and a tunic of brown silk when Ryan returned.

"The guard opened the pouch," Ryan reported. "He was surprised, I think. Impressed, anyway. He sent a messenger into the palace straight away. We should hear something soon."

"Good," Ambrose replied. "Lauren and I will stay here. You, Ryan, should leave. There is still great danger here. Go to Songhaven and tell Elisa all that has occurred here."

"Yes, Master Ambrose. I'll get there as quickly as I can."

I stepped forward.

"So, we part again, Master. I wish it had been longer, and under better circumstances."

"I, too, Lauren. Perhaps we'll meet again soon."

Ryan retrieved his pack and guitar from his own room and returned.

"May Garth guide your footsteps and put you on the path back to Mar," Ambrose said.

Ryan nodded and said, "I think that you'll need his protection more than I."

As he turned away, I said, "Safe travels, Master. If you see her, tell Peg that I'm thinking of her."

He nodded and slipped out the door. Once again, I barred the door behind him. Fear and anxiety touched me with icy fingers.

"What will we do when we reach the King?" I asked.

"I am not sure," Ambrose replied. "Sooner or later, I must confront this magician. I want you to stay back, Lauren. Say little and follow my lead when you do speak. If you watch, you may see something I miss."

I nodded and picked up my guitar. I stripped off its leather case, sat on the bed and tried to play. My concentration was disrupted by fear and the tunes came out badly. Frustrated, I set aside the instrument and stalked around the room in a rustle of silk. Ambrose sat patiently in the room's only chair.

Tension wound my guts into a knot, forced me to pace the little room like a caged bear. I froze when a loud knock shattered the silence. My eyes darted a quick look toward Ambrose.

"Who is there?" the prophet called.

"King's Guards, sir," a rough voice answered. "The King would see you."

CHAPTER SEVEN

A mbrose stood and went to the door. "A moment," he called as he lifted the bar. The door opened to reveal a huge man in the livery of Marc's household guard, a blue tunic and white trousers with silver piping at the collar and cuffs and a polished steel breastplate. I tensed. Ambrose's head came only to the mid-point of the man's chest. Unlike the men at the gates, this Guardsman was clearly a warrior in his prime and the leather-wrapped hilt of his massive broadsword was well-worn with use.

In a deep voice, the warrior asked, "You are the minstrel called Ambrose Kingmaker?"

"Yes," Ambrose replied quietly. "I am."

To my amazement, the huge Guardsman dropped to one knee, momentarily bowing his head. His action revealed two other Guards behind him in the hall. He looked up at Ambrose with awe in his face.

"I am Rogart, Captain of the King's Guard. I place myself in your service, Kingmaker."

I glanced at Ambrose. His face was unreadable as he motioned for Rogart to rise.

"My men are waiting in the courtyard," the captain said as he rose. "The King has sent horses for you."

Ambrose nodded and fetched his guitar. "And how is Marc?" he asked as we left the room.

I strained to hear as I stopped to settle my guitar across my back and to lock our door.

"Phelan says..." the captain started, but Ambrose cut him off.

"I don't want to hear what Phelan says." the prophet prodded. "What do you see, Rogart?"

The other Guardsmen fell into step behind us as I followed Ambrose and Rogart down the hall.

Rogart was hesitant as he answered Ambrose's question.

"He has changed much since the illness took hold," he explained. "Where he was once well-fleshed, he is now terribly thin. Perhaps, if Phelan could obtain what he seeks..."

"A unicorn's horn?" Ambrose asked dryly.

Rogart shot him a surprised look.

"How could you know that?" he asked.

"How not?" Ambrose countered.

I risked an amused smile but said nothing as we descended the stairs. We ignored Kaitrin's shocked look of recognition and the curious gazes of the patrons as we crossed the main room of the inn. In the courtyard, several more Guardsmen waited with the promised horses.

It was full dark now and the courtyard was lit by torches set in sconces. The air was a good deal warmer, the fog was clearing, and a light breeze was blowing. I glanced around nervously as I waited to see what would happen. I relaxed as I noticed the obvious deference being paid to Ambrose. Leather creaked as the Guardsmen mounted.

As we rode, the horse's hooves clopped loudly on the cobblestones. With Ambrose by his side, Rogart led the way back to the Great South Road. I stayed close behind them, trying vainly to hear their conversation over the noise of the horses. Our way took us north, into the heart of the city.

There was a large throng of people gathered at the gates as we neared the entrance to the King's estate. High overhead, black and silver clouds fled south, lit from behind by a moon just past full. Torches flared in the dim pre-dawn light. Someone in the crowd saw us approaching and shouted, "He's here! Ambrose is here!"

The shouts were quickly taken up by others in the crowd.

"Ambrose," they called. "Kingmaker!"

Someone grabbed my leg as our group carefully worked our way through the milling people. I looked down to see an old woman in a shawl, clutching at me.

"Is it really him?" she cried, hope lighting her face. "Will he heal the King?"

"It is Ambrose, and if it can be done, he will heal the King," I responded as compassionately as I could, and hoped that it was true. I pulled away from the woman and noticed that several others in the party were being similarly accosted. Rogart was at the gates, yelling for a guard to let us in.

A sleepy-eyed Guardsman opened the gate to admit us. Once inside, we dismounted and, at Rogart's instruction, the other Guardsmen led the horses away.

The huge Captain led the way down a path paved with flagstones. At the end of the walkway, I could see the lights of a large manor house. The path terminated at the foot of a broad flight of black marble steps. At the top of the stairs were doors, massive creations of oak and brass. The house itself was built of granite blocks, gray and weathered with age. Two guards flanked the doors, their blue and white livery ghost-like in the half light. They raised their swords in a silent challenge.

"Peace, Guardsmen," Rogart said. "I am Rogart, your Captain. With me are Ambrose Kingmaker and Lauren of the Minstrels. The King has summoned them."

"Enter in peace," responded the guard on the right. The formula complete, she relaxed and added, "Praise to Mar and the Keepers that you found him, sir."

Rogart nodded and we entered.

We entered a large hypostyle hall, separated from the throne room beyond by a wooden railing. The clatter of our boots on the black marble floor echoed within the vastness of the chamber.

As Rogart spoke softly to a sleepy-eyed page, I stepped quietly to one of the railings. The throne room, lit dimly by a minimum of lamps, was a place of shadows. The floor sank toward the center of the far wall where the throne, carved of the white Elfstone, was raised upon a dais of the same material. Behind the throne hung the banner of Amersford, a white cross on a blue field. A wide aisleway led down to the foot of the dais and, on either side of the aisle, there were tiers of seats. Each row was curved so that all faced the throne. Awe touched me; the throne room was only slightly smaller than the open-air amphitheater at Songhaven.

"It is impressive in the dark," Ambrose said, breaking my reverie. "In the light, though, it is a place of glory."

Something in the prophet's voice spoke of old memories. I turned to face him.

"It is here that I first proclaimed Aerman High King of the Federated Kingdoms," Ambrose said in response to my unspoken question. He paused, then said, "Come. The page has returned with the Chamberlain. We're to see the King now."

The page was back in his place by the doors and Rogart was speaking to a small, thin man dressed in dark blue. The captain gestured in our direction, and I caught the Chamberlain's look of relief as he recognized Ambrose.

"Duke Jaret," Rogart said formally as they approached. "I present to you Ambrose of the Minstrels, he who is called Kingmaker. His companion is Lauren of the Minstrels."

The Guardsman then turned to me and Ambrose.

"Sirs, I present to you Duke Jaret of Kerith, Chamberlain of Amersford. He will take you to the King."

"Thank you, Rogart," Jaret said. "Ambrose and I are acquainted. You may return to your duties now." He turned to Ambrose. "It is good to see you again, Ambrose, though I must confess that I wish it were under better circumstances."

I examined the Chamberlain. The man's thin features were worn with care and his green eyes darted nervously about the room, as if watching for spies. His tunic and trousers were cut of matching royal blue cloth and were trimmed at the cuffs in white. He wore a wide leather belt, dyed black, fastened with a buckle of silver, inlaid in white with the symbol of the Bridge. Over all was a black cape and his hands fluttered in and out of its folds like caged wild birds, unable to fly, but unable to rest.

"I also wish for better times," Ambrose replied. "But how are things with you, Jaret? I've not seen you in many rounds of the seasons."

"All was well until several weeks ago. Ambrose, Marc needs you." This last, said in a whisper, was so choked with fear that I shuddered.

"Then let us go," Ambrose answered.

Without another word, Jaret led us to a hallway that ran into the north wing of the manor house. I was amazed that a simple hallway could be so lavishly done. The floor was an oak parquet, highly polished. The walls and ceiling were made of blocks of the polished granite. Intricately worked oil lamps hung on silver brackets and there were richly woven tapestries every few feet down the length of the hallway. When we had traversed three-quarters of the length of the hallway, a passage opened on the left. A stairway led up to the second level. I followed Jaret and Ambrose through two right turns to stop outside a guarded door.

"Good morning, my lord Chamberlain," one of the two guards said.

"Good morning, Bran. I have brought Ambrose to see the King."

For the first time, the guard's eyes slipped past Jaret to take in the old man in the nondescript robe. His eyes widened in surprise. Quickly, he and his companion stepped aside to let us enter.

I quickly took in the wealth of the sitting room, then turned my attention to the men there. Several wore the green sashes of the Healers. I recognized none of the faces but noted the relief on each one as Ambrose's presence was seen. Quiet conversations stilled as the prophet entered and hopeful eyes followed him as he crossed the room to the King's bedchamber.

I followed Ambrose into the room. There was a writing desk and bookshelves against the wall to my left. Opposite me, three chairs formed a semicircle around the hearth of a fireplace, where a bright fire crackled. Briefly, I regarded the King's sword, mounted in finely wrought brackets above the mantel. Finally, I turned my attention to the right, where Marc lay wasting in his bed.

That the King was ill was obvious. Marc had the haunted, shrunken look of a hefty man after a long, painful illness. His salt-and-pepper hair and beard were cropped close, and his blue eyes were alert and glittering, though full of pain.

Jaret knelt beside the bed.

"Your Highness," he said in hushed tones. "May I present Ambrose of the Minstrels?"

The prophet bowed but did not kneel. Feeling awkward, I stayed back, quiet. Marc motioned for Jaret to rise.

"Jaret, if you would, wait outside," he requested in a voice stretched thin by suffering. "As you wish."

The Chamberlain closed the door as he left. For several moments Ambrose and Marc simply regarded each other in silence. Then Marc grinned and said, "Ambrose, my old friend. Come, sit beside me, and tell me how you've been."

Ambrose seated himself on the edge of the bed, watching Marc intently. "I have been fine," he responded. "What of you, Marc? What has brought you to this?"

The King smiled again and shook his head in mock disgust.

"Prophet, you haven't changed a bit. You never were one to let a little pleasantness get in the way of unpleasantness."

The minstrel chuckled. "You have not changed either, Marc. You never would take anything seriously."

"If I took seriously all the days you had me slogging through the mud and the battles I fought," the King spluttered in mock indignation. "If I took seriously the nights I spent without sleep, or women, or even wine, just so you could set a boy on the throne in Badon, I'd have you killed on the spot." The King laughed and pain twisted his body. He looked like a lost child as he straightened. "Ambrose, help me."

"If I can, I will," Ambrose said, his voice choked with emotion. He was silent a moment before he continued.

"Now tell me all that has happened."

In a voice that was little more than a whisper, Marc related his tale.

"Several weeks ago, I fell ill. It was bad, Ambrose. The pain in my guts was horrible. I couldn't keep any food down and, if I did, I got diarrhea. My Healers gave me draughts, but nothing seemed to work."

"It sounds like poison to me," Ambrose commented.

Marc nodded. I could see the muscles of the King's jaw draw tight as he fought the pain in his body.

"I thought of that," Marc answered. "I have all my food tasted. We've found no signs of poison."

"Go on," Ambrose urged. He took Marc's wrist, feeling for the pulse.

"After a week of constant pain, someone told me of a man, a lunatic some said, who claimed he could heal me. I was desperate, my friend, for at times the pain was so bad I began to hallucinate. I sent for this man. The potion he gave me lessened the pain. Phelan said that he needed one more magic ingredient for the healing to work. I told him to do whatever was needed. He is still seeking it."

Ambrose released Marc's wrist.

"That was not wise, my friend," Ambrose stated. "Do you know what he seeks, and what he has done to find it?"

"No," Marc admitted. "And no one will tell me. I've not left my bed in over a week. I think the Healers have warned everyone not to upset me. Ambrose, what has he done?"

A loud knock cut off Ambrose's reply. At the King's nod, I opened the door. The man who entered, I guessed, could only be the magician Phelan.

He was a small man who moved with sharp, quick motions, his black eyes constantly darting around the room. His long, dirty hair was in wild disarray and bits of food and other debris hung in his beard. Though his black robe was of the finest cloth, it was filthy and ill-kept, and covered with silver signs and symbols.

I stepped back from the little man in distaste. Phelan had the sour smell of a man who had not bathed in weeks. For the first time, I noticed that the magician held a goblet.

"Sire, I did not mean to intrude," squeaked the little man. "I have brought your draught."

"Very well," the King growled, his irritation plain in his voice.

Ambrose had risen to stand at the head of the bed. As he crossed to Marc's side, Phelan quickly noted, and discounted the old minstrel. He handed Marc the goblet.

"Soon, Sire," Phelan said. "Soon I will find what I seek, and you shall be healed."

Marc cast a skeptical eye on Phelan and prepared to drink.

"Sire," Ambrose asked. "May I taste the draught?"

Phelan exploded with indignation.

"To what purpose, minstrel?" he demanded, stressing Ambrose's profession. "Do you think I am poisoning the King?"

"Right now, no," Ambrose replied in a calm, steady voice. His smokey gaze never left the magician's face. "I merely wish to see what is in it."

"So? What gives you the right to come meddling in the affairs of Amersford?"

By the color rising in his face, I could see that Marc was angry. Ambrose remained silent.

"Well, singer," Phelan continued in a high, squeaky voice. "Why would you taste..."

"Silence, magician," Marc snapped. Phelan abruptly stopped. He looked surprised. "You overstep your bounds, Phelan. Ambrose could by right, wear the Healer's green."

Phelan's eyes widened as Marc handed the goblet to Ambrose. The little man backed away a step, saying, "I meant no offense, Kingmaker. I did not know who you were."

Ambrose regarded the magician coldly as he sipped from the goblet. Then, to Marc, he said, "When I was last in Amersford, men such as this were arrested and put to honest work, not brought to court."

The magician started to snap back but, with a visible effort, kept his mouth shut. He smiled slyly.

"And how is my draught, Ambrose of the Minstrels?"

Ambrose's green eyes narrowed in suspicion.

"I find nothing wrong with it," he admitted. "But neither is there anything magical about it."

"That will come later, when I find what I seek. Sire, by your leave I wish to return to my chambers."

The King nodded his assent and Phelan fled the room.

"He seeks the horn of a unicorn," Ambrose said quietly.

"What?" Marc snapped in surprise. He struggled to sit up, but pain forced him back against his pillows. "What?" he asked again, weakly.

"Lauren, tell the King what you heard," Ambrose instructed.

For the first time, Marc turned his attention to me. I stepped forward, feeling more awkward than before. I saw the questioning look that Marc shot toward Ambrose.

"Your Highness, I present Lauren, son of Dalach Egan-son. He was just recently awarded the blue."

I bowed. "I am honored, Sire."

"And I also," Marc replied. "Your father is a great warrior and a great friend."

"Thank you, Sire."

For an uneasy moment, I stood under Marc's speculative gaze. Despite my training and preparation for moments such as this, I broke out in a cold sweat; I'd never actually spoken to a king before. Then Marc smiled.

"Relax, son. Though I am a King, I'm still a man like you. I won't bite your head off." He gestured at his wasted body. "Especially in this condition."

His obvious joviality helped, and I relaxed slightly.

"I spoke with Aldus," I volunteered.

"The Captain of my Guard," Marc added. "I've not seen him in some time."

"He was dismissed," I replied.

"No," Marc denied. He looked from me to Ambrose, then back again. "Phelan?"

"Yes," I answered.

"Why?"

"He protested when the magician sent the army south to the Lellarin Plains, looking for a unicorn."

"The whole army?" the King asked, his face twisted with dismay.

"Most of them. The youngest and the best. Those who refused to go were relieved of duty and sent home."

The King hung his head. "What have I done? Mar's love, what have I done?"

"You were desperate," Ambrose replied compassionately. "The question is, what do we do now? I am sure you are being poisoned, but I do not yet know how. This potion could be a remedy for many things."

He handed the goblet back to Marc, who drank down the contents.

"You must recall the army, Marc. Larsen is preparing to move on the High King. He's gathering his troops and people are fleeing Meren. The High King will need you."

"But I cannot lead them like this."

"Leave that to us," Ambrose said. "I need to think. With your leave, we'll go to our rooms."

"Very well. But don't go back to the inn. I want you close at hand. We'll put you up here. Lauren, call Jaret back in here."

I found the chamberlain waiting patiently in the sitting room. He was speaking quietly with two Healers who were also waiting.

"Jaret, Ambrose and Lauren will be staying here tonight," Marc said as Jaret entered the room. "Please find them rooms and send someone to the inn for their belongings."

"Yes, Sire."

"Since Ambrose is here," Marc continued, "I'd like a formal morning meal to be served in the main dining hall. If need be, I'll be carried down there." He turned to me and Ambrose. "I trust you'll join me."

"Certainly, Sire," Ambrose and I said together.

Jaret, Ambrose, and I bowed and turned toward the door.

"Jaret, one more thing."

The chamberlain paused. "Yes, Sire?"

"Send the new Captain to me. And get someone to find Aldus. Bring him here as well."

"Gladly, Sire."

As we re-entered the sitting room the two Healers who had been waiting there stood and joined us as Jaret asked, "How is he, Ambrose?"

Ambrose glanced at the Healers.

"They can be trusted," Jaret replied to the unasked question.

"It is bad, Jaret. Marc is being poisoned somehow. I promise you; I will find out how."

The chamberlain nodded. "We've all suspected as much, but we have not been able to prove it. He has all his food and drink tasted. Is it magic, Ambrose?"

"I think not. But if you'll show us to our rooms? I need to think on this situation a little."

"Certainly."

Jaret led us out of the King's suite to another suite on the second floor. It had a small sitting room and two small bedrooms. The sitting room contained several chairs, a drysink and, in one corner, a washbasin. Exhausted, I flopped into one of the chairs and kicked my boots off. I leaned my guitar against the arm of the chair. Ambrose followed suit.

"I'm exhausted," I said.

"I am, also," Ambrose replied. "Let us turn in. Tomorrow promises to be an interesting day."

I felt as if I had just closed my eyes when a knock sounded at the door of our suite. I quickly climbed out of bed to answer it. Ambrose appeared in the door to his room just as I opened the door.

"I am to take you to the dining hall," a page announced when I opened the door. His eyes grew wide when he noticed Ambrose in the door to his bed chamber.

"Give us a moment, please," Ambrose requested. "We need to clean up just a little."

The page just nodded, a bit too awed to speak. Ambrose and I each took a quick turn with the wash basin and quickly dressed.

The page led us to the far wing of the manor. Along the way, we passed the throne room. Several workers were polishing the railings and benches. They looked up in awe as Ambrose passed. Then our party entered the dining hall. The room stretched away equally far to the right and left, and it was easily large enough to accommodate five hundred people. To the right, a fireplace was set into the wall, though there was no fire burning that day. Above the fireplace hung the blue and white banner of Amersford. In front of the fireplace was a table big enough for twenty people, set lengthwise in the room. Marc sat at the head of the table, closest to the fire. Beyond Marc, in the room's far right corner, was a small, raised stage. It was empty.

Long tables, set across the width of the room, filled the rest of the space. They were made of highly polished mahogany, as were the walls, and all were unoccupied. Brocaded curtains were drawn back, and the large windows stood open, allowing the cool breezes of the summer morning into the room.

Marc motioned to the page, and we were led to his table. Ambrose was seated at the King's right, and I sat to Ambrose's right. The chair to Marc's left was empty, but the one next to it was occupied by Jaret. I did not recognize any of the others who had joined the King in breaking their fast.

Shortly after we were seated, Phelan entered and took the vacant seat. A look of revulsion flickered across Jaret's face and was so quickly controlled that it seemed that only I noticed it.

The King raised his goblet.

"Welcome, my friends. Long has it been since I have eaten in this hall, but no less honor would be fitting for Ambrose, the Kingmaker."

All the rest of us raised our drinks in a toast to Ambrose. Stewards arrived with the food. I watched as Marc's was tasted by a tall, black-haired man, then fell to eating my own meal, which consisted of a large slab of ham, eggs, and bread with butter and honey.

Marc and Ambrose leaned close together to talk in whispers. As I ate, my gaze wandered around the table. Jaret consumed little; he was intently watching the King, concern etched in every line of his face. Phelan dined like a pig, slopping food and drink into his beard and down the front of his robe. Marc ate sparingly, pausing to talk to Ambrose between mouthfuls. I watched as the King used his knife to spear a slice of ham and one of the little bits of onion garnishing his plate.

"Onions?" I whispered to myself.

Quickly, I examined the other plates. Not one contained an onion. I laid a hand on Ambrose's shoulder.

"Ambrose," I said quietly, "why is Marc's plate the only one with onions?"

Ambrose glanced quizzically at me, then looked at Marc's plate. He froze and his face went white.

"Marc, no," he cried.

Marc froze in the act of putting the food in his mouth.

"What is it?"

Quietly, Ambrose responded, "May I examine that mouthful?"

Wordlessly, Marc handed over the knife. Ambrose removed the onion and sniffed it. Next, he touched it to his tongue.

Most people were quietly watching Ambrose as I glanced around the table. Jaret was pale, watching the prophet with great interest. Phelan betrayed no emotion, but his little dark eyes glittered.

"What do you think you've found, minstrel?" he questioned.

Ambrose ignored him.

"Sire, this is no onion," the prophet explained. "It is known as death camas, and it contains a most deadly poison. The effects are those that you have experienced: great abdominal pain and digestive upset. In addition, the heartbeat slows." At this point Ambrose looked pointedly at Phelan. "It is most fortunate, Sire," he continued, "that you were given a treatment for the symptoms before you took the poison."

If Marc noticed the look, he ignored it.

"Yes, I am very lucky. Jaret, bring the cook from the kitchens." The King motioned to a waiting page. "Fetch the Guardsmen immediately."

Ambrose took Marc's plate and began examining each of the apparent onion bits.

"Only a few of these pieces are camas," he said after a moment. "The rest are true onions. You've been getting a very small dose."

The rest of us sat in silence until the guards arrived and Jaret returned. The chamberlain led a non-descript old man who, by the stains on his clothes, was the cook. When they reached the table, the small man dropped to his knee and said, "How may I serve you, Sire?"

"Ralf, when did you begin using onions in my morning meal?"

Ralf looked puzzled.

"Sire, in the twenty rounds that I've served your family, I have never used onions in your morning meal."

"Then what are these?" Marc demanded, gesturing toward his plate.

The cook rose to examine the plate.

"Those did not come from my kitchen, Sire," he stated emphatically.

"Then where did they come from? No one else touched this plate except..."

Marc's angry gaze turned to the taster, who paled and stepped away from the table.

"Cray?" the King said, his voice low and menacing.

"Sire, I..." the taster stammered.

The look on Cray's face was enough for Marc.

"Seize him," he barked at the guards.

The Guardsmen fell on the taster like hawks. Marc forced himself out of his chair and stood swaying before the man. He grabbed the front of Cray's tunic, as much to steady himself as to threaten the taster.

"Why?"

Cray closed his eyes and trembled but said nothing.

"Cray, why?" the King insisted.

Again, the man said nothing.

Marc addressed the guards, his face blank.

"I want an answer," he said as he painfully returned to his chair. One guard held the taster, the other drew his sword. As the weapon rasped out of its sheath, the taster's eyes popped open.

"No," he cried in anguish. His knees buckled and only the Guardsman's grip kept him from falling. Cray turned an imploring face to Marc. "Sire, I was forced to add them to your plate."

"By whom?" Marc's voice was deathly quiet.

"I…" Cray's eyes darted wildly around the room. "He said he would curse my family as you have been cursed. Before beloved Mar and the Keepers, I did not know it was poison. He said that it was just onions."

"Who?" the King repeated.

The taster's face melted into a look of abject helplessness. He hung his head and sobbed once before he answered, "The magician. Phelan."

Phelan jumped up and levelled a pointing finger at Cray. He began yelling incomprehensible syllables. The guards released Cray, who slumped to the floor, and rushed the magician.

"Quiet," one yelled and, when the magician persisted, slapped him soundly in the face. Marc was on his feet again. The second guard had his sword at Phelan's throat.

"By the Seven, why?" the King roared.

In response, Phelan laughed. Even prodding from the sword brought no words from the little man's mouth. At last, Marc returned to his seat, his face red with exertion and rage.

"What now?" he asked Ambrose.

"Search his room," the minstrel suggested.

Jaret and a Guardsman were sent to the magician's room. We all sat in tense silence, awaiting their return. No one ate. After a short time, the pair returned, their faces grim.

"I found these, Sire, hidden in the bottom of a chest in his room," the chamberlain said.

Jaret tossed two pouches onto the table before Marc. By the sound, one contained metal. The King picked up the other and emptied its contents onto the table. They were small, onion-like bulbs. With a dark glance at the captive magician, the King opened the other pouch. It was full of gold coins. Marc examined one and then several more.

"These were minted in Meren!" he exclaimed.

"Now I understand," Ambrose said. "He is not a magician. He is a spy, sent here to rob Aerman of your support."

Marc turned to the Guardsmen. "Take him to your Captain," he ordered. "The charge is treason. Bring him before the throne this afternoon."

The guards nodded and dragged the unresisting Phelan away. Marc slumped back in his chair. He looked haggard.

"Ambrose," he said wearily. "Once again you have done a great service, both to me and the Federation. There aren't thanks enough for you."

"When you are returned to health, that will be thanks enough for me. It was, however, Lauren who first spotted the difference in your plate."

"Still, would you not be happy if we had a feast, or sacrificed a virgin in your honor?" Marc asked, his voice dry. I looked at him in wonder; even ill, he'd not lost his humor. Ambrose chuckled.

"That would be a waste of a perfectly good virgin, and I don't eat much."

"You're impossible, Ambrose. You do not appreciate the finer things in life. Lauren, how about you? Would you be happy with a virgin sacrifice?"

I smiled. I suddenly realized that the King was used to being outrageous and that few people responded in kind.

"Aren't there better things to do with virgins?" I asked, just as dryly as the King.

For a moment, Marc just stared at me, then he began laughing. As his laughter grew stronger, others joined in. Even the somber chamberlain laughed. Marc's laughs eventually became coughs. The King looked up at me then, tears in his eyes.

"Ambrose, there might be something to this young minstrel of yours after all," he managed to choke out.

When the laughter died down, Marc turned to Ambrose.

"One more favor, for today," he requested.

"You have but to name it, Sire," Ambrose replied.

"Would you and Lauren assist me to my room?"

Together, we half carried Marc back to his chambers.

"Ambrose, how long will it be until the effects of the poison wear off?" the King asked as we walked.

"Several days," Ambrose answered. "You should continue to take the treatment that Phelan was giving you. It contains thorn-apple, a plant that grows in Altiera. It contains a substance that helps counteract the effects of the death camas. I will give your Healers the correct dose. You should not take more than the amount I prescribe, though, because thorn-apple itself is a poison if you take too much."

The conversation paused as we struggled up the stairs. When we'd reached the top, Ambrose said, "There has been a tremendous drain on your body, Marc. It could be a month, or more, before you are yourself again."

"May beloved Mar grant that I have that long. I need to get my men to Badon to back the High King."

"With Phelan captured, Larsen may hesitate to act," I suggested.

"May that be true," Marc responded.

The sitting room in Marc's suite was empty. Once in his bedchamber, Marc collapsed into a chair. At the King's request, I opened the windows wide. As I settled into a chair, someone rapped sharply on the door of the outer chamber.

"Never a dull moment," I muttered as I stood to answer the knock.

A page stood in the hallway with a man in a gray robe and the white sash of a wizard.

"Master Olen of the Wizards wishes to see the King and Ambrose Kingmaker," the boy informed me.

At a sign from Marc, I stood aside to let Olen enter. The wizard had black hair and gentle, brown eyes set far apart in a broad face. He was of average build and without his sash, Olen could easily have been mistaken for a trader or innkeeper.

As I closed the door, the wizard went directly to Marc and Ambrose. He bowed to Marc, saying, "Greetings, Sire." He turned to Ambrose. "You are Ambrose the prophet?"

Ambrose nodded his affirmation.

"I am Olen, Master of the Wizards of Amersford."

"What of Crom, who was Master?" Ambrose asked.

"I am sorry to say that he died two summers ago. This is not a social visit, though, Kingmaker. Do you intend to see the High King?"

"Soon, yes."

"Then you must know this and pass it to Aerman Sorren. In our house is a book called *The Book of Kings*. It has several chapters concerning the last days of the Great War."

"I have read it," Ambrose commented.

"Then you will recall the last chapter. It speaks of the Keepers' confrontation with Lorrestian. The Elven King prophesied that, as a sign of the Lawbreaker's coming, the Dark Magic would wake."

"Yes, I remember."

I listened intently, struggling to recall all that Ambrose had told me concerning the Lawbreaker. Marc's gaze darted back and forth between the minstrel and the wizard.

"The standing stone in the center of *Aennsrhyd* is a thing of Dark Magic. During the Great War, the Keepers damped the power of that stone. It has been quiescent ever since. Yesterday it flared into life. Since then, some force – perhaps the Keepers, perhaps Mar herself – has quieted the stone. Even so, the wizards are convinced that the Dark Magic is waking."

Ambrose flicked one troubled look in my direction.

"Olen, are you sure?" he asked.

"Yes, Ambrose, we are sure."

My head was reeling. Ambrose and I had speculated that the Lawbreaker might be alive and active. Now the wizards of Amersford had independently come to the same conclusion. If the Lawbreaker was indeed alive, the Federation's days – the world's days – were coming to an end. We were all doomed unless the Lawbreaker could somehow be found and stopped.

"I must see Marc cured first," Ambrose said. He stood and began pacing the room as he spoke. "As soon as that is accomplished, we shall ride for Badon. Is there nothing more you can tell me?"

"Nothing that we can be sure of. Some of our number feel that the Dark Ones themselves are beginning to stir, but we have no real proof of that. Prophet, with your vision, have you seen? Are we doomed?"

Ambrose was facing away from us. He stopped in his tracks, and I could see his back stiffen at the question.

"If we are, I have not seen it," the prophet answered quietly.

Olen stood silent a moment, waiting for more.

"I must go," he said when no further response came from Ambrose. "We have been monitoring the stone since it woke. Soon, it will be my shift."

"Olen, I would ask a favor," Ambrose said, turning to face us.

"Name it, Kingmaker."

"Could we accompany you back to your house? I wish to read again from *The Book of Kings*."

"Certainly. Our library is open to you. By your leave, Sire?"

Marc nodded, but then said, "Ambrose, Lauren, a word in private before you go?"

Olen quietly left the room. Ambrose relaxed after the wizard left. Still, his face was a jumble of emotions. I was confused and overwhelmed.

"The High King must know," Marc stated.

"You must be cured first," Ambrose insisted. "You will be needed in the struggle."

"Without the poison I shall mend fast enough. This is grave news and Aerman must know."

Ambrose paced the room, obviously undecided.

"How about this?" the King asked. "The trial is this afternoon and I plan to have a celebration tomorrow night. Stay for that. That would give you two days to play nursemaid to me. Then you could leave for Badon and be there by the nineteenth. Surely the world won't end in the next six days."

Ambrose nodded.

"That sounds like a reasonable plan," he agreed.

Marc stood and staggered toward his bed.

"I need some sleep," he announced.

"Then we will go," Ambrose said. "We will see you at the trial this afternoon."

We joined Olen in the King's sitting room and descended the stairs to the first floor. As we crossed the entrance hall toward the doors to the mansion, footsteps sounded behind us. A rough hand fell on my shoulder.

"A far cry from the Black Dragon, young Lauren," a voice said.

"Aldus!"

"Aye. Back in my place and with all the thanks to you."

I smiled awkwardly.

"I really didn't do much. I just watched what was going on."

Aldus barked out a short laugh.

"Just watched, he says. Aye, and saw what no one of us ever did, though it was sitting right in front of us."

"It is good to see you again, Aldus," Ambrose said.

"Ah, where's my manners?" the captain replied. "It's good to see you, too, old friend. If I'd known who Lauren's friend was two nights ago… And good day to you as well, Master Olen."

Together we walked across the hall, our boots tapping hollowly on the stone.

"How goes the mustering?" Ambrose asked.

"Most of the men should be here in two days' time," the warrior responded. "It will take two days more to gather food and supplies and get them in some kind of order. We'll be in Badon just after the new moon."

We stepped out the main doors into bright sunshine. Long white shreds of cloud drifted across the sky.

"A beautiful day," Aldus said. "I go now to check on the provisioning for the army. Would you care to join me?"

"I think not," Ambrose answered. "We need to do some research in the wizards' library."

"Then our ways part here. I'll see you this afternoon."

Our way took us through the marketplace, where we had to fend off vendors of all stripes. We soon left the bustle of the market behind for the quiet of Wall Run and were soon at the Wizard's Corner.

A tall, thin novice was acting as doorkeeper. When Olen entered and announced who we were, the boy's eyes widened in awe, but he maintained his composure.

"Be welcome in this house," he said formally and bowed.

"Ambrose," Olen said. "I have some other matters to attend to, so I will leave you in Alun's care. Alun, please take them to the library."

"As you wish, Master Olen."

Olen nodded and strode off. The apprentice led us down several dimly lit hallways to a set of large double doors. He opened one and let us into the library.

I gasped. The collection of the wizards' library of Amersford was at least three times greater than the library in Songhaven, which was not small. The novice noticed my surprise and visibly swelled with pride.

"We maintain the largest library in the Federation," he informed me. "Much is preserved here that has been lost elsewhere."

"I can see that," I replied.

"Will there be anything else you require?" the apprentice continued. "Have you broken your fast?"

"Yes, we have," Ambrose answered. "You have our thanks though. We have all that we need for now."

"As you say."

The boy left us alone and Ambrose turned to me.

"Take a seat at the table and I will get the book we came for."

I sat and examined the library as Ambrose searched among the shelves. The room itself was not especially large, but every inch of space was crammed with shelves, each full to bursting with books. The only space left clear, a space just inside the doors, contained three tables. Golden shafts of sunlight shone through windows high on the walls, turning dust motes into tiny dancing stars. Ambrose gave a small exclamation of triumph and returned to our table, a book carefully cradled in his hands.

The lack of dust on the book was mute evidence of the wizards' recent inquiries, but its great age was apparent as Ambrose unrolled it on the table.

"In the language of the Elves, this is *Dor Kareth an Elmaren, The Book of Kings*. It was written by many different scribes, each setting down the record of his own King. Shortly after the Great War, it was translated by someone named Melcor, so that a record remained of the last King's prophecies."

Ambrose paused for a moment, then continued.

"I have spoken to you before concerning Lorrestian of the Elves. Now I would have you read for yourself the signs and portents he foretold. Begin here."

I bent close. The writing was small and cramped, the ink faded on the yellowing parchment.

"Please read it aloud," Ambrose requested.

"And it came to pass," I read, "that in the one hundred and twenty first round in his reign, King Lorrestian the Smith found himself to also be a prophet. In his visions, he saw war, the death of the People of the Stars, and the rise of the Keepers of the Alomar."

I looked up from the book.

"The one hundred and twenty first round?" I asked.

"Remember that unless they were killed, the Elves were immortal," Ambrose replied.

"I see."

I returned to the text.

"The King also saw a hope for his People. Far in the future would come a man of great power, a power great enough to shake the very foundations of the world. The Lawbreaker he would be called, for all natural law would be his, to bend to his will. This man would see the return of the Elves to the Kingdoms of the Alomar.

"Guided by his prophecies, Lorrestian forged a sword and a ring. The ring was of gold, worked in a wonderous design, and set with a stone of violet hue. The sword also bore a pommel stone of the same violet stone. Both jewels were dark and unreflecting of light. They would wake, the King said, when the Lawbreaker possessed them. Then, before the fires of war swept the Lellarin Plains, these tokens were hidden, to be found by the Lawbreaker in his need."

I looked up at Ambrose.

"Even the scribe didn't know where the sword and ring were hidden?" I asked.

"If he did, he didn't record it," Ambrose replied. "This book is the only mention that I've ever found of them. But read on, the next part is very interesting."

"What follows is not part of the original text," Melcor had written. "It is an eyewitness account of the final defeat of the Elven King, as seen by a common soldier who chanced to be in the throne room.

"Lorrestian stood in front of his ruined throne. The room was a shambles. Against him stood the seven servants of Mar, the Keepers of the Alomar. Cloaked and hooded in black, the Destroyer stood at their head.

"The Elven King spoke, his voice yet defiant. 'I know who you are Destroyer. I know who all of you are and I know who you serve. You may have defeated me and my people, but one day you, too, shall fall. Know this: I have seen the coming of the Lawbreaker!'

"The figure in black flinched marginally. The others turned toward each other in apparent confusion.

"Lorrestian continued, his voice full of contempt, 'Know this also, for these are the signs of his coming. Watch for them, for they are also the signs of your doom. The Dark Magic will wake and flood the land. The Dark Ones shall rise and walk again in the hills and on the plains. The People of the Stars will return and come against you. Then fear, Destroyer, for he will then be walking the earth. He will bear the tokens I forged for him; the ring *Elinaur* and the sword *Endolsar*. You, Destroyer, and all those who stand with you, shall fall and the world will be ended.'

"The black figure raised his arm. He said something in a harsh, grating tongue and clenched his fist. The Elven King's face contorted in agony, and he crumbled to the floor.

"So watch," Melcor concluded. "All of you future generations, watch for these signs. They spell doom for the world unless the Lawbreaker is defeated before he comes into his power. Be ever vigilant and call upon the Keepers for guidance should you find him. May the Love of Mar and the Grace of the Seven be with you always."

I looked up from the text.

"There is no comfort in this," I commented.

"None at all," Ambrose agreed. "Except for the hint that the Lawbreaker can be stopped. I do not see how, though, with all of natural law his to command."

At that moment, Olen entered. Behind him came another novice with a tray of food.

"Ambrose, Lauren, good day. I trust you found what you needed."

"Indeed," Ambrose replied. "Though it leaves us with heavy hearts."

"*The Book of Kings* can do that. I have arranged for someone to cover my shift monitoring the stone so that we could speak. I also took the liberty of bringing food. Would you care to join me in the midday meal as we talk?"

"Is it that late already?" I asked.

"It is," Olen answered.

"We'll be glad to join you, then."

"Good. Tadg, just place the tray on the table. Close the door behind you and see that we are not disturbed."

The boy nodded and did as he was bid. When he was gone, Olen joined us at the table.

"We shall eat as we talk," he said. "I feel the situation is grave, with no time left for soft words and formal phrasing, so I will be blunt. What do you know of this?"

I poured mead for each of us as Ambrose answered.

"Only what you have read in this book. I once had a vision concerning the Lawbreaker, but it showed me nothing that was not in *The Book of Kings*."

Curious, I asked, "When was that vision?"

"On the night that Colin, my Master, ga..."

Ambrose froze in mid-sentence, his eyes wide with alarm, then finished, "died."

"Ambrose," Olen challenged, "you said other than what you meant. This is no time for secrets."

I watched the Master closely. Though it was not overly warm in the library, he was sweating, and his pupils were wide and black.

"What I hide would cause more harm than good, were it known. Colin was dying before he revealed it to me, and I am bound by the same oaths as he. It would not help us in this matter. There is one thing we need to discuss, though."

"And what is that?"

Ambrose turned to me.

"Lauren, describe what happened to you in *Aennsrhyd* two days ago."

I swallowed a mouthful of mead before I answered.

"It was well past midday. We had entered *Aennsrhyd* through the South Gate. According to Ryan and Ambrose, it was too quiet, so Ryan and I went ahead to see if the garrison was still there. We came on the stone in the center of the city and just as I started past it, there was a clap of thunder. The world went black and seemed to spin around me. In the darkness, something or someone very powerful was looking for me. I could feel its desperation. Then everything returned to normal."

Olen listened to me intently and regarded me with a steady frown.

"You did not touch the stone?" he asked.

"No. I didn't even get close enough to touch it."

"And this Ryan, did he touch it?"

"No, he cautioned me not to."

"We suspect that the Lawbreaker woke the stone," Ambrose said. "And that Lauren simply got caught in the backlash of that waking."

"Perhaps," Olen replied, a thoughtful look on his face. "But why, then, did he get the sense that the being was looking for him?"

"His father," Ambrose replied, "is Dalach Egan-son."

"So," Olen said in surprise.

"We think that perhaps the Lawbreaker seeks him as a way to influence his father," Ambrose said. "He is also betrothed to the Princess of Han. If either Dalach or Houl were to be compromised, that could undermine our defense."

The wizard looked skeptical. He picked up his cup, leaned back in his chair and drank, and then turned to me.

"Lauren, you experienced the waking of the Dark Magic. It is strange to me that you felt it, yet Ambrose did not. How much do you know of the Dark Magic?"

Unwanted visions of a woodland shrine rose in my mind. I forced them aside and replied, "Very little. Such knowledge is forbidden."

"And well it should be. But we of the wizards must learn something of it, to avoid unwittingly following its paths. Still, I can tell you but little concerning it. When the Keepers bound the Dark Ones, the magic went dormant. We cannot fathom what woke it unless the Lawbreaker now lives."

The wizard leaned forward and refilled his cup, then did the same for Ambrose. I declined the mead but picked at the food on the tray.

"There is more," Olen told us as he set down the pitcher. "Crom once told me that, twenty rounds or so ago, in late in the second moon or early in the third moon of *Tymnagena*, there was a great disturbance in the magical sphere. Some huge power flared for an instant, then was veiled. Shortly thereafter, the Keepers instituted the *magenahr*. I, and several others, now feel that what Crom sensed was the birth of the Lawbreaker, and that the *magenahr* is part of their search for him."

"You could be right," Ambrose commented. "Are the wizards not more closely monitored than ever before?"

"We are, and I now feel that we know why. I am convinced that the Lawbreaker is alive and somewhere in the Federated Kingdoms. How do we find him, or the ring and sword, to prevent his using them?"

I leaned forward.

"Are there any of the wizards who could be the Lawbreaker?" I asked.

"Only a handful of my colleagues have gained the ability to light a staff, the final test of a Master. Her reputation aside, even the Morgan is not much more powerful than the rest of us."

"You have not answered the question," Ambrose commented.

"I'm thinking."

Olen bit into an apple, chewing thoughtfully. He shook his head as he swallowed.

"No," he said finally. "The training is too rigorous and the testing too thorough to hide that kind of power for long. He is none of the wizards."

"Who, then?" Ambrose pondered.

We were silent a moment, regarding each other.

"It could be anyone," Ambrose concluded. "From the High King to the most obscure beggar in the wilderness."

"Can we come at this another way?" Olen mused. "Could we find the ring and sword?"

I had my eyes on Ambrose. For one fleeting moment fear and panic crossed his face and then the look passed.

"Finding the sword would be like trying to find a needle that was hidden in a city. Lorrestian had all of the Alomar Kingdoms in addition to his own to hide it in."

"Then what would you have us do?" Olen asked.

"Bide our time. Think. Other than the waking of the stone yesterday, have any of you sensed the Lawbreaker's use of power?"

The wizard shook his head.

"Then he is untrained," Ambrose concluded. "Perhaps even unknowing of his strength. If the wizards are vigilant, his first trial of power may give us time to destroy him, before he can learn to use it."

"Such a course is risky," I noted.

"Indeed," Olen replied. "All we sensed yesterday was the waking of the stone itself, not the use of some power to trigger that awakening. Assuming that we could sense the Lawbreaker is unwarranted given what we know."

"Still," Ambrose countered, "I do not believe that it would be wise to disperse the armies of the Federation in a search for the ring and sword while Larsen marches into Badon to seize the throne."

"True," Olen admitted. "I had not considered the political implications. Now, it grows late and there is much to do. I must arrange to send word to the houses in other cities and the Morgan must be informed."

"Our thanks to you for your hospitality and for the use of the library," Ambrose said.

"And my thanks to you for your counsel. The minstrels will see to it that the Kings are warned?"

"Of course."

"Ambrose, Lauren, travel thee well," the wizard said. "May Garth guide your footsteps and put you on the path back to Mar."

"And may Mancier support your power in the service of Mar, Olen of the wizards," Ambrose answered.

We stood and Olen opened the door. I could see, in the darkened hallway beyond, the novice Alun, waiting.

"Alun will see you out," the wizard said. "Fare ye well."

Silently, Alun led us to the entrance. He opened the door and stood aside. When we had passed through, he closed it, all without speaking. Ambrose at once set off for the marketplace.

"Where are we going now, Master?"

Ambrose glanced back as he began to force his way through the milling crowd around the marketplace.

"To the Minstrel's Haven," he answered. "The word must go out across the Federation. Then we return to the palace for the trial."

The afternoon sun hung in a nearly cloudless sky. The day was not hot and there was a breeze, but I noted that Ambrose's tunic was darkened with sweat. I quickened my pace a moment and fell in alongside him.

"Master Ambrose, are you well?"

He did not slow as he answered, "My head aches, Lauren. When we return to the palace, I will take something for it."

Something in his manner convinced me that more than pain was troubling him. I also knew that it was useless to press Ambrose, so I let the matter drop.

A minstrel was playing in the courtyard of the Minstrel's Haven when we arrived. Ambrose, with me close behind, went directly to the small group gathered around her.

"Very well played, Anna," he said when she finished.

The woman's head snapped up, her eyes wide. Quickly, she regained her composure.

"Master Ambrose. I had heard that you were in Amersford. How may I serve you?"

Seeing that another song was not immediately forthcoming, the little group began to disperse amid awed whispers about the prophet Ambrose.

"There is a message that must be spread across the Federation," Ambrose replied. "Where are you bound?"

"Landfall," Anna answered. "My father is nearing his birthday and I go to mark the day with him."

"Can you contrive to get a message to Marwynn?"

Anna nodded.

"I am usually asked to play at the King's palace. What is the message?"

"Tell Marwynn that the Lawbreaker is alive and that Meren is planning to march on the High King."

"I don't understand. Who is the Lawbreaker?" the woman asked.

"Do not worry," Ambrose responded. "The King will understand. Anna, this message must reach all the Kings. Are there other minstrels here?"

"There are."

"We must get back to Marc's mansion. Will you talk to the others? Word must go to Marsden Forge, and someone should carry word to Elissa at Songhaven."

Anna brushed back her long dark hair. Her brown eyes were full of questions.

"You'll not tell me more of this Lawbreaker?"

Ambrose shook his head.

"I cannot. It is a matter for the Kings. Trust me, Anna. If this knowledge were released, it would cause a panic such as we have never seen before."

She was silent a moment, then said, "The message will go out."

"Travel thee well, then. May Garth guide your footsteps and put you on the path back to Mar."

"And you as well, Ambrose."

We turned to go. Anna began playing again and the sound of her guitar followed us out of the courtyard and a short way down the Road before the noise of the marketplace overwhelmed it. Soon we were back at the King's mansion.

The throne room was lit with the light of hundreds of lamps mounted in sconces on the walls and people were milling around, both in the throne room and in the hall, waiting for the upcoming trial. A page was waiting for us just inside the doors.

"The King has asked me to let you know that the trial will be starting in half an hour," the page said.

Ambrose nodded.

"Our thanks," he said. "You may let the King know that we will be there."

As the page scurried off, we quickly returned to our suite to change into formal attire. We spoke little as we washed the dust from the marketplace from our faces and put on fresh clothes. Someone had retrieved our belongings from the Minstrel's Haven and stacked them neatly in the outer room of our suite. I put on a knee-length tunic of brown silk over a shorter, cotton one. My trousers were of the finest samite. With pride, I tied on the bright blue sash that marked me as a minstrel. Almost without thinking, I picked up my twelve-stringed guitar. Ambrose was regally dressed in a robe the deep indigo blue of the midnight sky. I waited while he took a remedy for his headache. Then, guitars strapped across our backs, we strode through the halls of Amersford.

The throne room was full when we entered. Silver lamps had been kindled and light flared along the polished white walls and danced along the oak railings. Brightly dressed courtiers jammed the seats, restless as they eagerly waited to see their King healed and healthy once again. The buzz of hushed conversation rose and fell and chased its own echoes around the hall, then slowly ceased as Ambrose stepped into the room. Heads swiveled around and faces lit with hope as, motioning for me to follow, Ambrose strode down the central aisle.

At that moment, Jaret, clad all in white, stepped through a door to the right of the empty throne. Ambrose and I halted at the foot of the dais. For a moment, the chamberlain surveyed the crowd. Pitching his voice to carry, Jaret spoke.

"His Highness, Marc, by the grace of Mar and the support of the Keepers King of Amersford and Warden of the Amersford Bridge," he proclaimed. "All hail the King."

"All hail the King," the crowd responded.

Marc entered, clad in the white and blue livery of his army. The light flashed from his unadorned silver crown and from the gold hilt of the great sword at his side. Still weak, the King leaned heavily on the arm of a Guardsman, and I was pleased to see that it was Aldus, back in the blue and white livery of the King's Guard.

The crowd erupted with joyous shouts. "Hail Marc!" they called. "All hail Marc of Amersford!"

While they cheered, Marc moved to stand before his throne. Aldus and Jaret stood on his right. He gestured and Ambrose and I took up places to his left. Marc let the crowd yell just a while longer, then raised his arms for silence. The crowd quieted quickly and waited for the King to speak. Filled with the pulsing of the light, the hush grew. Marc drew his sword, the light flashing back from the great sapphire set in the pommel. He set the sword upright before him, his hands resting lightly on the jeweled hilt.

"My people, many forget that one of the titles of the King of Amersford is that of Warden of the Bridge," he said. "It is my duty to hold the Bridge against any invader. Like Han, we guard the gates of the Realm. It never crossed our mind to ward against those who we protect, yet it seems that we should have done so. One whom we trusted, one sworn to our service, endeavored to strike us down. Only through the efforts of Ambrose and Lauren of the Minstrels was our death prevented. We have summoned all of you here to witness the trial of one who is accused of being a traitor."

Marc signed to someone in the back of the hall. There was a slight commotion, then two Guardsmen appeared, dragging the magician Phelan between them. I risked a glance at Ambrose and noticed sweat beading on the prophet's forehead.

"Master Ambrose, are you well?" I whispered.

"My head is still aching, that is all."

Again, something in his tone gave lie to his words, but I could not press him in front of Marc's court. Phelan was now at the foot of the dais, still in the filthy robe he'd worn at the morning meal. Marc had drawn himself up to his full height, his kingship shining from him in the glory of the hall.

"Phelan," Marc said, his voice ringing with authority. "Do you have representation?"

The little man glared at Marc, his rodent-like eyes lit with the fire of hate. He shook off his guards and stood up straight.

"There is no one in this city worthy of speaking for me," he said, his voice dripping with contempt.

"You face death," Marc warned. "You may wish to reconsider that stance."

Phelan said nothing, but just stood there glaring at the King. After a moment, Marc continued.

"Very well. Phelan, you are charged with treason against the King of Amersford. You poisoned the King you swore to serve and, what is more, you did so as part of an alleged plan to overthrow the High King of the Federated Kingdoms of Alomar. How say you?"

"I do not deny it," Phelan said scornfully.

"I remind you, you face death."

Phelan laughed.

"You threaten me?" he asked. "I did what I did knowing the risk. But know this, mighty King of Amersford: I spoke truly when I said that your doom was upon you. You, and your precious High King, will fall. My only regret is that I will not be there to see it."

"So be it," Marc answered. "Phelan, you are sentenced to death as a traitor. Aldus, have a gallows constructed outside the North Gate. Tomorrow at sunrise, hang him. Now, get him out of my sight."

The Guardsmen hauled the magician up the aisle. Halfway up, the little man began to laugh, the wild, uncontrolled laughter of a madman. It echoed in the hall long after he was gone.

"Now listen, my people," Marc called. "With the help of Ambrose and Lauren, we have averted one disaster. Now another faces us. We believe that Larsen of Meren plans to march on the High King. Aerman will need every man who can wield a sword. I have recalled the army from the plains. All of you, return to your homes. Rally your men, empty the towns and villages. The Federation is at stake. The cavalry will ride for Badon in two days with the infantry to follow as soon as possible. We need you. Go now and ride like the wind. The Federated Kingdoms are in your hands."

The throne hall erupted in shouts of "Hail Marc!" and "Amersford for the High King!"

As the crowd filed out, Marc sheathed his sword and sat down on his throne. I watched with concern as Ambrose used a sleeve to wipe his sweaty forehead. The King saw my look of concern and focused on the prophet.

"Ambrose," he said. "You're as pale as a ghost. Are you well?"

"It is nothing," Ambrose denied. "Just a sore head. It will pass. How are you holding up, Marc?"

"Fine, Ambrose. Never better. Strange, what not eating poison does for a man."

The King idly pushed back his crown.

"Ambrose," he said. "Once again, I thank you."

Marc undid a pouch at his waist and held out the ring that Ambrose had sent to the guards two days before. "I want to return this to you." He turned next to me. "Lauren, I am in your debt as well. Is there anything you would ask for?"

I bowed and said, "It was an honor to serve you, Sire. I ask for nothing in return."

Marc snorted his disapproval.

"Ambrose has taught you too well. Take this anyway."

The King placed a ring, twin to the one Ambrose possessed, in my hand.

"Thank you, friend," the King said quietly. "This gives you complete freedom in my Kingdom."

I dropped my gaze to the ring in my hand.

"Sire, I..."

"Aldus," the King cut me off. "See to the gallows. Jaret, see what you can do about rounding up food for the army as it gathers. How go the preparations for tomorrow's celebration?"

As Jaret replied, Ambrose took my arm and led me from the dais. At the foot of the stairs, I hesitated. I held up the glittering sapphire ring, tears in my eyes.

"Ambrose, I didn't know what to say. I didn't even thank him."

"There is no need, Lauren. He understands. That was a rare display of emotion for Marc. Come, we should practice for tomorrow's celebration. I am sure that we will be asked to play."

My heart swelled with gratitude, and I glanced up at the King, who was giving orders necessary to mobilize his forces. Then I turned to accompany Ambrose to our suite.

We were awakened the next morning by a page knocking insistently on the door to our suite.

"Master Ambrose," he said. "The King requests that you break your fast with him in his suite."

"Very well," Ambrose replied. "We will go at once. Would you seek out a Healer and have them send a treatment for headache to the King's rooms for me."

"I will, sir."

As we walked, I asked, "Your head still hurts?"

"It does."

"Master, in the last day, you've gone through all of the remedies for headaches that you possessed. I don't mean to pry, but that does not seem normal."

"It is nothing to worry about, Lauren."

"But Master..."

"It is nothing to worry about," he insisted, emphasizing the word "nothing."

The outer door to Marc's suite was open, though still warded by two Guardsmen. We announced ourselves to them and they let us pass. Marc and Jaret were seated at a small table in the center of the room going over some report. Jaret was pointing out a particular set of numbers on the paper as we entered. The table was covered in various papers, quills, and inkpots. In the center of the table was a cut glass pitcher full of water. The light coming in the open window flickered as the breeze stirred the leaves of the trees and the pitcher echoed it, seeming to flicker as if lit with some inner flame.

"Ambrose, Lauren," Marc said as he spied us. "Join us. The food will be here soon. Until then, I'd like to speak with you about tonight's celebration."

Ambrose and I sat. The Master seemed distracted by the pitcher of water and didn't seem to hear when Marc said, "I'd like both of you to perform tonight. Is that asking too much after all that you've done."

I had turned my attention to Marc when he began speaking. In response to his question I said, "I'd be honored to per..."

Ambrose screamed.

I flinched. Ambrose sat rigid in his chair, his head thrown back in seeming agony. As I watched, he collapsed to the floor. Instantly, I was at his side.

"Master Ambrose," I cried, panic raising my voice.

I glanced around the room. Marc knelt on the other side of Ambrose and the Guardsmen had rushed into the room along with several pages. Marc rolled Ambrose onto his back.

"Jaret," he said calmly. "Bring me one of the pillows from my bed. Someone fetch a Healer. Tell the Healer to bring a draught for a headache. A strong one. And get him some wine." There was no worry on the King's face as he placed the pillow under Ambrose's head.

"Sire, what is wrong with him?" I asked.

The King looked at me strangely and said, "You don't know?"

"No."

Marc chuckled.

"Then you've never seen Ambrose prophecy before?"

I shook my head.

The King nodded his thanks as a page handed him a goblet of wine.

"Fear not, Lauren. He'll come out of it and, when he does, he'll want wine and something for a headache. For now, all we can do is wait to hear what he saw."

Ambrose groaned and everyone in the room pressed closer. Only Marc's angry glare held them back. Ambrose grasped at his chest and moaned again. His eyes opened and I could see that his pupils were enlarged well beyond normal.

"Lauren?" he croaked.

"I'm here, Master."

"Wine."

Marc held the goblet to Ambrose's lips, and he drank deeply. Slowly, his eyes returned to normal. As they did, he saw Marc, then focused his gaze on me.

"Lauren," he said weakly. "If we do not reach Badon soon, the High King will die."

CHAPTER EIGHT

My mind went blank, and my world narrowed to Ambrose's face. I sank back until I was sitting on my heels. Several of the people in the room cried out in dismay. Marc dropped the goblet and, ringing dully, it rolled around in the spilled wine.

It was the King who broke the silence.

"What?" he breathed.

Ambrose struggled to sit up. Marc and I helped him into a sitting position. For a long moment, Ambrose sat with his head down, breathing heavily, then spoke. His voice was raw and strained.

"Death marches toward Badon," he said, his voice just above a whisper. "I saw a figure cloaked in black murder the High King in his throne room. If we do not reach Badon in time, Aerman Sorren will die."

Marc spent a moment intently studying Ambrose's face. Satisfied with what he saw, he nodded and stood.

"Jaret, you stay here," he ordered. "Guards, return to your post. Speak to no one of this."

The Guardsmen simply nodded and returned to their post in the hallway.

The King continued, "One of you pages – you Rory – find Aldus and bring him here at once. Thom, you get my Healer and send him up here with the strongest headache draught he has. Then find General Oscon and likewise bring him here. Both of you say that the matter is urgent but say nothing about what you've heard here. Now, go."

The pages practically ran from the room. The King bent and helped Ambrose to his feet and then we settled back into our chairs. I felt shaken. Ambrose was white with fear and the painful aftereffects of prophecy. Only Marc seemed totally in control as he focused on Ambrose.

"What do we do now?" the King asked.

Ambrose did not answer. Marc and I glanced at each other, then back at the prophet.

"Ambrose, what do we need to do?" Marc insisted.

"Marc, a moment," Ambrose pleaded. "It is difficult to think through this pain. Normally I take something for the pain and go to sleep after seeing."

Marc sprang to his feet. The color had risen in his face, his large, lumpy nose was red, and his pale blue eyes glittered from their deep sockets.

"Ambrose, I am sorry you are in pain, but the Federation is at stake. I need to know what you need from me."

The King stood in front of Ambrose, his jaw set, his salt-and-pepper beard jutting out. Ambrose just hung his head. When he spoke, his voice was strained.

"*Mirdl*," Ambrose said, the first time I'd ever heard him swear. "Marc, you know how it is after a vision. I will try. But please, send for a Healer. I need something for the pain."

Marc's mood softened.

"It has been done," he said. "One should be here soon."

"My thanks," Ambrose said, his voice a raspy whisper. "We'll need horses," he continued. "Best would be permission to use the horses from the posting stations. Our animals can walk all day, but we need speed now. Lauren, we'll carry only some clothes and our guitars. Marc, can you bring our horses and the rest of our things when you come?"

"Of course."

Someone knocked at the door.

"Come," Marc called.

A Healer stepped in bearing a wine goblet. With a nod to the King, he stepped across the room to hand the goblet to Ambrose.

"It is an honor to serve you, Kingmaker," the man said.

Mumbling words of thanks, Ambrose took the goblet and downed its contents. Marc gestured for the Healer to leave.

"I had them make it strong," the King commented as the Healer left.

"My thanks to you," Ambrose said, a grateful expression on his face.

Another knock sounded at the door.

"Now what?" Marc grumbled. "Come," he snapped in irritation.

Aldus entered and bowed to the King.

"You wished to see me, sire?"

Marc nodded. "Aldus, have someone ready two of the swiftest post horses. Ambrose and Lauren will ride within the hour."

"As you wish," Aldus responded. "The fastest are Stormwind and Challenger. They will be ready within that time."

"Excellent."

At that moment, another man entered. He was of a height with Marc and, going on appearance alone, could have been related to the King. He was dressed in the formal white and blue livery of the Amersford army.

"Oscon," Marc said, noting the man's presence. "Meren is preparing to move on Badon and there is going to be an attempt on the High King's life. We will be needed to either save the King or defend his son. You must accelerate the mustering of the army. We must march as soon as possible, even if it means leaving before everyone is back from the plains."

The warrior nodded.

"Aye, sire. I'll do what I can to speed the mustering."

"I want every available cavalryman ready to go the day after tomorrow. I will lead them myself. You'll stay here to bring the infantry when they're ready."

Ambrose cut in.

"Marc, you are in no condition to ride, especially under the conditions required for this ride."

"Ambrose, you've told me what needs to be done. Now let me do it. I will not send my men into battle if I'm not willing to go myself. Not only that, but I'm on the High King's Council. No one else here is. In the coming fight, a council member might be as important as soldiers. I will be there if I have to have them tie me to my saddle."

The two men stared intently for a moment, then Ambrose just nodded slightly.

"Oscon, get to it."

"Aye, sire."

Jaret stepped forward.

"What may I do, sire?" he asked.

The King turned to Ambrose.

"What else is required?"

"You must be in Badon with as many men as you can as soon as you can," Ambrose replied. "Other than that, there is little else."

The King turned back to the Chamberlain.

"Jaret, please share with the Queen what has happened and make plans with her for the two of you to keep things running while I'm gone."

"Very well, sire. I shall be with the Queen if you require anything further."

As the Chamberlain left, Ambrose stood. His thin face was still pale, but he was steady on his feet.

"That draught was quite effective," he stated. "You must thank your Healer for me. Lauren, come, we must pack. Sire, we shall see you before we depart."

Marc just nodded as I followed Ambrose from the King's suite.

"Ambrose," I asked. "How long will it take us to reach Badon?"

He answered without slowing.

"Normally it would take us almost four days, but we'll be using the High King's posting system. The horses are bred for speed and there are posting stations every twenty-five miles between here and Badon. So, we should be there before sunset tomorrow."

Once back in our suite we quickly packed. I changed back into my traveling clothes and jammed my dress clothes and a change of everyday clothes into my shoulder pack. I put my guitar back into its leather case and announced to Ambrose that I was ready to travel. A moment later, he was ready as well.

We quickly returned to the King's suite. Marc was sitting at his desk, writing furiously. He finished his letter and pressed his signet ring into the hot wax of the seal.

"I have a letter for you," he said as he stood. "It authorizes you to use the post horses. Are you ready?"

"Yes," Ambrose responded as he took the letter.

I glanced out the window. All I could see was a small patch of the morning sky through the trees. I thought of the long ride ahead of us and weariness washed over me. It was going to be another sleepless night.

"I don't think I'm going to enjoy this," I said to no one in particular.

Marc laughed.

"Lauren," he said. "Before you left Songhaven with Ambrose, someone should have told you that riding with the Prophet of the Federated Kingdoms means very little sleep and absolutely no fun."

I laughed briefly at that. Ambrose just smiled and turned to the King.

"We must go," he said. "Follow us as quickly as possible."

"We will," the King replied. "Once again, old friend, the Federation is in your hands. May Garth guide your footsteps and put you on the path back to Mar."

For just a moment, the two men stood regarding each other.

"Your horses should be ready at the gate," Marc finally said.

Ambrose nodded and gestured for me to follow him. Together, we all but ran to the gate of the palace grounds. There we found Aldus waiting for us with two saddled horses.

The captain handed Ambrose the reins to a great black stallion.

"Ambrose, this is Stormwind. He has a temper, but you should be able to handle him."

My mount was a slightly smaller chestnut stallion.

"This is Challenger," Aldus informed me. "He'll be no problem at all. These are the fastest horses currently in the stables. Ride them well. May Garth speed your journey and put you on the path back to Mar."

"And may he be with you, when you march," Ambrose replied.

I mounted the stallion, who was so much larger than my Windsfoal. The horse pranced nervously as he picked up the tension from the humans around him.

"There is some food and skins of water in the saddlebags," Aldus informed us. Then he opened the gate, and we spurred our mounts through. A few moments later, we passed through the North Gate of the city and Ambrose paused.

"The first posting station is in twenty-five miles," he said. "The horses will be exhausted by then, but we must not spare them."

We spurred our stallions forward and the nightmare ride began. Soon, all I was conscious of was the bunching and release of the great horse's muscles and the steady pounding of hooves on the road.

Without stopping or even slowing, we thundered through the town of Hindon. The townspeople heard us coming and moved to the side of the road. I caught glimpses of curious or frightened faces as we flashed by, then we were past and back on open road.

The sun was nearing its zenith when we reached the first posting station. A surprised looking attendant stepped out of the office section of the building as Ambrose leapt from the saddle. As I dismounted, somewhat more slowly, Ambrose handed Marc's letter to the attendant, who took one look at it and instantly perked up. He yelled for a stable hand to saddle two horses and bring them out then handed the letter back to Ambrose.

"We'll have the horses out in a moment," the attendant said and then went to assist.

"We should eat a little while we can," Ambrose said to me.

I nodded numbly and returned to my horse. Only then did I notice the condition of our mounts. Their flanks were heaving with the effort of breathing and foam dripped from their muzzles. Their heads hung low and sweat poured down their sides. I was shocked and felt guilty for having asked so much. I patted Challenger on the nose.

"You ran well, Challenger," I said soothingly. "Now you can rest. You did your very best for the Federation."

I dug into the saddlebags and brought out the travel bread, cheese, and apples that Aldus had stored there. I broke off some of the bread and cheese and then stuffed the rest, along with the apples, into my pack. I was chewing on the bread and cheese when the station attendants reappeared with fresh horses. I quickly stuffed the rest of my food in my mouth and fetched the water skin, which I stored in the saddle bag of my new mount. Ambrose and I mounted, shouted our thanks to the attendants, and spurred our horses northward, gradually building to a gallop as they warmed up.

A stiff breeze sprang up as we rode, bringing an increasing number of clouds with it. The land here was mostly flat with just a few gentle hills and very widely scattered stands of trees. Near the small villages that we passed through, the land was cultivated; in between the towns the hills were covered in tall grasses, swaying in the breeze. I found myself regretting not taking a drink during our stop. The water skin in my saddle bag was impossible to reach at the speed we were going.

At our next change, I noted that the edge of the King's Forest was visible in the distance. The King's Forest was a huge tract of land set aside for the High King's hunting. Cresswell was nestled into the southern-most part of it. For the rest of the day, I could make out the forest to our right. As we mounted our fifth mounts of the day, the sun was nearing the horizon and, an hour later, we were riding in the dark.

We had to wake the attendant at the next station, but once he was up, he quickly brought us fresh mounts. He also gave us each a bowl of stew, left over from his own evening meal. When we dismounted at the station after that I could hear a loud shushing sound from beyond the station as if a great wind was blowing through a forest of evergreen trees. When I asked about it, the attendant told me that it was the rapids of the Camm River. I had never seen a river rapids and I longed to see them, but it was too dark to see the river from the road. I couldn't stop yawning as the attendant readied our horses. We changed horses once more in the small hours of the morning and then the sun rose. At the next station after that, the attendant shared some freshly made farina. All through the day we rode with the King's Forest in the distance on our right and the Camm River in the distance on our left.

Throughout the day, the easterly breeze continued to blow, and ominous black storm clouds were filling the sky to the east. We reached the posting station at the Camm River Bridge just as the attendants were sitting down to dinner. Nearly three hours later, we reined in at the foot of Badon Hill.

Badon Hill stood alone in the gently rolling terrain of the central Alomar lands, a giant sentinel watching over all the surrounding countryside. The sleepy Camm River rolled by the eastern foot of the hill. Badon Hill had been holy long before the Alomar had fled across the mountains. Before the Great War, a chapel dedicated to the Old Ones had stood on the east side of the summit. After the war, the chapel had been rededicated to Mar, but most people avoided it because of its association with Dark Magic. As a result, a temple to Mar had been built next to the chapel.

The first High King, Sorren, known as Stronghand, had built a city atop the hill. The innermost wall compassed an area of nearly two acres and was the site of the High King's palace and the ancient chapel. Each successive wall enclosed more of the hill until the last, the fifth, circled a city capable of housing thousands. The outer wall, made of granite hauled down from the Breton Mountains near Han, was made to withstand the most determined of assaults. Only two gates pierced the outer wall, one north, one south, and each gate was warded by two towers. Below the wall, ditches circled the hill, their bottoms lined with sharpened stakes.

I looked up the hill at Badon, the heart of the Federation, its walls etched in weathered gray lit up by the late afternoon sun against the sable backdrop of the storm clouds building to the east. Brightly colored banners hung from the walls. To the left of the gate there were two: a rampant lynx done in gold on a red background – Canim's banner – and a black ax and a brown oar crossed above an acorn cluster on a gold background – Meren. To the right of the gate was the banner of Marsden Forge, two crossed swords done in gold on a black background. The High King's banner hung from each tower, a golden eagle outlined in deep green on a field of vertical stripes in the colors of the six Alomar kingdoms: indigo, pale blue, gold, red, sky blue, and black.

I looked at Ambrose, who was staring up at the banners.

"Those," I said, pointing at the banners, "would only be displayed if the petty kings were here, right?"

"True," Ambrose replied. "But that makes no sense. If Larsen was planning treason, he'd stay as far away from Badon as he could until he planned to attack."

"You said that the High King was in danger. Could Larsen be the figure in black?"

Ambrose's face blanched.

"We must reach the High King at once."

We spurred our horses up the hill. Their hooves thudded loudly on the wooden bridges over the ditches. The gates were closed, and three guards stood there. All were wearing the standard uniform of the High King's army: green tunics with gold piping at the cuffs and collars, green trousers, and a gold tabard. Two of them crossed their spears across our way as the other, with a single red band around each arm that indicated a sergeant's rank, stepped forward.

"Who would enter Badon," he challenged, "and why would he do so?"

Ambrose urged his mount forward a step.

"I am Ambrose of the Minstrels. With me is my companion, Lauren of the Minstrels. We come to see the High King on urgent business."

The guard's eyes widened in surprise at Ambrose's name, then twisted into a strange expression, a combination of surprise and grief.

"Kingmaker," he started, but his voice broke as from some great grief. He closed his eyes for a moment, obviously fighting to control his emotions, and then started again. "Kingmaker, I regret to inform you that High King Aerman Sorren was murdered this morning."

Darkness threatened to overcome me. Horror displaced my weariness. Despite Ambrose's vision, we'd come too late.

"How?" Ambrose demanded, his voice raw with exhaustion and disbelief.

"I was not there, but rumor says that he was struck down by a black-cloaked figure as he held court this morning."

"Has anyone been arrested?"

"Not that we've heard. Again, according to rumors, the person struck down the King and then vanished."

"Vanished?" Ambrose asked. Without waiting for an answer, he continued, "No matter. Aerman is dead and I must see the prince."

He shook his head in disbelief. He hung his head for a moment, all spirit apparently gone from him. Then, visibly pulling himself together, he raised his head and asked, "What is your name?"

"Galvin, sir, sergeant in the High King's Infantry."

"Galvin, who is in charge in the palace?"

The guard shrugged.

"I do not know. We have been on duty here since sunrise. No word has come down except orders to increase the number of guards at the gates."

"Will you accept my orders?"

"Willingly, Kingmaker."

Ambrose straightened on his horse, the gold flecks in his eyes kindling.

"Seal the city. No one in or out until we have secured the succession."

"It shall be done," the guard replied. "You should know, however, that Larsen of Meren sent riders out this morning after the attack. We've also received a report from the Rangers that the army of Meren is camped but a day's march away."

"Destroyer take him," Ambrose exclaimed. "Are we to lose the Federation after all?"

"Kingmaker?"

"I fear that treason is marching on Badon, Galvin. Ready the city for a siege. Do so quietly but prepare. Know that Amersford is on the way. Should need be, we will have to hold out until they get here. If you need me, I will be at the palace."

"As you say, sir," Galvin responded.

He signaled his companions, and they lifted their spears. They opened the gates, and in the company of Ambrose the Kingmaker, I entered Badon for the first time.

The outermost walls of Badon were thick. The gate was set in a great arch between the two watchtowers. The gates were fashioned of oak bound with Marsden steel. As we entered the arch, I could almost feel the weight of the granite walls bearing down on me. Darkness closed in around me and then just as quickly dispersed as we entered the first level of the city of Badon.

Everywhere I looked there were people, some shouting at each other, some hawking their wares, and some just shoving their way through the throngs on their way to some-where. Buildings crowded the road on either side. Shabby inns stood side by side with tiny shops and ramshackle houses. I saw some stables and, here and there, the tents and quick-made stalls of Badon's less permanent vendors.

As we pushed through the bedlam, I was deluged by the noise. I had to fight the urge to cover my ears. People were shouting at me. One was hawking jewelry of "the very finest gold." Another, in ragged clothes, was begging alms. One woman shrieked at me to watch where I was going with my big filthy horse and reminded me – in colorful terms – that there were other people there, too.

At last, mercifully, we reached the Traveler's Gate in the second wall. The men who had built Badon built not only a city to rule from, but one that could be defended if need be. The three lower walls were each pierced by only two gates, the fourth and fifth by only one each. None of the eight gates fell on a line, so an attacker who breached one gate would have to engage in a great deal of street to street fighting to mount an assault on the next gate.

The second level of the city was quieter; the open marketplace was mostly confined to the first level. The second level did, however, offer some specialty shops catering to a somewhat more refined clientele. The inns we passed were in better condition, as were the homes, which tended to be somewhat larger. Many of the buildings were barracks for the High King's army.

We wound our way ever upward, passing through the third wall by way of the West Gate. The third level was a quiet residential area with few people out on the street, so we were able to quicken our pace. The Wizard's Gate through the fourth wall led us into a section of the city where ornate homes sat behind ornamental walls on large plots of land with fine, well-kept gardens.

Ambrose pointed out a large cluster of buildings just inside the gate.

"The Wizard's College," he informed me.

Men in the sable and gold livery of the High King's guard challenged us at the King's Gate, the entrance to the fifth level. When they learned Ambrose's identity, they passed us through. Inside the gate, Ambrose reined in, and I pulled up beside him. There was a stable built against the wall to our left and a pair of stable hands came out to take our horses.

The fifth level of Badon was roughly oval in shape, its axis oriented roughly southwest to northeast, and flattened on the northeast end. King's gate was located at the center of the south side of the oval. Directly ahead of us, a fountain stood in the center of a paved circle. Broad paved walkways quartered the area and between the walkways were immaculately kept gardens, filled with a profusion of flowers and ornamental trees. I recognized phlox, geranium, lavender, and daylilies. I also saw lilac and felt a pang of longing for Peg.

On the opposite side of the oval from King's Gate was a large building that Ambrose said was a mausoleum where past High Kings and their families were interred. As we neared the fountain, I could see that it was a statue as well as a fountain. In the center of the pool that formed the base of the fountain a woman stood on a small island of stones, a slight smile on her serene face. Her arms were raised to shoulder level and were spread slightly more than shoulder width apart, her palms angled down. Water flowed from her palms. Ambrose said that the woman was meant to be Mar. I said nothing, but to me she looked like *Tael*.

From the central circle, there were walkways to the right and left. The one to the right led to Mar's temple. It was a large white marble building similar in design to the one I'd seen in Amersford. There was a smaller building to the north side of the temple – quarters for the priests and pilgrims – and another to the south, nearly hidden amid a very old stand of trees and shrubs: the ancient shrine of the Old Ones. Though it had been rededicated to Mar and the Keepers, it was clear that it was not often visited, if it was visited at all. To the left was our destination, the palace of the High King. It was also constructed of white marble and on a pole in front of it hung the banner of the High King, the golden eagle on its multicolored field. Several sable and gold clad guards warded the doors.

Standing there by the fountain, I felt terribly out of place. My clothes were rank with sweat and stained with the dust of the road. My eyes felt dry and gritty, and I had no doubt that they were red with my exhaustion. My voice sounded hoarse when I spoke.

"We're not going in there, are we?"

"Why would we not? That is what we came to do."

I gestured at the state of our clothes.

"Master Ambrose, look at us. We'll most likely get thrown out as beggars."

"I doubt that. In any case, there's no time to clean up. The High King is dead by the hand of an unknown assailant and the prince is in there with the power-hungry king of a rebellious kingdom."

Just then, one of the guards left his colleagues and strode purposefully toward us, his hand on the hilt of his sword.

"Sir, I am Sloane, First Lieutenant of the King's Guard," the guardsman said, "I am sorry to be so brusque, but I must require you to state your name and business before you may approach the palace."

"I am Ambrose of the Minstrels," Ambrose replied. "I came to see High King Aerman Sorren, but I have learned that I am come too late. I must, therefore, see Prince Anders."

"You can prove what you say?" Sloane asked.

Ambrose nodded and dug into the pouch hanging at his side. He pulled out a gold medallion on a heavy chain and handed it to the guard. The guard's eyes widened as he examined it, and he sank to his knee.

"Kingmaker," he said in awe. "I meant no disrespect. Forgive me."

He offered the medallion back to Ambrose, who took it and said, "Please get up, Sloane. There is nothing to forgive. You are simply doing your duty. Had I been thinking, I would have displayed the medallion before approaching."

The guardsman rose and nodded in my direction.

"And your companion is?"

"This is Lauren, also of the Minstrels, and son of Dalach Egan-son."

The guardsman smiled.

"I thought you looked familiar," he said. "You have the look of your father."

He turned toward the palace.

"Come. I will take you to the prince."

We followed him to the palace and mounted the wide marble steps to the door. Four additional guardsmen barred our way.

"Who would enter the High King's palace," one challenged, "and why would he do so?"

"This is Ambrose Kingmaker," the lieutenant replied. "With him is Lauren of the Minstrels. They seek an audience with the prince."

Quickly, the guardsmen stood aside and allowed us to enter. Sloane led us down several brightly lit corridors, the walls of which were adorned with paintings and, in special niches, statues. As far as I could tell as we went by, the artwork was exquisite. Between my exhaustion and my attempts to get a better look at the art, I soon lost track of the route we were taking. I do know that we passed through several turnings before stopping before a door guarded by two more of the High King's Guard. They challenged Sloane and, when satisfied with our identities, stood aside to allow us to enter.

The room we entered was clearly a meeting room. The walls were of mahogany and were hung with the banners of the High King and the six Alomar kingdoms. Most of the floor was covered with a hand woven Altieran rug, oval in shape, with concentric rings of brown and beige that perfectly accented the walls. The only furnishings were a long, highly polished mahogany table and a number of chairs, some against the walls – obviously intended for guests – and the rest arranged around the table. In the corner to our right a young scribe sat at another small table, obviously ready to take notes for a meeting. At the far end of the room at the head of the table sat a young man who was clearly the prince.

Anders Sorren had long light brown hair bound back by a gold coronet, plain except for an enameled eagle fixed to the front. He was very slim and, even sitting, gave an impression of grace. His eyes were ice blue, and at the moment, they glittered dangerously.

Standing over the prince stood a tall, well-muscled man whose face was flushed with anger. His clothes were dusty, as if from travel, and he was unshaved and deeply tanned. On his head was a silver coronet set with emeralds. He turned as we entered and snapped, "What now?"

"I could ask you the same thing, King Larsen" Ambrose replied, quietly but firmly.

The king and the minstrel faced each other for a moment, the king obviously angry, Ambrose calm. Then a silver-haired man stepped forward from where he stood in the corner to the prince's left.

"Welcome to Badon, Ambrose. Once again you have come in our hour of need," he said. He had the highly polished voice of a courtier and sketched a brief bow in Ambrose's direction.

"Would that I had arrived sooner," Ambrose replied. "But we are here now, and we have information that I believe you need to hear. Ashlin, may I present Lauren of the Minstrels and son of War Duke Dalach Egan-son." He turned to me. "Lauren, this is Ashlin, the High King's Chancellor."

"It is an honor to meet you, sir," I said.

"And an honor to meet you," the Chancellor replied. "Your father is a close friend."

He turned to Sloane.

"Thank you, Lieutenant. You may return to your duties."

After the door to the room closed, Ashlin spoke again.

"We were about to convene a meeting of the Council," he informed us. "The prince and I wished to wait until all members of the Council could be present, but King Larsen reminded us that the Council's procedural rules set the quorum for a meeting at four and, conveniently, four of us are present. Ambrose, you probably know most of the people in the room, but some of them will be unknown to you or to each other, so I will introduce everyone."

"You, of course, know Anders, Prince of the Federated Kingdoms."

The prince stood, confirming my impression of grace.

"It is good to see you again, Ambrose," he said in a quiet, confident voice.

"And good to see you as well, my prince," Ambrose replied. "I am very sorry about your father. He was a good man."

The prince nodded as Ashlin continued around the room. "You also know Larsen, King of Meren." He then gestured to a woman and man standing in the far-left corner of the room. "And these are, of course, Mairy, Queen to Aerman Sorren and mother to Prince Anders, and Roth, King of Canim."

The queen was a middle-aged woman with long dark brown hair and large doe-like eyes. She contrasted sharply with the King of Canim, a grizzled old man who wore an eye patch over his left eye. When he turned his head, I could see that he was missing his left ear as well and that a jagged scar ran from the patch to where his ear had been.

Ashlin next indicated two men who were seated in the center of the right side of the table, one in the sable and gold of the Guard and the other in the emerald green tunic and gold tabard of the High King's army.

"Hagen, Captain of the King's Guard and Burke, Captain of the Rangers. At the other end of the table is Moireach, Queen of Marsden Forge."

I studied the queen of Marsden Forge. Moireach was very young, younger even than me, perhaps seventeen or so. She was very thin, but her arms were roped with muscle and both her hands and her arms were scarred by sparks from her forge. She had black hair, cut very short, and a fair complexion. Her coronet was a plain circle of iron. She looked just a bit scared.

"It is good to see you again, Ambrose," Larsen said harshly, "but if you'll just move on, we have pressing matters to attend to."

"The succession?" Ambrose asked.

"What concern is that of yours?"

"Calm down, Larsen," Roth ordered gruffly. "He said that he has information we need to hear."

"According to our procedural rules, only members of the Council may participate in the discussion of matters before the Council," Larsen said.

Before Roth could answer, Ashlin spoke up.

"King Larsen, your newfound enthusiasm for the Council's procedural rules is refreshing, but I would remind you that those rules also say that the chair of the Council can allow non-members to speak. In the absence of the High King, *I* am chair of the Council, and I would hear what Ambrose has to say."

Larsen looked as if he was going to object, but before he could speak, Ashlin continued.

"If everyone present would take a seat, I shall call the meeting to order."

As we sat, Larsen shot a cold, calculating look at Ambrose and me.

"Stay then," he said and slammed himself into the chair to the prince's right.

Prince Anders returned to his seat at the head of the table and Ashlin sat to his left. I took a few steps to sit next to Queen Moireach. Ambrose sat to my left and Queen Mairy on his left. Roth took the empty seat between Ashlin and Hagen. When we were all settled, Ashlin spoke.

"In the absence of the High King and in the presence of a quorum of four of the seven Council members, I, Ashlin, Chancellor of the Federated Kingdoms of Alomar, call this meeting of the High King's Council to order on the evening of the fifteenth day of the first moon of Tymnacynn in the one thousand and sixteenth round since the founding. The purpose of the meeting is to discuss the death of High King Aerman Sorren and to determine a course of action concerning the succession."

"Before we begin," he continued, "I request that we observe a moment of silence in honor of our fallen king."

We sat for a moment, our heads bowed in respect. I found myself thinking of Anders, who was having to deal with this after having lost his father just hours before.

"My thanks to you all," the Chancellor said, and we all raised our heads. "Your Highness, I would like to begin with you. Would you tell us what you witnessed this morning?"

"My father was slain this morning," Anders said. "His assailant was covered in a black hooded cloak. My father was sitting on the throne, about to hear a petition from the Kings of Meren, Canim, and Marsden Forge." The prince shot a questioning look at Larsen, but the King said nothing. "Those Kings have since refused to disclose what they were going to ask the High King, but I digress. The figure appeared from nowhere, standing directly in front of my father and stabbed him to death with a sword as he tried to rise. Before anyone could lay a hand on the assassin, he vanished. I refer to the assassin as a man, but I cannot know that for certain. It could easily have been a woman under the cloak."

The prince paused for a moment.

"The identity of the figure is unknown, as is his means of entrance and exit. I suspect, as do several of you, that magic was involved. An investigation has been launched."

"Chancellor Ashlin," Ambrose said. "May I ask a question?"

"Please do."

"Are there any thoughts on the identity of the assassin? Are there any clues at all?"

"None, really," Ashlin replied. "As the prince has said, the manner of entrance and exit suggests magic, but none of the wizards possess the ability to transport themselves in such a fashion."

"None that will admit it, anyway," Larsen mumbled, just loud enough to be heard.

Ashlin shot the king an annoyed look and then continued, "The only other being known to commonly wear a hooded black cloak is the Destroyer, but none of us can conceive of a reason why the Keepers would execute the High King."

"There is another possibility," Ambrose said quietly.

"And what would that be?" Larsen demanded.

"What we say now must not leave this room. The kings are all aware of the writings concerning the Lawbreaker. Hagen, Burke, you must keep this information confidential." They both nodded their assent and then Ambrose continued. "Lauren, please describe what happened to you in *Aennsrhyd*."

Once again, I described the sudden waking of the stone. When I finished, the room was silent.

"The wizards in Amersford also sensed the waking of the stone," Ambrose said. "After consulting with them and *The Book of Kings*, I am convinced that the Lawbreaker is alive and is somewhere in the Federated Kingdoms. He could be the one who murdered the High King."

We sat in silence a moment as the others considered that idea. Larsen broke the silence.

"That's the information that was so important that you had to intrude on a Council meeting?" he said scornfully. "You want us to believe that the High King was murdered by an Elven fairy tale?"

"Is it just a fairy tale, King Larsen?" Ambrose asked. "Why did the stone wake? And we've all heard for rounds about strange things happening all over the Federation: animals born twisted or behaving in strange ways. Those could all be attributed to the Lawbreaker. As could the murder of the High King."

Larsen started to respond, but the prince cut him off.

"Ambrose, if it is true, that is dire news, indeed. I believe we will have to consider carefully what must be done. However, we have a more immediate concern. That concern is whether I will succeed my father as he wished. That is the question that we must answer. I would wait until the full Council is present, which would require waiting just a few days, but that wish has been overruled."

"As we have heard, Council rules say that four of the seven members is sufficient to conduct business," Larsen observed smoothly. "There is no need to wait for the others. The Federation must have a confirmed ruler as soon as possible."

Larsen now turned his attention to the rest of us.

"These are troubled times," he said. "The incursions by the Kelmar are increasing. There is trouble of an undefined kind in Amersford. While I have no doubt that Prince Anders is as well prepared as may be, we need someone with experience guiding the Federated Kingdoms. I say that we confirm him as the next High King but let a regency council rule until he reaches his majority."

"Chancellor, may I speak?" Ambrose asked. At the Chancellor's nod, he continued. "What you say is true, King Larsen. There is trouble in the Federation. And Prince Anders is young, it is true, but his preparation to rule has been thorough and his majority is but a few short moons away. What we need now is the rightful ruler on the throne, not a council that argues over every move."

"You call up the past," Moireach said. "We are not the same regents who sat on that previous council. We need someone with experience."

"You call for experience," Ambrose said. "My long experience has taught me that a council is ineffective in ruling the Federation. We need our king."

"He is too young," Larsen insisted.

"That is your opinion, King of Meren."

"That is fact!" Larsen yelled.

Suddenly they were all trying to speak at once. My head was spinning with confusion. Larsen was pounding his fists on the table while screaming at Ambrose. The captains were talking over each other and Moireach and Roth, both in support of Anders. The Queen sat with her face buried in her hands, sobbing. Only Anders and I were silent. We locked gazes for a moment and then, with a look of resignation, Anders sprang to his feet.

"Enough," he shouted.

Instantly there was quiet, and everyone turned to look at the prince. He glared at the members of the Council for a moment, then continued in a quiet voice.

"I think that perhaps you all make Ambrose's argument for him," he said. "This squabbling is senseless. We must act..."

"You are correct," Larsen said, cutting off whatever the prince was going to say. "We must act. As a member of the High King's Council, I move that until Anders Sorren reaches the age of majority and can serve as High King that the Federated Kingdoms be ruled by a regency council consisting of the rulers of the Federated Cities."

"I second that motion," Roth said.

Anders slowly sat, a stunned look on his face. Ashlin looked around the table, with tears welling up in his eyes. It was clear that the vote would be three to one in favor of a regency council.

"There is a motion to establish a regency council consisting of the rulers of the Federated Cities to serve until such time as the prince reaches the age of majority," the chancellor said in a voice choked with emotion. "Is there any discussion?"

Larsen looked smug as he spoke up.

"I believe that as the one who made the motion, I have the right to speak first. I wish to do so. I do not seek to deprive the prince of his birthright," he said. "I merely contend that he is at present of too young an age to govern successfully in the face of our problems. We need an experienced general at the head of our armies to combat the ever-increasing Kelmar incursions. A regency council could hold the Federation in trust until the prince reaches his majority and then he would be crowned King. That is all I wish to say."

Ashlin looked around.

"I would speak," Moireach said.

Ashlin nodded.

"My opinion," she started, then paused as if her throat was dry. She swallowed once and started again. "My opinion is simple. I agree with the King of Meren. The prince is too young to govern effectively. I realize that this may sound hypocritical in light of my own youth but consider this. I rule over but one kingdom. My decisions affect only one small part of the Federation. The High King, however, governs us all and could easily lead us to ruin with an inexperienced decision. I favor a regency council."

Ashlin again looked around the table. When no one spoke, he asked, "Roth, would you care to address the motion?"

"I would not."

"I would address the Council," Ambrose said as he rose from his chair. "May I speak?"

"You may," Ashlin replied.

"My thanks to you," Ambrose replied, with a slight bow to Ashlin.

"Before we go further, I must inform you that the city has been sealed."

"On whose orders?" The King of Meren snapped.

"Mine," Ambrose replied quietly. "Captain Hagan, I apologize for usurping your authority."

"Why have you done so, Kingmaker?" Hagan asked.

Ambrose turned to the captain of the Rangers.

"Captain Burke, the guardsmen on the first level told me when we rode in that the Rangers had brought back a report. Could you tell us what that report was?"

"I have been waiting for the opportunity to do so," Burke said. "The report came in this morning, just after the High King's murder. An army under Meren's banner is but a day's march away from the city."

"Beloved Mar protect us," Ashlin said, his voice barely above a whisper.

I looked around the room. Ashlin and Mairy were white with fear. Anders' face was hard and defiant. Larsen still looked smug, but Roth looked angry and Moireach looked even more frightened. They both frowned as they looked at Larsen.

"Now I must tell you what I came here to tell you," Ambrose said. "Larsen mentioned 'trouble of an undefined kind' in Amersford. Lauren and I have just come from there and we can define that trouble. Marc was being slowly poisoned, and the person charged with treating him usurped royal authority to disperse Amersford's army. That person was a spy; both the poison and payment from his master were found in his room."

"Who paid him?" Anders asked, his voice quiet, but full of threat.

"Meren," was Ambrose's reply. "During the trial, he admitted the whole thing in open court; boasted of it, actually."

Everyone was silent for a moment, then as one turned to the King of Meren.

"Larsen," Roth said, anger rumbling like thunder in the background of his voice. "What have you done?"

"I did what needed to be done," Larsen answered. "What we have been saying is true: we do need a strong leader. I am no longer convinced that any whelp from the line of Sorren can be that leader. We need a change. I was promised that I'd be that change."

"You've involved us in treason," Moireach said, disbelief in her voice.

"Who promised you?" Anders demanded. "Who are you working with?"

"Change is coming, Anders Sorren," Larsen said, a sneer on his face. "A new world is being born. Pray that you will be part of it."

At that moment, there was a commotion out in the hallway. The door was flung open, and my father strode into the room. I'd never seen him in the livery of the army before and the green and gold of the High King's service suited him. His gaze darted around the room, lighted for a moment on me, then went to the prince. He bowed to Anders.

"My liege," he said. "The beacon fires have been lit. Han is under attack."

CHAPTER NINE

The only place where a sizable group of people can easily pass through the Breton Mountains is the Aeran Pass near the northern end of the range. Thousands of rounds ago, the Alomar fled Mar's anger through the Pass and for generations afterwards the Kelmar sent their armies through the Pass to exact Mar's retribution. To protect themselves, the Alomar built the fortress city of Han in the narrowest part of the Pass to block the Kelmar attacks. Since then, whenever the weather allowed it, the Kelmar sent small raiding parties through other places in the mountains, but it had been hundreds of rounds since a Kelmar army had set foot on Federation soil.

To summon aid should an attack on Han occur, Adelene, the first High Queen, had a series of beacon towers built every fifteen miles between Han and Badon. The beacons allowed a summons to reach Badon even faster than the fastest post message. Now, for the first time in living memory, the beacons had been lit.

Prince Anders stood and addressed my father. His voice was quiet, but his tone rang of authority.

"War Duke Dalach Egan-son, where lies your allegiance."

My father didn't hesitate.

"With you, my liege."

"My thanks to you," the prince responded. "No one – especially King Larsen – is to leave this room without my express approval. Do you understand?"

My father's hand settled on the hilt of his sword.

"I do," he answered.

"Excellent. Please send one of the Guardsmen to bring more men. I believe that we will have need of them."

My father took several steps back until he stood in the doorway and began issuing instructions to the men outside. The prince returned to his seat. His ice blue gaze swept the room. I found it hard to believe that he had only thirteen rounds of the seasons.

"Now, where were we?" he asked. It really wasn't a question.

"My prince, this Council has a motion under consideration that was properly made and seconded," Ashlin said, missing the point. "We must deal with that motion before we can move on to other matters."

"This has gone too far," Roth said, glaring at the King of Meren. "Larsen has played us all false. I withdraw my second."

"I also withdraw my support for Larsen's proposal," Moireach said. "I regret that I listened to him. I now agree with you that the full Council should be present for a discussion of the succession, but until such time as that meeting can be convened, I follow you, Prince Anders."

She paused and looked at the prince, a question on her face.

"If you'll have me," she finished.

Anders simply stared at her for a moment and then nodded. He then turned his gaze on Larsen.

"King Larsen, I believe that I asked you a question. Who are you working for?"

Larsen said nothing but crossed his arms and leaned back in his chair.

"Might I suggest that we send for a wizard and have him Read?" Ambrose said.

Larsen sprang from his chair and advanced on Ambrose.

"Stay out of this, minstrel," he said. "I will not submit to a Reading."

I'm not sure why, but I stood. Perhaps I meant to protect Ambrose. In any case, just as I got within arm's reach of Larsen, he pulled a concealed dagger out of his sleeve, turned, and lunged toward the prince. I leapt after him and we fell to the floor in a tangle. Before I knew what was happening, I was on my back with Larsen astride me. Both of my hands were wrapped around his knife arm pushing back against his attempt to slit my throat. I heard the rasp of a sword being drawn.

"Larsen," my father said. "Stand down or I'll have your head off your shoulders."

To make his point, my father tapped Larsen on the head with the tip of his sword. Larsen stopped pressing toward my throat, dropped the knife, and raised his hands.

"I'll thank you to get off of my son," my father said.

Larsen carefully climbed off me. My father gestured toward one of the chairs against the wall with his sword.

"Sit," he commanded.

As Larsen sat, my father reached out with his left hand to help me up.

"It's good to see you, son," he said.

"It's good to see you as well," I answered. "My thanks to you for your help."

"I see you've taken the blue. Much has happened in the last seven rounds. We should talk soon."

"Lauren," the prince interrupted. "You stopped Larsen's attack on me. You have my thanks for that. Are you injured?"

"No, my prince."

"Thanks be to Mar for that."

At that moment, several more guardsmen entered the room. Anders pointed to Larsen.

"I want King Larsen restrained," he ordered. "He is under arrest for an attempt on my life and possibly for additional acts of treason. One of you men, please go down to the wizard's college. We need someone up here to Read him. Now, we have many things to discuss."

Anders returned to his seat. My father sheathed his sword and resumed his position by the door. Two of the guardsmen took up positions on either side of Larsen and the rest moved out into the hallway. Anders turned to Larsen's guards.

"Men, anything you hear in this room stays in this room unless I personally give you leave to discuss it. Is that clear?"

They both nodded.

Everyone around the table looked expectantly at the prince.

"As I see it, we have two linked problems," he said. "We need to send help to Han, and we need to get that help on the way as soon as possible. However, we also have Meren's army camped on our doorstep, and we don't know what they're planning to do. So, what are our options?"

"We cannot leave Badon undefended," Hagan said. "Not with Meren's army so near."

"Indeed," Ambrose added. "It seems a little too convenient that Larsen showed up with an army just as Han is attacked and the High King slain."

"Badon will not be undefended," my father noted. "Our response to Han must be quick and that means that only the cavalry will be going. The infantry will remain here and can ward the city."

"True," Anders said. "However, I wish to mount as many archers as we can and take them with us. Their aid will be invaluable in the defense of Han."

"I have a suggestion," Roth said.

Anders looked at him, skepticism on his face.

"My prince, I know that you have little reason to trust me at this point, but I ask that you hear me out." At the prince's nod, he continued, "Donal, the general in command of Meren's army, is married to my daughter. I believe I can convince him to set aside whatever orders Larsen gave him and submit to your command."

At that moment, there was movement in the hall. A member of the guard spoke quietly to my father, who stepped aside to allow the woman in.

"Your Highness, Leannan, Morgan of the Wizards, is here."

"Send her in please," Anders instructed.

The guard withdrew and the wizard entered. Leannan was an old woman, older even than Ambrose, with skin the color of aged parchment. Her shoulder length hair was thin and wispy and white as snow. She was a short woman, her arms spindly, and her body almost lost in her black wizard's robe. Power filled her, though, and her deep brown eyes had the same compelling, unsettling quality as Ambrose's. She bowed to Prince Anders.

"You sent for me, Your Highness," she said.

"Leannan, my thanks to you for coming so quickly. I have need of your skills. Within the last hour, King Larsen has made an attempt on my life. In addition, he has brought an army to Badon, and his purpose in doing so is unclear. According to Ambrose of the Minstrels, he is complicit in poisoning the King of Amersford. He also let slip that he is working with someone but will not reveal who that person is. I need to know what you can learn from him. Will you Read him for me?"

"I will, my prince." She turned to the men guarding Larsen. "Please bind him, arms and legs. I must make physical contact and would prefer that I not be struck while doing so."

"I do not agree to this," Larsen said to Leannan. "Doesn't that matter to you, wizard?"

"It does, King Larsen," Leannan replied as the guardsmen bound the King's arms and legs. "Respect for the autonomy of an individual is an essential principle governing the actions of the wizards. However, the respect that you would normally be afforded has been suspended due to your actions."

Leannan took a chair from the table and sat facing Larsen.

"Further," she continued, "Given what you have done, I find it somewhat odd that you presume to lecture me concerning ethics."

Larsen made no reply, but simply glared at the wizard. Leannan took her ash staff in her right hand and leaned forward to put her left palm over Larsen's eyes and forehead.

"Please everyone, be silent this next little bit," she said and closed her eyes.

A faint light seemed to play along the length of her staff. No one said anything. Someone – the queen I think – coughed. There was a quick, very quiet conversation out in the hallway. Then Leannan sat back in her chair and sighed. We all waited several more moments, but the wizard said nothing.

"Leannan?" said the prince.

"I got a great deal," the wizard replied. "Most of it you already know. He hired someone to poison Marc and to do what could be done to ensure that Amersford could not respond effectively upon the High King's death. He was well aware that the High King was to be assassinated. He has spent months convincing Roth and Moircach that a regency would be needed if anything happened to Aerman, but he never informed them of the plot to kill the king. The intent was to keep matters confused until his army could get here, then he planned to kill you and install himself as High King. He believed that the being he was working with promised him that."

"Being?" Anders asked. "Not person?"

"Your Highness, the being that Larsen was working with was cloaked and hooded in black. They always met in darkness and the being's face was shadowed. That being on several occasions demonstrated sufficient power to convince Larsen that it could set him on the throne. He never knew, however, the individual's name nor could he even determine whether the individual was a man or a woman. It never spoke to him in anything but whispers. Even with an outsider's perspective, I could not learn anything more of its identity."

I could feel the intense interest of everyone in the room. Leannan had just described the being that had murdered the High King.

"Can you tell us anything more?" Ambrose asked.

"Just this," Leannan responded. "Larsen did not know that Han was going to be attacked. He believed that the being was working with the Kelmar to increase the number of raids into Federation territory in order to demonstrate that Aerman Sorren was ineffective in defending the Federation. There was never talk of a full out attack."

"My thanks to you, Leannan. Guards, take Larsen to a cell. I'll decide what to do with him later. Keep him fed and reasonably comfortable, but without my express permission no one is allowed in to see him, nor may he send messages or letters to anyone."

"We will see to it," one of the guardsmen said.

The prince looked around the room.

"We have many things to discuss," he said. "Dalach, close the door and join us please. Leannan, would you mind staying?"

"Not at all, Your Highness."

My father and Leannan took seats at the table as the prince continued.

"I believe that the being that Larsen was working with is the same one who killed my father. Has anyone heard anything tonight that might suggest who that being is?"

"Your Highness," Ambrose said, "I am more convinced than I was before that the being that we're talking about is the Lawbreaker. In the vision that led me from Songhaven to Amersford I heard a whispering voice very much like the one that Leannan just described. That, along with the other signs that we discussed earlier, supports the idea. The Lawbreaker is alive and working against us."

"What other signs?" Leannan asked.

Quickly Ambrose recounted the waking of the stone in *Aennsrhyd*, my sense of being hunted by a being very much like the one that slew the High King, and the wizard's independent conclusion that the Lawbreaker was responsible. The wizard nodded her head.

"All of that sounds reasonable to me," she said.

"Any other thoughts?" the prince asked.

"If this is true," Ashlin asked, "what can we do?"

"If I may, did anyone get a good look at the sword that was used to kill Aerman?" Ambrose asked.

"It was quite plain," Anders said. "The kind of weapon that would be issued to a common soldier. Why do you ask?"

"*The Book of Kings* says that the Lawbreaker's sword is adorned with a violet-colored pommel stone," Ambrose answered. "According to *The Book of Kings*, he will not face the Keepers until he has it. If he does not yet have it, we may still be able to forestall whatever he is planning."

"Then we should find this sword," Roth said. "Is there any record of where it is?"

"None that I have ever seen," Ambrose replied. "And no real clues about where it might be. All that *The Book of Kings* had to say on the matter was that Lorrestian forged both a ring and a sword and that the Lawbreaker would bear them when he faced the Keepers."

"We should begin a search," Roth suggested.

"I do not believe that would be a good use of our time or men," Ambrose replied. "We have no idea where to look. Lorrestian could have hidden the sword anywhere within the Elven Kingdom or somewhere in the Federated Kingdoms. For all we know it could be somewhere in Altiera or even in the Kelmar Empire."

"Would it even help to find the sword?" Moireach asked. "If it was in fact the Lawbreaker who killed the High King, he did it with a plain sword. It seems that he can do a great deal of harm without it."

"But how much more could he do with it?" Roth asked.

"If we had it, could we use it?" my father asked. "What does it do?"

That stopped the conversation, and everyone focused on my father.

"I do not know," Ambrose replied, his tone thoughtful. "No one has ever asked those questions before."

"Ambrose, Leannan, I would like you to explore the issues surrounding the sword in the next few days," the prince instructed. "I'd like to hear what you've come up with when I return from Han. Aiding that city is the most pressing issue right now. Dalach?"

"Yes, Your Highness?"

"I think Roth's plan is a good one, but I would like you to go with him. Take twenty of our mounted men with you. I'd very much like to get you back should the negotiations go wrong. Before you go, arrange to have the cavalry and as many mounted archers as possible gathered outside Northgate by sunrise. I want you back by then and ready to ride with us. I'll meet you there."

"Very well, my Prince. I'll see you at sunrise. Roth, you're with me."

The two men moved toward the door. I quickly stood.

"Father?"

He stopped and turned to me.

"Be safe."

He nodded.

"You, too."

"Hagen," the prince said. "You, Ashlin, and Rhys should see to the defense of Badon should Roth not be successful. Moireach, would you be willing to work with our smiths to prepare weapons and armor?"

The queen rose and bowed to the prince.

"I am honored that you're allowing me to help," she said. "I hope that in doing so I can begin to win back your trust."

The prince nodded and turned to the captain of the Rangers.

"Burke, I will want a company of Rangers with us when we ride for Han. Now, can anyone think of anything else that we need to do tonight?"

"My Prince," Ambrose said.

"Yes?"

"Lauren and I could really use a bath and a place to sleep."

Anders smiled.

"Of course. Ashlin, see to it please."

We were up the next morning before dawn to meet with the prince just outside Northgate. I was doing my best to stifle what seemed to be an unending series of yawns. Neither Anders nor Ambrose said anything when they noticed, but they both looked far more amused than I thought was warranted.

Nearly two hundred of the High King's soldiers were mounted and awaiting the order to set out. Of those, one hundred and sixty constituted the entirety of the High King's cavalry, but their numbers were augmented by archers who usually fought on foot with the infantry. They had all set aside their gold tabards for gold-plated chain mail, but their emerald green and gold uniforms still looked more suited to a group preparing for a formal parade than a group preparing for a grueling ride followed by a battle. Near us, a small group of mounted soldiers waited for the prince: ten in the sable and gold of the High King's Guard and one cavalry man bearing the King's standard.

The prince was giving final orders to those of us gathered around him: me, Ambrose, and Ashlin.

"Ambrose," he said, "I want you and Lauren to ride out to meet Marc when he gets here. Welcome him to the city in my name. Ashlin..."

At that moment, a lookout called out that a mounted force was approaching on the road from the north and uneasiness rippled through the prince's forces. Then it became clear that the lead riders were my father and King Roth. Most of the soldiers following them were wearing the brown and gold uniforms of Meren. The riders from Meren stopped at the edge of the High King's forces, but my father and Roth rode up to us and dismounted.

"Your Highness," my father said, and he and Roth both bowed to Anders.

"War Duke," Anders acknowledged.

"We were successful in convincing Donal to stand down," my father said. "He gave his word that he will not advance on the city unless summoned to its defense. I did, however, leave several scouts in positions to monitor the movements of Meren's forces. Badon will be warned if they move toward the city."

"Excellent," the prince responded. "It looks as if you've brought additional forces to aid Han."

"I did. I am reasonably convinced that these soldiers are loyal and were simply following the orders of their King. You should know, though, that several groups left the Meren camp last night under cover of darkness. Their whereabouts and intentions are unknown, but I suspect that they were those who are still loyal to Larsen."

"That's good to know," the prince said. "Ashlin, you'll need to get some of the Rangers out to locate them."

"I will, Your Highness."

"Ashlin, you are in charge until I return. You have good advisors; Ambrose is here as are Hagen, Rhys, and Leannan. Marc of Amersford will be arriving in a few days. Make use of them and prepare to defend the city. You shouldn't need to do so, but if things in Han go terribly wrong, you should be ready. And keep an eye on Moireach. I think we can trust her, but I don't want to be surprised if it turns out that I'm wrong."

"We will be ready, Your Highness."

The prince nodded and then said, "Gentlemen, let's mount up. It's time to go."

As the prince and Roth mounted their horses, my father glanced my way, nodded, and then turned to mount his own horse. The prince's standard bearer moved to the prince's right and my father to his left. The guardsmen spread out to surround the prince and his companions as they all moved to the head of Badon's forces. In moments, the whole company was in motion. We watched until they were no longer in sight.

In the morning of the third day after the prince rode out, we received word that Marc and his forces were nearing the city. During those three days, Ashlin and Hagen had been working with Rhys, the commander of the High King's Infantry, to prepare defenses for the city. Meren's troops had been moved to defensive positions along the road east of Badon. Burke and his Rangers had been hunting the soldiers who left Larsen's camp after learning of their king's arrest. It appeared that most of them had headed back to Meren, but several small groups conducted raids on some of the villages and towns around the city and then went to ground. The Rangers continued to search for them.

Ambrose spent a great deal of time with Ashlin. It was clear now that there would be no regency and the two were planning a coronation ceremony to be held upon the prince's return. I found myself with a great deal of time on my hands. I spent some of it in the High King's library, but nothing held my interest for very long. I also spent a great deal of time wandering through the city.

At midday on the first day, I purchased some fruit from a street vendor and found an empty bench in a park where I could eat and enjoy the day. Just as I sat down, one of the Repentant entered, ringing a handbell as he walked. He paused near a fountain.

"Wayward children of Mar, gather round," he said. "I would share a tale of Mar's love."

The Penitent was wearing the black robe and gold sash of those who had devoted their lives to Mar's service. His, though, were cut from the finest cloth, which was unusual for one of the Repentant. In most other ways, he was quite ordinary; he was of medium height and had brown hair and brown eyes. His face was brown from long hours in the sun and that was also unusual for a Penitent. He waited while a small crowd gathered around him and then he began his story.

Many rounds of the seasons ago, when men still remembered Mar's mercy in sending the Keepers to deliver them from the Elves, a king by the name of Jorlith ruled in Landfall. Jorlith was a devout man, steadfast in his love for the great goddess Mar. Jorlith knew well the sinful nature of the Alomar and each morning he gave thanks to the goddess for her forbearance towards his people. For the people of Landfall, sullied by their contact with the Altierans, were lax in their worship of Mar, withholding from her the love and devotion she was due. The people of Landfall traded with the Altierans and grew wealthy, and they hoarded their wealth to themselves, failing to use their good fortune to glorify Mar.

The Penitent paused and looked around at the crowd, frowning slightly at its small size.

> *Mar became aware of their apostasy and in her pain at the loss of her children, she grew wroth. She summoned the Destroyer, her strong right hand, he who administered her justice, and bade him to cleanse the city of the faithless. But Nordel, the Dream Giver, the beloved patron of the Repentant, implored Mar to withhold her justice for, he reminded her, "You have given the Alomar into our Keeping. Allow me to try to return them to your worship."*

I had finished my fruit by that point and the sun was growing uncomfortably warm. I wanted to leave, but it was unwise to walk away when a Penitent was reciting a story.

> *And so did Nordel come to Jorlith and said unto him, "Jorlith, thy people are in peril. Despite your example, they stray from Mar's worship, seeking only wealth for themselves and denying the goddess their love and devotion. She was prepared to wreak justice on Landfall, but I begged her to show mercy. Thou hast one moon to return your people to Mar's grace, or justice shall fall upon them."*
>
> *Jorlith was sore afraid for he had seen the might of the Keepers unleashed against the Elves. He spent the moon given him imploring his people to return to Mar's worship, but they heeded him*

not, tending each day to their business dealings instead of praising Mar. At the very instant the moon expired, the Destroyer appeared, ready to bring down Mar's justice on the people of Landfall. But Jorlith fell to his knees saying, "Mighty Destroyer, I beg you, withhold Mar's justice from my people for it is I who have failed. My devotion to Mar was insufficient to turn them from their wicked ways. I must pay the price and would do so willingly if it will save my people, for they are as children in the ways of the goddess."

The Destroyer stayed his hand and shared Jorlith's plea with Mar. The goddess was pleased with his love for her and agreed to forego punishing the people of Landfall if Jorlith would consent to be her slave. The King readily agreed, and the Destroyer carried him to Surmasifa, *the goddess' great palace. Jorlith spent the remainder of his days serving the goddess according to her whims.*

"And so, you have seen the love that Mar has for us," the Penitent concluded. "Go now and give thanks for her love."

Several people stepped forward then to speak with the Penitent and I took the opportunity to slip away.

In the afternoon on the second day, I was alone in the gardens outside the palace when motion caught my eye. It was a heron. Surprised to see one in the city, I watched as it landed in the basin of the fountain, where it stood watching me. We stayed frozen like that for long moments, then the heron looked at the statue in the center of the fountain before it took wing and flew off over the ancient shrine.

I looked back at the statue. Again, I was struck by its resemblance to *Tael*. I looked across the gardens to where the shrine was nearly hidden amongst the trees and bushes. Before I realized what I was doing, I was halfway to the edge of the thicket surrounding the structure. Mindful of the fact that my guitar was slung across my back, I began to push my way through the dense growth. It was a matter of minutes before I reached the building.

Despite uncounted rounds of obvious neglect, the structure was in good condition. There was a clear space about the width of my outstretched arms all around the building. A few dead leaves rested atop the bare soil, but nothing grew there. The air was damp and smelled of soil and growing things; the light was tinged green from filtering through the foliage. The building itself was constructed of native gneiss, so that the shrine looked almost as if it had grown there rather than been built. The end of the building facing me was completely open, with but two square columns to support the gable. The side walls were only about the height of my waist and were topped with columns that supported the roof. From outside, I couldn't make out much of the interior, so I stepped inside.

I could feel a change almost immediately. Inside, the air was still, and sounds were hushed. There was a sense of presence in that place, but unlike the unclean presence that surrounded the stone in *Aennsrhyd*, this not only felt ancient and unhuman, but also somehow right and natural. It evoked a sense of awe and reverence. Those who had attempted to repurpose the shrine had erected a statue of Mar in the center of the building, but it had not weathered well and was covered in mold and lichen. As my eyes had adjusted to the gloom, I could begin to make out details of the back wall. There were five empty niches carved there; I suspected that they had once held statues of the five greatest of the Old Ones. I just stood there for long moments. There was a sense of peace in that place, but also a vague feeling of loss and sorrow. I felt a light breeze waft through the shrine and my guitar strings hummed faintly, an odd minor sounding chord that sent chills down my spine.

Later that evening Ambrose and I stood on the wall above Northgate. It had been a warm day, but the sun was nearly at the horizon and stiff breeze was blowing out of the west, so we were quite comfortable.

"The prince should reach Han tomorrow," I said. "He took so few people with him. Will they be enough?"

"I hope so," Ambrose answered. "But I did not foresee any of this." He paused for a moment, seeming to consider whether he wanted to go on, but then he continued. "Lauren, there are some things I must tell you."

The wind tugged at his long gray robe and set his hair to dancing around his head.

"In the last few days, I have tried several times to see," he said, his voice carefully neutral. "Each time, I succeeded, or seemed to. Each time, though, I saw something different. The first time, I saw the world laid waste, towns and fields and cities scorched and burned. Homeless people wandered aimlessly, obviously dying, and piles of dead bodies were everywhere. The next time, I saw peace. The world was intact but changed somehow. I could not define the change, but it was there. The third time was similar to the second, but a large force of warriors rode through my vision with a priest of Mar at their head. Even in the vision, I was afraid."

"Master, what do they mean?" I asked.

"I do not know for sure," he answered. "Each vision was different, yet each had one thing in common with the others. Before each, I was shown a sword. It was standing upright in some kind of altar, and it was lit with an eldritch light. I am certain that what I saw was the sword of the Lawbreaker."

"Could you tell where the sword was," I asked.

"No. But I believe that my visions are true. I believe that they are confused because the future is uncertain. What will happen depends on whether we can find and defeat the Lawbreaker."

A strong gust of wind howled around the towers. Ambrose was silent, but I could hear the snap and crack of the High King's banners above us. My hair whipped about my face and tiny bits of dust brought tears to my eyes. Silently, I considered everything that had happened over the last few weeks and the implications of Ambrose's visions.

"I feel so insignificant," I said at last. "There is so much happening all around me, and I've done nothing. Since we left Songhaven, I've trailed along behind you like a piece of useless baggage. I really don't know why I'm here."

Ambrose regarded me silently for a moment, as if weighing what to say.

"You are not a useless piece of baggage. Do you truly not see what you have done?" he asked. "In Amersford, you are the one who detected how Marc was being poisoned. Had you not done so, we might still be there trying to cure Marc."

"And if we were still there?" I asked. "Would that change what happened here? Even with your vision, the High King was still murdered."

"But Anders would also be dead," Ambrose pointed out. "It has been overlooked in the confusion, but you were the one who stopped Larsen from killing the prince."

I was staring off into the distance. I had no reply to what Ambrose had said but felt that someone else would have done the things he credited me with.

"Lauren," he said.

When I didn't respond, he tried again, more forcefully.

"Lauren."

I turned toward him.

"I spent all those rounds teaching you what I did for a purpose. I brought you with me for a purpose. I cannot tell you what that purpose is at this moment. Soon, I think, but not now. I can tell you that it is more important than you can imagine."

He paused and then said quietly, "I tried to see your future."

That surprised me.

"What did you see?"

Ambrose's gaze was intense. The gold flecks in his eyes glittered like tiny stars.

"Nothing," he replied. "Though I tried again and again and with all my strength, I saw nothing. Your future is hidden, and some power prevents me from seeing it. But I came away from the attempt with the conviction that you are more intimately tied to the fate of the world than anyone else. That is, perhaps, why the Lawbreaker seeks you."

Again, I had no answer. We stood in silence, each lost in his own thoughts, until a page found us and reported that a messenger from King Marc had arrived. Amerford's cavalry would be arriving in the late morning of the next day.

I was thinking of that conversation as Ambrose and I rode out to meet Marc. We were accompanied by ten of the High King's soldiers, though the Rangers had yet to find any trace of the rogue Meren forces to the south of Badon. The day was bright and clear, and only a few puffy white clouds drifted in the sky. The day was promising to be hot but wasn't uncomfortable as we rode. A gentle breeze stirred the grass, which was going a bit brown, on the side of the road. We were planning to meet Marc about five miles from the city on the south side of a small wood that straddled the road. The wood would offer a cool shady place to await the arrival of Marc and his troops.

We were halfway through the wood when we heard a faint whisper of sound, and half our party fell with arrows protruding from their bodies. At the same time, soldiers in the brown and gold of Meren boiled out of the trees. Several who were mounted on horseback blocked the way forward and back. A couple of our soldiers who had fallen tried to rise but were hacked down by foot soldiers with swords. Our guards who were still mounted moved to attack the soldiers on foot, but another flight of arrows took down two more of them.

At that moment, my training as a minstrel kicked in. I yelled to Ambrose to dismount, and we stood back-to-back using the horses as shields. That worked for a brief period, but some of the soldiers of Meren prodded at the horses with swords until the beasts panicked and pulled the reins out of our grasps as they fled. A man in the sable and gold of the Guard inserted himself between an attacker and Ambrose, but I found myself alone facing the soldier who had driven off my horse. Over his shoulder, I saw soldiers in the colors of Amersford fall upon the attackers at the south end of the fight. My attacker seemed unaware of the newcomers and slowly advanced on me. I retreated and nearly stumbled over one of our fallen guards. As I stepped back over his body, I noticed that his sword was lying across his chest.

My attacker saw the direction of my glance and smiled.

"Go ahead, kid," he said. "I'll let you pick it up. It won't make a difference, but at least you'll die with a sword in your hand."

Carefully, not taking my eyes off the soldier, I stooped and picked up the weapon. I hadn't held a sword in nearly eight rounds, but I hoped that I remembered enough to hold him off until someone could come to my aid. I managed to parry his first attack and the next couple after that, but then a particularly vicious blow knocked my sword from my hand, and it fell to the ground at my feet. The soldier didn't pause even to gloat but swung a killing blow that I simply could not stop.

Time seemed to slow. I felt something pass out of me and my skin tingled. The soldier's sword flashed brilliant white and disappeared and at the same instant, the soldier himself was flung back away from me. He hit the ground with a sickening crunch, and I knew that he'd not be getting up.

At the same moment, I heard Ambrose scream in pain. I looked his way. With one hand he was clawing at something under his tunic. His scream had distracted the man protecting him and the attacker drove his sword through the guardsman's chest. Quicker than I would have thought possible, the man freed his sword, stepped past the falling guardsman, and drove it into Ambrose's gut.

My whole focus narrowed to the sight of Ambrose falling to the ground, blood staining the front of his tunic. His killer yanked his sword free, turned, and ran toward sudden shouting to the south. I half stumbled, half ran to Ambrose's side. I couldn't seem to catch my breath and tears were streaming down my face. I knelt by his side and took his hand in mine. He opened his eyes and turned his head to me.

"Lauren," he said weakly. "I do not have much time. Listen."

"Master Ambrose, no."

"You must listen. I am dying and you must hear me. There is a chain around my neck. Pull it out."

I reached under the collar of his tunic and found a fine gold chain. I pulled it out.

"Take it off me," he instructed. "Break it if you must."

I couldn't immediately see a clasp, so I used both hands, snapped the fine chain, and pulled it free of Ambrose's clothes. It held a heavy gold ring set with some dark stone.

"Lauren, listen. This is the ring of the Lawbreaker. It was given into the hands of a minstrel centuries ago. We have kept it hidden, passing it on only at death, and only to someone who was carefully chosen. I had it from my master Colin. Now you will have it. Keep it secret. Keep it safe. You must keep it from the Lawbreaker."

"I will Master."

"You must swear to do so."

I started to speak but became aware of the sounds of fighting and turned toward them. Men from Amersford were fighting with the last of the Meren soldiers. I turned back to Ambrose.

"Marc is here, Master," I said. "He'll have a Healer with him…"

Ambrose was shaking his head weakly.

"It is too late for me," he said. "Quickly, before Marc approaches, hide the ring."

I'd broken the chain, so I could not wear it around my neck as Ambrose had. I dropped the ring from the chain into my hand. As I did, the dark stone woke, glittering violet with highlights of red and blue.

"No," Ambrose breathed. I heard footsteps behind me.

"What is it, Master?" I asked.

"Merciful Mar preserve us," he said. "It is you. You are the Lawbreaker."

Cast of Characters

Aldus (ALL-dus) – captain of the King's Guard in Amersford.

Alun (AL-uhn) – a novice wizard in Amersford.

Amie (AY-mee) – a young woman, formerly of Badon, who moved to Cresswell to marry Clay.

Ashlin (ASH-lin) – the High King's Chancellor.

Bran – a member of the King's Guard in Amersford.

Burke – Captain of the Rangers, a division of the High King's Army.

Cadal (CAH-dul) – stable master at Songhaven. Exuberant. Somewhat horse-like in appearance.

Clay – a young man from Cresswell.

Clel – son of Harl. A boy from Cresswell.

Cray – King Marc's food taster.

Creighton (CRY-ton) – a man from Cresswell. Oversaw care of the village's livestock.

Crom – a wizard. Master of the House in Amersford.

Dalach (day-LOCH)– Son of Egan and Lauren's father.

Dane – Lauren's friend in Cresswell. Son of Govran, the blacksmith.

Denny – son of Harl. A boy from Cresswell.

Donal (DOUGH-nul)– a general in the army of Meren.

Egan (EE-gan) – Dalach's father and Lauren's grandfather.

Elinore (EL-in-or) – Lauren's mother.

Galvin (GAL-vin) – a guard in Badon.

Govran (guhv-RAN) – the smith in Cresswell. Father of Lauren's friend Dane.

Hagen (HEY-guhn) – Captain of the High King's Guard.

Helori (hi-LOR-ee)– the innkeeper in Cresswell.

Jaret (rhymes with "parrot") – Duke of Kerith and Chamberlain of Amersford.

Jarl (rhymes with "Carl") – weapons master in Cresswell.

Kaitrin (kay-TRIN) – an innkeeper in Amersford. Owner of the Minstrel's Haven.

Kayne – Warder of Songhaven.

Kendal – a travelling merchant.

Keri (pronounced the same as "carry") – Lauren's aunt.

Leannan (LEE-ann-an) – Morgan (head) of the Wizards.

Mairy – wife of Aerman Sorren and mother to Anders.

Olen (oh-LEN) – a wizard in Amersford.

Oscon (AHS-cahn) – the General in charge of Amersford's army.

Paul – an innkeeper in Amerford.

Phelan (rhymes with "felon") – a long-ago smith who made the gates of the Twin Cities or a "magician" in Amersford.

Ralf – King Marc's cook.

Rhys (rees) – Commander of the High King's Infantry.

Robeson (robe-SON) – an employee of Kendal.

Rogart (ROW-gart) – member of the King's Guard in Amersford.

Rory (ROAR-ee) – a page in Amersford.

Sloane - First Lieutenant of the High King's Guard in Badon.

Tadg (pronounced as "tie" with a g on the end) – a novice wizard in Amersford.

The Kings of the Alomar

Aerman Sorren (The ae is pronounced as a long "i" sound as in "aye", so ayer-MAN SOAR-in) – High King of the Federated Kingdoms of Alomar.

Anders Sorren – Aerman's son.

Houl (rhymes with "cool") – petty king of Han

Larsen – petty king of Meren.

Marc – petty king of Amersford.

Marwynn (mar-WUHN) – petty king of Landfall

Moireach (MOY-rick) – petty queen of Marsden Forge.

Roth – petty king of Canim.

Minstrels

Anna – a Minstrel of Alomar.

Ambor (am-BOAR) – a Minstrel of Alomar.

Ambrose (AM-broz) – a Minstrel of Alomar. Master of the College of Minstrels and a prophet.

Avery – one of Lauren's fellow students.

Denys – one of Lauren's fellow students. Sings duets with Rachel

Dermot – a Minstrel of Alomar. Son of Perrin. Met Lauren on the road to Amersford. Later played in Cresswell.

Elissa (eh-LIS-ah) – a Minstrel of Alomar. She teaches at Songhaven.

Katryn (cat-RIN) – a Minstrel of Alomar. Peg's Master at Songhaven.

Pegara (pe-GAHR-a) – one of Lauren's fellow students. Daughter of Houl of Han. Usually called Peg.

Rachel – one of Lauren's fellow students. Sings duets with Denys

Ryan – a Minstrel of Alomar. Lauren's Master at Songhaven.

Taran (TAIR-an) – a Minstrel of Alomar. The Master Crafter at Songhaven.

Tavis (TAH-vis) – one of Lauren's fellow students.

Keepers

???? – The Destroyer. Patron of warriors. Wears a black robe. Most powerful of the Keepers.

Garth – Patron of the minstrels and protector of travelers. Wears a blue robe. Second only to the Destroyer.

Mancier (man-SEE-er) – Patron of the wizards. Wears a white robe.

Acknowledgements

Many thanks go to my first readers: Stephanie Slocum-Schaffer, Marian Gleba, and Stephen Sherlock, with a special nod to Stephanie and Steve for long conversations about whether what I had written made any sense at all. Thanks are due as well to Stephanie, Sandi, Marian, and Benjamin for listening to me ramble on about the trilogy – for years – and for encouraging me to actually finish it (and, yes, the other two books are finished). Special thanks go to the team at Damonza who took one of my vague ideas for a cover and turned it into something absolutely amazing. I'd also like to thank all the people who have worked in the Shenandoah National Park and who labored over the decades to preserve Virginia's beautiful Blue Ridge Mountains, the inspiration for my Breton Mountains.

About the author

Larry Daily was born in Covington, Kentucky and currently resides in the eastern pan-handle of West Virginia. He holds a Ph.D. in Psychology and teaches psychology classes at Shepherd University. *The Minstrel and the Prophet* is his first work of fiction and is the result of a decades long love of fantasy inspired by J. R. R. Tolkien, Ursula K. Le Guin, Patricia McKillip, and Mary Stewart. In his spare time Larry builds HO scale model trains, plays folk music on six- and twelve-string guitars, and devours fantasy novels.